# THE CONTENDERS

# THE
# CONTENDERS

A NOVEL BY

JOHN WAIN

READERS UNION
MACMILLAN
1959

Philip's

Success is the necessary misfortune
of human life, but it is only to the
very unfortunate that it comes early.

ANTHONY TROLLOPE

# I

This is the story of two men, Robert Lamb and Ned Roper. I know them both and I'm going to tell the story as I watched it happen, straight through from the beginning to – well, I can't quite say 'the end', because it hasn't ended yet, but at any rate as far as it's gone. My name's Joe Shaw. At least, my Christian name isn't really Joe; it's an absurd name that I always detested and wouldn't let anybody use, so my friends had to find some other name for me, and being rather fat and easy-going I'm the kind of man who does tend to get called things like Joe or Fred or Alf.

The story starts when we were all at school, in the Sixth; before that, I hadn't really got to know either Lamb or Roper very well, though we had come up the school together, and had all been in the same form ever since we could remember, more or less. But the School Certificate, as it was called in our day – I understand it's got another name now, but I'm talking about the middle thirties, when we took ours – the School Certificate is the Lethe of school life, the frontier which, as you cross it, takes all the meaning out of the past. About four-fifths of the boys leave, the others split up into Science and Arts, and within those groups they re-align their lives. Look back across your schooldays and I'm pretty sure you'll find yourself dividing your friendships into two categories, those you made before and after getting into the Sixth. I mention this, which might seem a trivial detail to put on the very first page, to bring out an important point; namely, that Robert and Ned and I first got to know each other at the age of about seventeen, just at the point where the rat-race of adolescence quickens its pace and boys begin to see life in competitive terms – as opposed to girls, who seem to see life in competitive terms from the age of about ten minutes. Robert and Ned weren't really aware of each other during the main part of their boyhood; it was only after we all found ourselves in this small enclave, this self-conscious aristocracy, that they bumped up

5

against one another's personalities, and this seemed to give the tone to everything that followed.

That time of life is, of course, the period when you do begin to explore other people's characters; you are all growing up and the outlines of your real characters are beginning to show through the spiritual puppy-fat that used to hide them; also, normal school discipline is very largely relaxed, and you have time to sit about and gossip. In my own case, for instance, it was at this period that I first realized the most important truth about myself; namely, that I'm non-competitive. The urge to go one better than the next man, which seems to dominate most people's lives in one way or another, is something I just didn't have built into me. As I think over it now, I can see just how much of a puzzle I was to my schoolmasters; in spite of the fact that I didn't give much trouble and worked fairly steadily I was disliked by nearly all the people who had charge of me. What must have needled them most was that I was incapable of absorbing the one lesson they were all put up there to teach – that life is a competition. The bait they were continually dangling in front of our eyes was the sense of having snatched at something which the others hadn't been quite smart enough to see first. From the day our schooldays began, we were taught, implicitly, that every other boy was a potential rival and that we must all get down to the sacred task of outdoing one another. For instance, every fortnight the formmasters had to tot up the marks scored by each boy and write out their names in a competitive list; these were known as 'fortnightly orders', and the top five of each form were read out by the headmaster; you were supposed to applaud. When, years later, I read about the methods used in Russia to boost production in the factories – wall-charts and so on – I could never understand the smug tone in which the English newspapers described them, much as if saying, 'Thank God we don't have this kind of thing'. They can speak for themselves: I had eight years of it. And then when we got into the Sixth it continued in a subtler form. 'Marks' were left behind, of course, with the rest of our childhood's paraphernalia; but competitiveness was still the sacred law. What most of the Sixth were after was a scholarship at Oxford or Cambridge, and in the end most of them got one, largely owing to the ferocity of the methods employed. You picked a subject that not many other candidates would be taking, which in practice meant something not worth doing, and then you crammed it up from notes which were the same for everybody. Over the top of this you put your own bit of garnish; the garnish was the only thing that varied, because you used your 'general reading' for it, and it depended on the stuff you were generally reading. I dropped out right at the beginning, and said that Higher Cert. was good enough for me and they could keep Oxford and Cambridge. (We didn't try for anywhere else, by the way; the other places were thought to be *infra dig*.)

We had, in a word, the perfect training for careerists. I really think any boy who wasn't a fully qualified careerist when he left that school must have been abnormally well protected against it, either by having a safe job in the family business to go to, so that he didn't have to *have* a career, or by laziness, or stupidity, or something. Not that the competitive spirit, thus fostered, had necessarily to come out in the form of pushing for the best jobs. It could be social, or personal. In at least one case it was sexual. We had a chap called Stocker in the Arts Sixth, a thickset, shock-headed type with a pallid bruiser's face that looked as if it were made of rubber; you felt he couldn't possibly feel it if you punched him on the nose with all your strength. He was quite amiable with everybody, but a trifle distant, because he never gave them more than half his attention. The other half was always devoted to thinking about sex. Not in the abstract, but in the form of specific plans and speculations which concerned individual girls. That was the difference. We all, at that time of life, spent a lot of each day thinking about 'sex' and having vague reveries about girls, but Stocker thought about this or that waitress or shop-girl and what, in the concrete, he intended to do with her. And he did it too. He didn't talk about it much (have you noticed that men who *do* it don't talk about it?), but we knew, from his laconic accounts of his campaigns, that he was already having a fair amount of *bonne fortune*. And what struck me, even then, was that he had a competitive spirit about it. He went out for a kill, achieved it, chalked it up, and passed on to the next. It was success he wanted in his own way, just as much as the fantastically hard-working scholarship-hunters wanted it. If they were going to swot for examinations they were going to pass them. If he was going to be a lecher, he was going to be the lecher of all time.

This was the sort of thing that made me feel out of it, even then. I'm the type, anyway, who would rather be the first man in a village than the second in Rome. When I left school and went on to the local paper, I did so with the knowledge in my bones that I was capable of becoming a better journalist than anyone else they were likely to get, and that being a whale among minnows would suit me better than if I were to move to London and find myself crowded by a lot of other whales.

Now I've mentioned the word 'London' I'd better explain where all this took place. But here again I have to do some hedging before I can get on with the story. In England so much depends on where you live. At least, for the working class it doesn't; for them, it's simply a choice between town and country, and a working man who lives in Hammersmith, say, doesn't have a much different life from one who lives in Wolverhampton. But for the *bourgeoisie* there's the fatal dividing-line; if you're in the London telephone book you're in town, and if not, you live 'in the provinces'. Well, we were in the provinces, and no error. I mustn't name the place, because there's this fool convention in English publishing that you don't name the place you're writing about, in case the unpleasant characters in the story turn out to resemble the mayor's in-laws or whatever. Neither, on the other hand, am I going to follow the idiotic custom of calling it Bruddersfield or Grimchester. If I can't name this town, I'll just call it 'the town I mustn't name'. Anyway, it's that place you stop at on the way to Manchester – the one where you look out of the train window when it's slowing down, and think, 'Well, at least I don't live *here*.' We did live there, however; for that matter I still do, working, as I said, on the local paper. Yes, people actually do live in this place. All English towns fall into one of two categories: those that people live in because they like them, and those that people live in while they make enough money to be able to leave and go and live in the other kind.

For the moment, I'll just make the obvious point. That the mere fact of being brought up in a town where everything was shabby, dirty, dwarfish, peeling and generally lousy was another thing that helped to make most of us competitive. You looked round you as you stood waiting for the bus to take you to school, and you thought, 'If I don't do well I might have to end up staying *here*.' You thought of schoolboys like yourself, all over England, who were standing waiting

8

for the bus to take them to school, only the difference was that some of them were doing it in pleasant places like – well, Brighton, say. I hadn't travelled much, at that age, but I'd been to Brighton for a holiday, and I thought it was bang-on. It was my favourite town, Brighton, all through my schooldays, on the strength of that one visit. I used to think of boys standing and waiting for the bus at Old Steyne, Brighton, while I had to stand and wait for it in Campbell Place in the town I mustn't name. No wonder I grew up full of self-pity. And if it made me feel like that, what did it do to someone like Robert Lamb?

Even as a boy he never left the rest of us in any doubt that he wasn't staying. He was very good at drawing and painting, and used to go about saying he was going to be an artist, but he lived with his grandparents, and the old people were too cautious, or rather just too plain scared of life, to let him go into any such 'daft game', as they would have called it. The reason he lived with his grandparents was that his father had bunked off and left his mother when he was a baby, and shortly afterwards his mother had got ill and died. I don't know any more about it than that, so don't ask me whether she died of a broken heart or anything. For all I know she may have died of joy at seeing the back of her husband. Or she may have had a minor internal operation and the surgeon may have left a rubber glove inside her and killed her that way. There are plenty of ways people can die. Anyway, Robert lived with his mother's parents, whom I seldom saw because, for one thing, I disliked them. They seemed to me an unnecessarily fussy and worried old couple. I never saw either of them look happy or confident for one minute. His grandfather looked like a walrus, with his bald head and moustache, and his grand-mother looked like a seal. She had the little puckered-up face of a seal, very worried-looking. I'll give them this, that they had plenty to worry about. It was the early thirties, remember, and times were bad. And when times are bad in a place like the town I mustn't name, they're bad. Practically everybody is working-class – the middle class are just represented by a skeleton staff, as it were, to do the doctoring and the lawyer-ing and so on, and the upper class not at all – and when there's unemployment they all get rattled, even the ones in fairly safe jobs. Always remember, when I'm describing this place as it was in my boyhood (I'm thirty-seven now), that I'm talking about the period of what they politely called 'the depression'. A lot of the miners and potters were out of work, and as there isn't anything to do in that place but work, they were uncomfortably conspicuous, loafing about the streets. Then again, times being 'bad', there was never a quid or two to spare for putting a coat of paint on anything, or giving some of the kids a pair of boots that kept the water out, or doing anything about the cripples and morons who lolloped about the streets. Don't ask me why there was never any money. If you do, all I can do is to look up the figures and find that we were the richest country in the world at that time. The richest country. Pardon my hiccups. You wouldn't have thought so if you'd seen that place when I was a boy. Even today you can't help noticing, when you go there, that most of the men over thirty-five have got bow legs, or are midgets, or hunchbacks, or some damned thing. That's because the government we had in those days, when we were the world's richest country, didn't give a damn whether the kids grew up with rickets or not. I suppose they were too worried about making sure the Reds didn't murder them in their beds, or something. Politics.

Anyway, Robert Lamb's grandparents were just like a seal and a walrus, worrying about the North Pole getting too hot for them or something. Of course he mustn't be an artist! In any case the word 'artist', up there, has a special meaning. (Most words have.) It means someone who works in one of the pottery factories – it's the industry there – putting the designs on crocks. As such, they get sacked just as easily as anybody else when times are bad, and the main object of the old couple's lives, the one thing they still had to do before they could die in peace, was to guide Robert into a job where he'd be safe from the sack. Say, school-teaching. That was how people thought, at that time. They didn't ask whether such and such a job would suit the boy. They just went all out for the one that wouldn't get snatched away every time trade slumped. The mere idea of Robert as a schoolmaster is of course a screaming rib, and it wasn't any less of a screaming rib when he was sixteen. He wouldn't have lasted a day – not a morning. But he did have the sense to play along with it to the extent of going into the Sixth. It gave him a couple of years' breathing-space before he set off to conquer the world, using nothing but his paintbrush, his personal magnetism and his elbows.

At the time I'm speaking of now, the Sixth Form time, he

didn't have much need for the elbows; by comparison with what went before and came after, he had very little occasion to feel himself in direct competition with anyone. Still, it was bred in the bone, so to speak, and it had to come out now and again. And the one person who never failed to bring out the spirit of competition in Robert was Ned Roper. They were the strongest personalities among us, for one thing, and for another they were such contrasting types. Robert was dark and thickset, moody and often angry, but given also to bursts of manic high spirits; Ned was tall and fair, and by temperament the kind who keeps everything under control and drives steadily towards a set purpose. The two of them felt themselves to be in essential opposition, and yet they never actually quarrelled. Perhaps they needed each other; the rivalry between them, which was never openly confessed, may have been an important driving-force in their lives from the start. They needed me too, and were always bringing me in as a kind of buffer state. I remember one instance in particular.

It was right at the beginning – the first winter we were in the Sixth. We were all out on the cross-country run. Not a cross-country run; the cross-country run. The school organized one mammoth one, each year, and everybody entered. When the lists were first drawn up, about six weeks ahead, you put your name down mechanically, feeling you might as well turn out with the others. As time went on, the more athletically inclined began to train, at first shamefacedly and in out-of-the-way places, but later openly; you'd meet them out for runs in the evenings, padding along the country lanes. You joined in the general laugh at this, but slowly the thing began to infect you; a week from the date you began refusing second helpings, turning in early, and the rest of it – though you wouldn't have admitted even to yourself that you cared about 'the Cross'.

Anyway, this year 'the Cross' had come round, and we'd been through all the stages, the day was here and we were off. I'd been running heavily along somewhere at the rear of the field, for a couple of miles, when I saw ahead of me two figures in shorts and singlets rather elaborately 'resting' on a stile. I plodded up and saw it was Ned and Robert.

'Getting breath for a sprint, eh?' I wheezed, halting.

Ned smiled loftily and Robert said, 'Sprint, my foot. We're just waiting about to make sure the whole field gets in front of us so that we can come in last. That'll show them our attitude to this footling Cross.'

'What's wrong with it?' I asked. 'Why'd you enter if you don't hold with it?'

'Oh, never mind arguing,' said Robert impatiently, swinging his body backwards and forwards on the stile. I could see he hadn't really any grudge against the Cross except for being something he hadn't thought of himself. 'Come along with us, Joe. Let's have three dead-heating for last place – what about it, Ned?'

'By all means,' said Ned, as if they were discussing whether to take me with them on a tour of the Riviera.

A few more kids trailed past, and then a very young one, who really oughtn't to have been allowed to enter, limped up to us. The distance was already too much for him, after a couple of miles. He'd got a blister on one heel, and seemed to have fallen into a ditch; anyway, he was pretty wet, and there was a keen wind blowing. He looked about ready to burst out crying.

'What's been happening to you, kid?' Robert asked, kindly but rather roughly. He was obviously annoyed that the child had happened along, and was no hand at concealing it.

'Nothing, Lamb – I – fell over,' the boy stammered. 'I couldn't see where the others had gone and – I was afraid I was –'

He was going to say 'lost', but didn't finish the sentence because if he had brought out the word it would probably have made him cry. He was as young as that.

'Well, my God,' said Robert, looking at him. 'Somebody slipped up, letting you enter.'

'I thought I – might not be last,' the kid said and at that he really did start crying. A tear dribbled down his nose.

'Well, it's quite simple,' said Ned, getting down from the stile with a single forceful movement. 'What the boy wants to do is to drop out and go home on the bus.'

'Yes, but what about our –'

'Exactly,' Ned went on, cutting Robert short. 'We mustn't have any retirements, or else it'll spoil our whole gesture when the list comes out.'

The list! I saw how their minds had been working. They had a vision of the long list of placings that was always posted and stayed up in the main corridor for the rest of the term.

They coveted that nice conspicuous place at the bottom: 150th equal (or whatever it was), Roper and Lamb. A couple of cards, everyone would say. Probably they had had the idea quite spontaneously since starting the race; but in any case they both had to be equally involved in it. And now here was this kid, obviously about to retire and in all probability mess the list up.

'There's only one thing for it,' Ned continued. 'We'll have to carry him.'

'All the way?' I quavered.

'Yes, obviously it's the only thing we can do,' said Robert, snatching up the idea just too late to give the impression that he'd thought of it simultaneously 'Then, twenty yards from the finishing line, we'll put him down and let him walk over by himself, ahead of us – '

'And then the three of us can link arms and – '

' – just *stroll* across – '

' – what a gesture!'

They were crowing with laughter, skipping about and slapping one another on the back. Somehow it left me cold. I began to wish myself out of it.

'Well, you seem to have it all worked out,' I said. 'All the details nicely in place. I think the best thing I can do is jog on ahead and leave you to it.'

They both spoke at once: Ned with 'Oh, come!' in a calmly reproachful way, Robert with a loud squall of reproach. The kid, meanwhile, was standing looking from one to the other of us with a half-interested, half-frightened air. The tear he had shed had left a rivulet of cleanliness down the middle of his muddy face.

'Now, we can't have any of your nonsense, Joe,' said Ned firmly. 'Of course you must come along with us. It'll make the effect all the better.'

The trouble was that I had just enough intelligence to know what he meant by that. For two such live wires as Roper and Lamb to loaf across the finishing line just behind a small boy, and not only that but in the company of an amiable fat oaf like Joe Shaw – naturally it made the effect all the better. I wish I could put it on record that I felt any resentment at this, but I didn't. It was the role they had cast me for, and I accepted it; looking back, I don't remember any inward struggle at all.

'Well, let's go,' I said, bending down for the kid to climb

on to my back. Which he did, with an evident surge of high spirits. I couldn't see his face, but from the way he was wriggling and digging his heels into me, I deduced that the little chap was full of glee.

We walked doggedly along, keeping up a good pace because we couldn't afford to be so late that they would all have gone home. I did my best to shirk my share of carrying the lad – that was the idea of coming forward to have my turn first – but the others kept me to it pretty sternly. As it happened, I was carrying him as we turned into the road where the school was. We had about a quarter of a mile to go, and at any moment we should be recognizable to people clustering about the finishing line.

'All right, Joe,' said Ned. 'I'll take over.'

I hadn't been carrying him long, so I said, 'I can manage the rest of the way now, thanks.'

Robert glanced at Ned sharply, and said, 'Besides, it isn't even your turn to carry him.'

'Never mind,' said Ned easily. 'I've got plenty of energy to spare. Hand him over, Joe. You've got your fat to carry.'

The kid had stopped wriggling and was sitting quite still on my back.

'That's true,' said Robert. 'Joe's too fat to lug him any more. I'll take my turn. Jump off, kiddy.'

Idiots! I thought. The one who's actually carrying the kid when we get to the finish would naturally have the extra bit of limelight; some of the sillier spectators might even jump to the conclusion that he had tenderly carried the little fellow all the way. Like Tom Brown and Arthur – that kind of thing. And here they were, ready to quarrel over it.

'You heard me, laddie,' said Robert. 'Jump off.'

We'd been trudging along, and by this time people at the finishing line were craning towards us, wondering what was happening. I decided to put a stop to the farce. I swung the boy down, bent over him and said in his ear, 'There's the tape ahead of you – run!'

He looked dazed for an instant, then set off like a scared rabbit. He seemed to have forgotten about the blister on his heel; before Ned and Robert could react, he was out in front of us, going hard. The onlookers sent up a ragged, ironical cheer.

I turned to the other two and said, 'Now let's – '

Before I could get any further Robert had gone. One instant he was walking along with us, the next he was sprinting, and going so fast that he had already half closed the gap between us and the flying little figure.

The cheering died down. Amid a puzzled silence, Robert thundered after the kid, swooped on him five yards from the finishing line, and swung him up on to his shoulder. He stood there with a benign smile, but I could see, as we hurried up, that he was holding him very tightly to prevent any monkey business.

He waited for us to get level with him and then said, in a voice that he tried to make light and friendly, 'Now. We're all here, so let's cross the line together.'

Ned gave absolutely no sign of having heard. He just walked steadily onwards, neither speeding up nor slowing down. Robert and I fell in beside him and the three of us, with the kid sitting aloft and looking very puzzled, walked over the line.

I didn't know how to carry it off. There was a certain amount of clapping, and laughter and what-not, but I fancy it would have been heartier if Ned and Robert had done anything to encourage a spirit of fun. But the moment we had crossed the line they both seemed to forget all about the Cross, each other, me and the kid. Robert just put him down and they walked off to the changing rooms, a few yards apart, not ostentatiously ignoring each other but not speaking either.

'Well, you finished,' I said to the kid.

'Yes, Shaw,' he said, beginning to feel a bit of a hero. 'And I wasn't *last*, was I?'

'No,' I said. And I meant it, because I knew who had come in last in that particular race. I had. Robert and Ned had simply engulfed me, as they were to go on doing.

That was one of the times, I'd say, when Ned had the best of it. Under the pressure that bore down on them both he kept his nerve better than Robert. It was the same all the way along; he had the external world under much better control.

In contrast to Robert, he had all his family living and there seemed to be about two hundred of them. If you ever went round to his house, your first thought was that the Ropers had moved and sold the house to another family, because the person who let you in would be someone you'd never seen before, and so, probably, would the first ten or a dozen people you saw when you got inside. They lived, or rather swarmed, in a biggish house, very dark and shabby, and the way they ran in and out, and crowded together in the rooms, it was just like a rabbit-warren. And there were other branches of the Roper family scattered about the neighbourhood, all equally numerous. They ran about a dozen businesses, none of which paid. One lot had a haulage business – i.e. owned a beaten-up old lorry, which probably cost more in spares and fuel than it earned. Another branch were pottery manufacturers, and had a 'works'. That sounds grand, but if you know this town at all, you'll know that a lot of the factories are tiny little concerns, hidden away in side streets, employing a handful of work-people and unable, or unwilling, to expand. They seem to be exempt from the usual law that governs businesses – expand or go under – and able to remain stationary from one genera-tion to another. Twenty years ago this was more true than it is now; there were some very small and primitive 'pot-banks' at that time, and I dare say the Ropers' was the smallest and most primitive. The branch of the family that Ned Roper actually belonged to were 'dairy-farmers', if that isn't an absurd way of saying that they had a few broken-down old cows and used to milk them and go round with a cart selling the milk out of churns. I suppose they produced other things on their bit of a farm too, but the milk-round is the only thing I ever remember seeing them do. Ned used to swank about it when he was smaller, when we were all young enough to think him lucky because his father used to take him on the round on holidays and Saturdays, but of course at the time I got to know him better the milk-round was never discussed, and indeed I'm sure Ned never had anything to do with it. He was the white-collar one of the family, the one who was going to make good and redeem all their fortunes. One odd thing, considering that the Ropers bred like mice, was that he hadn't any brothers. He had about two dozen sisters, but no brothers, as if the force of his personality had frightened all the other embryos so much that they had turned into girls so as to avoid competing with him. This wouldn't sound so fanciful to you if you knew Ned. He certainly had his family under control, better than any boy I ever knew. He'd managed, right from the start, to get them to accept him at his own very high valuation of himself. Perhaps this was the reason for the impressively no-nonsense manner he always had; he had assumed it in order to terrify his family, and then found it impossible to get rid of. More likely it was the other way; his manner was just him, and his family kow-towed to him quite naturally because of his strong character. At all events he was much the same at seventeen as in later life; forceful, a bit grim, not wasting words, always neat and methodical, as if everything he did had got to be done quickly, to allow him to get on to the next thing, and also thoroughly, so that it *stayed* done. I can see him now, a tall, fair-haired youth, coming in for a history period with the Bloater, and unstrapping his bag and getting out just exactly the books he was going to need and putting them in exactly the right order on the table in front of him.

I'm aware that this makes him sound insufferable. And of course most boys of seventeen who are methodical and very grown up in their ways *are* insufferable. Ned, however, was very likeable. The way he did things generally was pretty deadly, but the things he did were all right. I mentioned the Bloater just now. That was the master who took us for history in the Sixth Form. He was good at his job, and he needed to be to keep it, because there was no doubt that he was an unpleasant man. He had an evident grudge against the fate that had made him a schoolmaster instead of a university lecturer, and to do him justice he was quite good enough for a university. I suppose the reason why he didn't get an academic job was just because nobody could stand his guts. Anyway, the Bloater was a proper old bar-steward, as we used to say. He was there to drill us so that we got good marks in scholarship examinations, and, as he saw it, that didn't involve him in having to pretend that he *liked* us. This sounds all right, but actually it's no use teaching boys of that age unless you *do* like them; most adolescents are very hungry for approbation from adults, and if you take away that bait – if you make it clear that however well they work you still won't care whether they live or die – they'll turn rebellious.

Did I say 'rebellious'? Were we rebellious with the Bloater? That's an understatement. We really slammed hell out of him. But nobody was better at this than Ned. He really put all his efficiency, his thoroughness and dislike of muddle, into organizing the struggle against the Bloater, and the rest of us just naturally accepted him as the organizer and co-ordinator of our efforts; we recognized that his ability, in this sort of direction, was greater than ours. The rest of us except for

Robert, I should have said. Robert's attitude was quite consistent; it wasn't that he wanted to rival Ned in his position of administrative chief; he just didn't want any part in it. Nobody was going to organize him. I can never remember his coming in on one of Ned's concerted schemes for making the Bloater's life hell, unless he could contribute an idea that he had thought of himself and could carry out independently. If Ned could find some means of integrating his contribution in the general framework, all right; if not, so much the worse for the general framework. He was the complete anarchist.

Take the case of the Book, for instance. Ned decided, at the beginning of our first summer term in the Sixth, that it was time we codified and placed on record the experience of Bloater-baiting that we had amassed during the winter. So he produced a large exercise book, in board covers, and drew up a title-page. It was to be called 'the Book of the Bloater-bait', and we were all to contribute articles on our own special line. That's another thing Ned was very keen on, at seventeen: specialization. He used to hold that the stupidest person could get skilful at one task if he did it all the time. This infuriated Robert, who had an instinctive dislike of that kind of attitude, though he was not good at rationalizing it. When they disputed, Ned could always riddle Robert's arguments and it nearly always ended in a row, with Robert losing his temper. He was thickset, with an easy scowl, and this gave Ned an unfair advantage of looking the more reasonable of the two; he was tall and fair. Anyway, to get back to the Book of the Bloater-bait. Ned, the general editor, led off with a general survey of the objectives to be aimed at – I remember, across the years, that his opening sentence ran, 'While we cannot make the person hereinafter described as the Bloater stop being a bastard, it should be possible in certain ascertainable ways to make him *sorry* that he won't stop being a bastard' – and the rest of us chimed in with short accounts, illustrated with diagrams, charts, and what-not, of various individual ways we had developed of needling the poor old sod. I could never be quite sure how far Ned took all this seriously. To the rest of us it was a joke, pure and simple; but Ned, though there were undoubtedly times when he saw it as we did, would often get into a very solemn mood about the Book. 'We'll bequeath it,' he used to say. 'Each new generation coming into the Sixth will have this body of experience handed on, and they'll be able to make their own contribution and correct things that have become obsolete with time.' He saw a glorious future ahead, in which Bloater-baiting would be established on really firm lines. 'A flexible tradition' – that was another favourite saying of his. 'We must have a flexible tradition – nothing hidebound,' he wrote in his essay. 'With the passage of time it may be that the Bloater will develop new phobias and manias, and it is up to the generation currently at work to exploit each new symptom, seeking always to convert every passing manifestation of strain into a permanent mental flaw.' That was the kind of phraseology he went in for, as nearly as I can reproduce it now. He used to say that if the Bloater could be driven out of his mind altogether before his retiring age came, he would have to resign before the age limit and thus forfeit his pension.

Robert, though not at all backward in the attack on the Bloater, showed very little interest in the Book. How could he? It was Ned's idea, and to contribute to it would look like placing himself under Ned's leadership. Ned had enough common sense to see this, and refrained from pressing him to contribute; he just included Robert in the general invitation and that was that. As a matter of fact, Robert's attitude towards the Bloater was an inconsistent one. He was much more self-centred, much less aware of what went on around him, than the rest of us, and for weeks on end he would appear hardly to notice the Bloater's presence. Then the Bloater would tread on his toes in some way and the result would be a flaming row; Robert would lose his temper and go to far greater lengths than anyone else would have dared. Because, as I should have mentioned before, the Bloater *was* formidable. This was no silver-haired recluse living for his books and pictures and music, forced to teach for a living, whose life we were wantonly crushing with our adolescent malice. To begin with, he stood about six feet and had plenty of bulk to go with it; his voice was unpleasantly dry and sarcastic, except that when he was really giving someone the rough edge of his tongue, which happened about a dozen times a day, he raised the pitch and barked like a St Bernard. He was about two hundred per cent stronger than any of us in repartee, and when you add to all this that he had a permanent grudge against us, because he hated teaching us, you get the picture. I suppose it was good for us, at that age, to have somebody of his strength of personality

19

against whom we could measure our awakening powers; at any rate, I don't think it did us any harm. But I mention these characteristics of the Bloater to make it clear that when Robert went for him bald-headed, as he did now and again, his attacks were attended with a certain risk – it wasn't just a question of cheeking a schoolmaster.

One rather drowsy afternoon, I remember, we were sitting about listlessly while the Bloater droned out some stuff we were supposed to be taking down. Most of us were half-heartedly trying to get down the gist of it, if only for something to do to keep us awake, but Robert had found a better way of evading the general boredom. He had given up listening altogether and was delightedly grinning to himself over a pen-and-ink drawing he was making. He often doodled, in fact all his exercise books were covered with scribble, but this was the first time I had noticed him really drawing something. I didn't want to lean over and peer at it, though I was sitting next to him, for fear of making it obvious that he was ignoring the Bloater's discourse. But after a few minutes he evidently felt the urge to show it to someone. Turning to me, he pushed the paper half-way along the table (we didn't sit at desks, in the Sixth) and nodded down at it, as much as to say, 'Look at this!'

I'm not likely to forget that drawing. It was the first piece of really characteristic work by Robert Lamb that I ever saw. There were some things of his pinned up in the art-room of course – he had always been the star turn at 'Art' – but as far as I was concerned, this was the moment when he found his characteristic manner. What he was showing me was a rapid but tremendously energetic sketch of the Bloater on skates, skimming over the surface of a lake. In the left foreground was a star-shaped hole in the ice, with a boy clinging desperately to the straining surface round it: the sort of thing that used to get a laugh in Punch about 1905. The drawing made it clear that the Bloater had seen the boy and just couldn't be bothered to do anything about helping him. He was sweeping past, skating very stylishly on one foot, and obviously in the middle of some intricate figure that left him with no energy to spare for saving lives. The thing that struck me, and has stayed with me ever since, is the extraordinary precision of comment in the drawing. There was the Bloater, with his nose up in the air, his eyes popping in a supercilious way, his mouth exactly like that of a fish, and his whole being expressive of self-admiration

20

and lack of concern for anyone who had been fool enough to fall through the ice. It isolated *exactly* those qualities in the man which we all disliked.

'It's great,' I whispered. Across twenty years I remember the exact words I used, because it's always seemed to me prophetic that I should have used that word, 'great.'

Then a shadow fell across the sunlit table, a tweedy arm came down between us, and the next second the Bloater had snatched the drawing and borne it off to his corner. Robert's chair went back with a loud scrape, and he half rose, then sank down again, tensely.

'Artistic creation,' the Bloater said in his horrible dry voice. 'Our friend Lamb is well known to be the fortunate possessor of a talent.'

Everyone looked and listened.

'You will perhaps forgive me for saying, however, that this is hardly the purpose for which we are assembled. My claims on your valuable time, Lamb, are made, you will recall, on the pretext of furnishing your mind with some historical facts.'

Then he dropped his eyes to the picture and, I suppose, saw it clearly for the first time. All he had realized till that minute was that Robert had played into his hands by drawing a picture instead of taking down notes. But now he saw *what* he had been drawing, and the full force of that moral diagnosis caught him across the face like a whip. I swear I actually heard him catch his breath. It's a long time ago, and we were on opposite sides of a fairly large room, but I heard him.

I expected a tirade, but for the moment the Bloater could think of nothing to say. He just tore the drawing across, then laid the two pieces together and tore them across. Then he laid the four pieces together and tore *them* across. About simultaneously with the second tear came the clatter of Robert's chair going over, and Robert was on his feet.

'You didn't have to do that,' he said quite quietly; he had not had time to feel anger yet – for the moment he was just shocked.

'Certainly I had to. It is a duty to maintain some sort of discipline.' The Bloater looked as if he were breathing more easily now that he had asserted himself and the picture didn't exist any more.

'Tearing up drawings isn't discipline,' said Robert. He began to advance towards the Bloater, looking fixedly at him.

'Making them isn't learning history, I might remind you.'

'Remind me nothing. A moment ago there was a drawing, and now it's a torn-up bit of paper. I did that drawing. I should have been listening to your tommy rot.'

'I won't stand insolence, Lamb!' the Bloater shouted. He took a step forward and the two faced each other, scowling.

'I should have been listening to your messed-up drivel,' Robert went on. 'But I did a drawing. So what. Punish me. Send me to the headmaster. But don't tear up drawings.'

'Don't say another word, Lamb, if you want to continue to be a pupil at this school,' the Bloater barked in his St Bernard voice, which was really terrifying. 'Get back to your place and I'll see if I can bring myself to overlook your insolence, your – '

'I said don't tear up drawings!' Robert shouted. 'Don't ever do it again, don't ever do it again, do you hear?'

They went on shouting 'Get back to your place!' and 'Don't tear up drawings!' for what seemed about ten minutes. They both had powerful voices and the room was absolutely full of noise. I was sure the whole school would drop what they were doing and come racing to see who had gone mad. Then, quite suddenly, the tension dropped. Instead of attacking one another, Robert and the Bloater began arguing in more or less normal voices.

'What am I to do when you ignore my efforts to teach you?'

'Destroying a work of art can't by definition be anything other than a swine's trick.'

'Setting aside whether this impertinent scribble was a work of art – '

'I won't set it aside. I won't agree to set it aside. It was a drawing I was pleased with, and I drew it. That makes it art.'

'Trying to educate you is already a thankless task, without finding that instead of paying the slightest attention you're scribbling impertinent caricatures.'

'Some of the greatest drawings were done as caricatures, and we don't even recognize the people any more. It isn't a question of impertinence – '

'Lamb!' The Bloater was beginning to shout again. 'Allow me, if you please, to be the best judge of what constitutes impertinence on the part of a pupil!'

'And allow me to be the best judge of what's art and what isn't art,' Robert snapped.

For a moment I thought they were going to start another bawling-match, but at that moment the bell rang for the end of the period, and the whole situation suddenly became obsolete.

Afterwards I couldn't tell how much Robert cared about the loss of his drawing. I did make one effort to commiserate with him, but he didn't seem interested in the incident from an ordinary point of view. His feeling about it seemed to be mainly a superstitious one.

'Bad luck,' he said, with something like a shudder.

'Yes, it was rotten luck,' I agreed. 'That's the trouble with –'

'You don't understand!' he said. 'To have one of my drawings torn up, by a lout like him – to let his insensitive, horny hands destroy something I'd made . . . it's asking for trouble.' And he stared at me.

'What kind of trouble?' I asked. But he just shrugged, as if it wouldn't be any good explaining. Looking back, I can see it was some sort of numinous bad luck he was thinking of. The gods had given him the power to make something, and it was his duty not to let his creation fall into the hands of the enemy. His indignation must have sprung from fear – fear of offending the Powers on whom he depended for his gift. As I say, I can see that now, but at the time I didn't yet know how his mind worked, and I certainly didn't realize how superstitious he was.

I never saw Ned, or anyone else, take the Bloater on in that sort of way. And the funny thing is that Robert didn't seem to have any special grudge against the Bloater after that; he reverted to his usual indifference to the man's existence, punctuated by rows, though never as violent as that one. In the end too he decided to contribute an essay to the Book of the Bloater-bait; he took the Book home one evening, as if merely wishing to look through it, and brought it back the next day with the addition of a very long and elaborate essay, much the longest of the lot, on 'The Technique of the Pseudo-quotation'. He had developed a method of rattling the Bloater by larding his essays with phony quotations which he attributed to people like Hilaire Belloc. There were always enough genuine ones to keep the Bloater guessing, and if he demanded precise sources Robert would make up some marvellous book titles. 'It's from Chapter III of *The Inception of Protestant Europe*,' he would say loftily, 'published in 1910'; or, 'I thought that was a book you'd mentioned to us yourself – *The Crusades, from the Beginning to the Dominant Phase.*' His contribution to the Book was the best of them of course. It had to be. It was the only way he could avoid looking like one of Ned's team.

As for me, I contributed a one-and-a-half-page essay on 'Strategic Coughing – Summer and Winter'. Mine was the worst contribution.

# II

At first sight it may seem odd that Robert and Ned ever saw anything of each other after we all left school. They seemed destined to follow utterly different paths if ever two youths did. Beyond the accident that they went to the same school, you would have thought there was nothing that could have caused their lives to touch.

But in fact this intertwining of their lives, like most things, loses a lot of its strangeness when you come to look at it more closely. Robert was an artist; that is, although he still had many a long journey to go before he had mastered his art, he already had, at eighteen, the fully developed mentality of an artist; he saw himself as one, and recognized the impossibility of his being anything else. He might have entered some sort of art school, but for one thing times were bad, and there wasn't the spare cash for him to go on being a non-earner after leaving school; for another, his grandparents would have received any such suggestion not merely with opposition but with outright incredulity. The problem would have been to get them to believe their ears. Robert to go and have an expensive training to be an *artist*? To convey any such idea to them, you would have had to repeat it in a monotone about five thousand times, at the same time writing it on a blackboard, flashing it on an illuminated screen, feeding it through on ticker-tape, and playing a musical version of it on a gramophone record. As there would not have been the slightest question of getting them to *agree* to the proposal once you had driven it into their heads, it would hardly have been worth the trouble.

Given this situation what did an artist do next? Obviously he made use of the fact that the local industry used people who could paint and invent designs. To be employed, earning money, as a visual artist – of whatever kind – was the most convenient send-off Robert could have given himself.

So, when the day came, we left school (all of us about equally grateful that, whatever the future held, *that* nonsense was over), and nobody was surprised when Robert joined Ned's firm as a designer, any more than they were surprised at my going on to the local sheet as a reporter. To grasp the kind of business relationship they had in mind, you have to picture the cosy family way these small-scale pottery businesses are run. It might seem odd that Ned, just leaving school and going into the business, should take along a youth of his own age on the more or less explicit understanding that he was going to spiral up to being head of the design department as soon as he got used to the way things were run. But then, for one thing, there wasn't a 'design department'. There were one or two fellows about the place who thought up ideas of their own in the intervals of overseeing the girls who sat at trestle tables and did the painting. Chiefly a man called Baxter, a harmless bore of about thirty-five who had risen from the ranks, so to speak, and had the gift of thinking up designs that were hideous enough to sell in the usual markets. All Baxter had to do was to work out a design that he, personally, would like to see on his crockery at home, and it was a seller. He was so representative. It's depressing to think how much all the industries depend on their Baxters, but they do. Robert, of course, hated Baxter's insides from the first. He could hardly bring himself to speak to him. But Ned worked it so that they didn't tread on each other's toes. He did this, chiefly, by tying different labels on them. Baxter was the Man Who Knew What Folks Want. Robert was the Genius. This went over with surprisingly little trouble, because Robert, like Ned, had succeeded in getting those about him to accept him at his own valuation of himself, i.e. that he was a Genius. Baxter could look after the average department, and Robert would look after the things that needed Genius. And quite a lot of things were going to need Genius, because it was Ned's idea to break away from the old channels and go in for a more chic, not to say chi-chi, line of stuff altogether. While the others were playing safe with chamber-pots and coronation mugs, he was going all out on ash-trays shaped like banana leaves – that kind of thing.

So Robert got the Genius department. I used to look in now and again and spend half an hour watching him at it. The Genius Room was a little cubicle in one of the painting shops, made by erecting a few fibre boards and putting a door in. The door didn't have Robert's name on it; to have your name on a door is a thing of mystical significance in any factory, implying that you have ceased to recognize any limit to the power you can wield within the structure of the place. It was just 'Mr Lamb's place'. Mr Lamb being the Resident Genius. What he seemed to be doing most of the time was doodling on cups and saucers. He'd have a pile of crocks round him, unglazed ones so that they had a kind of porous surface he could paint on, and tubes of colour, pots of water, bits of sponge, and all the rest of the gear. Then he'd pick up a teacup, go into a trance, and start smearing his brush against it. All the time he was doing this he'd keep up a long, snarling monologue, usually about Baxter. I particularly remember one afternoon, about six months after he had started work.

'Know how Baxter does his designs?' he was saying. 'He gets a piece of paper and draws a flower on it. Sometimes it's a daisy and sometimes it's a bluebell.' He dragged his brush across the saucer he was holding in his left hand. 'If he branches out any more I expect it'll be pixies or doggy-woggies. So right. He gets this piece of paper. And he makes a nice little design on it, about an inch and a half across, measuring in all directions. Just the right size for a transfer. Because his idea is that if one daisy or bluebell is all right, then a string of them, equally spaced, is going to be all right.' He drew the brush across the saucer again, meanly, as if wishing to humiliate it. Some sort of pattern seemed to be growing. 'And he goes in and leaves these designs on Ned's desk. The poor sod. I don't feel angry with him, Joe. I just feel sorry for him.'

'Yes?' I said.

'Sorry,' Robert repeated, stabbing his brush angrily at the saucer. 'His vision. It's so tragically limited.'

'Get off,' I said. I should explain that 'Get off' is an expression

26

much used in North Staffordshire as an ironic rejoinder to obvious remarks.

'Yes,' said Robert. 'He doesn't realize that this is an integrated activity.' He wasn't looking up at me; he was staring angrily at the saucer, spattering and twisting colour on to it more and more rapidly. I began to realize that he needed this grumbling as an accompaniment to his work, as some artists need to smoke or chew something or have the wireless on. It didn't matter whether or not I was listening or agreeing with him. 'He thinks that if you draw something on a bit of paper you can tell just by looking at it whether it's any good. He doesn't realize that the physical sensation of holding a cup or plate in your hand is all part of it. Something's flowing through the nerves of the hand that's holding the thing, something that your brain needs to make the design valid. In fact, the mere eyesight that Baxter puts his sole reliance in, the poor bastard, is probably the least indispensable element. I bet I could do some interesting designs blindfold, as long as I could hold the cup in my hand and knew what colours I was putting on. Here' – he jumped up – 'let's have a go.'

He began to arrange his pots of colour and his brushes where he could pick them up easily, and to rummage for a suitably shaped cup.

'This one'll do,' he said. 'Here, Joe, tie this behind my head.' He gave me his handkerchief.

'Why not put the paint on with your tongue?' I asked. 'The taste papillae are probably the most receptive centres.' But I did as he told me. One always did.

'Right,' he said, as soon as the blindfold was in place. 'Now just let me get the feel of the cup.' He began to fondle it in a way that I can only call lascivious. 'There's a special rhythm of design that goes, integrally *goes*, with this shape and weight.' He poised his brush.

Then a flat voice spoke from the doorway.

'Mr Lamb,' he said. 'Don't you think you ought to be getting on with some work instead of just wasting the firm's time?'

Actually he pronounced it more like 'faarm' and 'weark'. I can't be bothered to work out phonetic equivalents for these things. But imagine a self-righteous, though quite polite, voice, with the flat, nasal accent of North Staffordshire. Baxter, of course, rather pleased at having caught Robert making a fool of himself.

27

Robert looked up, although he couldn't see. I had turned to look at Baxter, but he was gazing past me, keeping his eyes on Robert's blindfold as if he were trying to see his eyes through it. They stared at each other, one sightless, the other full of accusing vigilance. I felt out of it somehow. What they call *de trop*.

'Do me a favour, Baxter,' said Robert, jigging the cup up and down in his hand. 'Scrub off. Take a powder.'

'It's the firm's time,' Baxter insisted.

'He's carrying out an experiment,' I put in. I think that was what damaged the situation beyond repair. Baxter just thought I was ribbing him. One of Robert's ne'er-do-well friends, hanging round and encouraging him to play the fool in the firm's time. He shot me a look of distilled hatred, but declined to waste his breath on me.

'It'd be better all round if you'd take that thing off your eyes, Mr Lamb, and get on with your work,' he said, the honest, bluff John Bull. The effect was spoilt by the fact that he was only about as big as a rat. Actually I didn't feel annoyed with him. He must have felt that the firm had to be protected from people like Robert, to say nothing of people like me; and from where he stood it must have looked pretty queer.

'Oh, Baxter, for God's sake run along,' Robert snapped. 'You're dissipating my creative mood.'

'Creative mood,' Baxter shouted. 'It's honest bloody work as we want here, not fooling about with a bloody cloth over your eyes and calling it creative mood!'

Robert snatched off the handkerchief and jumped up. The cup bounced on to the floor. His eyes, suddenly appearing, made all the difference to his face.

'Look, Baxter,' he said between his teeth. 'You and your honest work. You're the sort of person who'll keep this factory down in the mud, turning out cheap trash and getting a bare living out of it, for as long as you're – '

'Cheap trash!' Baxter shrieked. 'There's no cheap trash turned out from here! But that's you all over, isn't it? Decent bloody stuff that's good enough for sensible – ' He choked. 'Stuff that's done by artists that keep their bloody eyes open when they're painting. . . . That's what you'd call cheap trash – well, it was good enough before you ever – '

By the time he had got as far as the word 'sensible', Robert was shouting too, and some of the girls had left their tables and were coming down to see the show. The two of them kept shouting more and more loudly, and I put in an occasional volley to try and silence them. The noise was just at its peak when Ned appeared, framed in the doorway. Neither Robert nor Baxter saw him, and the first they knew of his presence was when he stepped quickly and decisively into the gap between them, which was by now a narrow one, and gripped each of them by the shoulder. They fell silent and he turned his head to look into their faces one after another; first Robert's, then Baxter's.

He was a head taller than either of them, which meant that he had to look slightly downwards to meet their eyes. The three of them made an extraordinary tableau – Ned, tall and fair, holding and dominating, thickset, dramatic Robert and weedy, angry Baxter.

'I won't ask you what it's all about', he said, 'because I'm not interested. I know it can't be anything but damn foolishness because any dispute between you two can't be anything else but damn foolishness. You're not here to quarrel. There's plenty of work for you both to do – work that's been specially laid on in such a way that you don't tread on each other's toes.'

He let go of their shoulders, and let his arms fall to his sides. Then he turned and looked across at me. The force of his personality, when he brought it to bear fully on a situation, was so blasting that for a moment he had me feeling that I was in for a dressing down myself – although my conscious mind knew perfectly well that I didn't work for him, and hadn't been doing anything wrong, and all the rest of it.

Anyway, he said nothing, just nodded to me and walked out. Almost on his heels, I walked out too, not waiting to see how Robert and Baxter went about putting the pieces together. It was none of my business.

That was the way things went on: quite exciting, with new ideas flowing out (though I never heard any more of the painting-blindfold idea), but really too stormy, too up-and-down, to last.

Quite often during those months I had the impression that Robert would have been glad of something that pushed things over the edge and made it inevitable for him to leave. I don't say 'gave him an excuse to leave', because he wasn't the kind of person who looked for excuses to do things; if it got to that stage he just did them. Things didn't get to that stage, or even very near it. But all the same Robert didn't like working for Ned, and, no matter how clever Ned was at not making him feel like an employee, things were always cropping up – that row with Baxter was an example – which forced Ned to demonstrate who was the boss. Robert was a success at his job; some of his designs are still selling; but I think they both shared my feeling that it couldn't last for ever.

Even so, it might have dragged on for years, because Ned was far too clever to have anything like a quarrel with Robert, or to allow anyone else to. The thing that finally wrenched them apart was a spoilt kiln. I'll explain what I'm talking about, but first let me set the scene.

I was round at Robert's house one week-night. We were going out for an evening on the beer, and he had asked me to pick him up. I timed it so that I arrived about ten minutes later than he had said, because I wanted to be sure he would be there and ready to go. This was because his grandparents, the walrus and the seal, got me down so much. I wanted to work it so that I didn't get asked in, or at any rate no further than the hall. That way, there would be no danger of having to start up some stumbling conversation with one or both of them, keeping it moving as fast as possible, however disjointedly, for fear of giving them a chance to introduce their favourite aria, which was called Things Are Bad. They always had some fresh illustration of how Bad Things Were, and were ready to slap you with it. I had found, on my few previous visits, that the walrus-grandfather was slightly easier to deal with than the seal-grandmother, because it was sometimes possible to head him off; he did have one other topic that interested him, and that was the career of Stanley Matthews. I found I could side-track him into Matthews quite easily, so of course I always did. I always had a few gambits ready, and I varied them cleverly. For instance, when Matthews had just signed on as a professional, the walrus obviously expected me to talk about that, but did I? No, siree. I talked about his father's hairdressing business and how valuable it must be, from the point of view of heredity, for a footballer to have a barber for a father. All those close shaves, that delicacy and lightness of touch. To say nothing of the physical toughness required of a barber, a man who had to be on his feet all day. Tireless men, barbers, one and all. I really threw that at him, I remember. He never got a chance to bring in how Bad

Things Were that evening. 'Have you ever seen a barber looking tired?' I asked him, challenging him to overthrow my thesis. He moved his big bald head about, anxious and puzzled, trying to fathom why I was talking such a lot of rubbish.

Anyway, on this particular night I wanted to cut all that out. So I went slightly late. But, as it turned out, it was no use. The seal opened the door to me and said that Robert was not back yet. They'd expected him over an hour earlier and kept his tea but he hadn't come. There was nothing for it but to go in and wait: she led me into the sitting-room, with her feet slapping the linoleum of the passage just like a seal's flippers.

I went in, and there was the walrus, sitting by the fire. It looked quite a cosy little domestic picture, but by way of greeting he started straight away to grumble about having to have a fire at all.

'More than half-way through April,' he said, poking fretfully at the coals. 'I can remember when we never needed a fire after the end of March.'

'And coal wasn't such a price then,' the seal struck in, 'if we had needed one.'

That set them off. I took out a packet of cigarettes and offered the walrus one, hoping to stem the flow a bit, but he accepted it and lit it without breaking his conversational rhythm, except to say, in an aside, that he thought I was a bit young to be smoking.

'I've seen good times and I've seen bad times,' he said, puffing cautiously at my cigarette (he did everything cautiously). 'And the only way I've been able to pull through even as well as I 'ave' – he only dropped his aitches when speaking with unusual emphasis – 'is by taking care to let a bit of brass stick to my fingers. And my advice to any young man,' etc.

I said that whatever happened it must be a relief to them to see Robert settled into a job and doing well.

'Doing well,' the walrus echoed, eyeing me carefully. 'That's 'ow it looks to you, I dare say. But just think 'ow it looks to me. Robert's in the pottery trade. So far, that's good. That's what I'd have advised him myself. But he's in it the wrong way about, so to speak. This designing, it's not as secure as the other branches. When a firm's got to shed a few men to get through a difficult patch, they often reckon they can do without a designer for a bit. One manufacturer even

31

told me, once, as he reckoned he could replace a designer, no matter 'ow good he was, easier than he could replace a good works foreman.'

The seal had been nodding her sleek grey head to all this, listening as attentively as if she had not already heard it scores of times. I relaxed and let his talk drone through the air round my head like a tired-out bee.

How long he kept it up about the insecurity of a designer's job I don't know, but I do remember that I was beginning to think Robert had forgotten all about our arrangement and that I had better go. I was vaguely searching my mind for some formula to excuse my departure, when we heard the front door open, Robert's footsteps came rapidly down the passage, and he burst in, looking pretty wild about the eyes.

'You're late, lad,' said the walrus, not unkindly but stiffly. 'Your gran's been keeping your tea waiting.'

'Got held up at the works, sorry,' said Robert offhandedly. 'Can't always foresee these things. It'd be one thing if we had a telephone here.'

He might have known that this sort of remark wouldn't do any good, but I could see he was in no mood to be tactful. The seal and the walrus went into a 'You-seem-to-have-no-idea-about-money' routine, which Robert utterly ignored; in fact he barely waited for it to finish before turning to me with, 'Coming, Joe?'

'What about your tea?' his grandmother piped.

'I'm not hungry, gran,' said Robert. He turned to her and tried to give her a flashing smile, to counterbalance the bad mood this would put her in, but his face was tense with strain and all he could manage was a really terrifying grimace.

'Not hungry?' The old man took him up. 'Are you ill or something?'

'I feel all right.'

'Well, all I can say, if you feel all right, is, you ought not to waste good food – not to mention the trouble your gran's taken to – '

'Three hundred and sixty-five!' Robert suddenly yelled, half an octave above his normal pitch. 'Three hundred and sixty-five times a year I come home and eat my tea and don't waste the good food and do think of all the trouble that's been taken . . . And just once when I come home a bit late and say I'm not hungry and – '

It was one of those typical, silly family rows that blow up over nothing and leave everyone shaking with rage. I could sympathize with them all round; I could see that from their point of view Robert was being pretty impossible, and yet I could also see that if I had to live with the seal and the walrus I should be impossible at times. But this wide-ranging sympathy, though no doubt it did me credit, didn't do anything to make me less uncomfortable. After a brief but sharp exchange of views on all sides (except my side), Robert swept out, more or less dragging me with him; and as the front door closed behind us, I'll guarantee I was feeling as chewed up as he was.

Neither of us said anything until we got to the pub. Possibly with some idea of showing that we were masters of ourselves, we didn't just dive into the nearest one, but doggedly trudged on till we got to our 'usual', about a mile away. It was still early and we had the private bar to ourselves. I remember the cheerfulness of the gas-fire and the empty ash-trays laid out neatly on the little tables.

We ordered pints and solemnly held up our tankards in salutation before taking the first draught. We hadn't been drinking beer very long, and to take a pint mug in one's hand still seemed a wonderfully adult thing to do (it was to be several years before that glow quite faded), but I noticed that Robert just drank his as if it had been water. Obviously there *was* something the matter; or, more precisely – for he hadn't exactly the air of a man in *trouble* – some very important issue was taking up all his attention. I was about to ask him to spill it, when he spoke first.

'You're a news-hound, Joe,' he said.

'A newspaper reporter,' I substituted, not caring to stand any insolence about the Fourth Estate.

'And yet here you stand, with your foot on a rail,' he went on, 'all unconscious of a piece of important news in the local industry.'

'Let me guess,' I said. 'You've devised a new aesthetically integrated spittoon.'

'No,' he said, and looked at me unwaveringly to let me know he wasn't joking. 'A spoilt kiln.'

I whistled. 'Not at Roper's?'

'At Roper's.'

In the pottery industry a spoilt kiln is the disaster of

disasters. When the ware is ready for firing they stack it in the kiln (pronounced 'kill' locally, for some reason) and keep it at a fantastic temperature for about thirty hours. This temperature has to be even and the art of firing is to feed the coal in so that it doesn't vary; if it wanders up and down, the entire contents of the 'kill' come out distorted and have to be thrown away. And that means several hundred pounds' worth of pottery.

I thought quickly. Roper's, like any small firm at that time, was already riding pretty low in the water; an extra burden like this could sink it, unless Ned could be clever about getting help from the bank or something.

'This isn't good,' I said.

'Cheer up,' said Robert. He drained his pint sturdily, as if suddenly waking up to the fact that it was beer and deserved to be swigged with an air. 'It'll be a valuable lesson to Ned at the outset of his career. It'll teach him to employ good workmen who know how to fire a kill.'

'Anybody can spoil a kill now and again, and you know it,' I said. 'This won't teach Ned anything except how to grow ulcers.'

Robert laughed, and called the landlord over to fill our mugs. His whole bearing had altered suddenly.

'Fortunately I can help him,' he said, turning to me with my mug in his outstretched hand.

I was too startled to think of taking it. 'Help him?'

'Save him some money.'

'Oh.' I took the beer. 'So it is an idea of yours that's the news scoop.'

'In a way,' Robert smiled. He raised his glass. 'Wish me luck.'

'Doing what?'

'Going to London.'

I was disappointed. Why, even people like me, who didn't expect to have any colour in their lives, went to London. I had been several times. 'How long for?' I asked him.

'For good, you ass. I'm leaving Ned's.'

'Dash my rags,' I said. I looked at him attentively, but he obviously wasn't fooling. Some of the wild look had come back into his eyes too, as if the seriousness of what he was doing was building up a pressure inside him. Yet he seemed quite steady.

'I give you a toast,' he said. 'My London period.'

'Your London period,' I said, and we drank.

In the silence that followed, we thought of London, the impossible London of the provincial adolescent, the smoky swamp full of jewelled toads, the dirt-track where racing taxis full of millionaires skid together in a shower of sovereigns, the pallid aviary of bank-notes flapping their wings in time to the cunning chimes of Big Ben.

Still, we couldn't stay inside this reverie for long, in the face of the pressing realities, and after a minute or two I asked Robert to try and explain his motive in going.

'Don't start telling me it's a case of pure consideration for Ned,' I said. 'It's nice of you to spare him the expense of your wages, but that can't be all.'

For an instant Robert looked as if he were about to flare up, and either tell me to mind my own business or insist that the whole thing *was* pure altruism; but before a word came out he had changed his mind, and he merely turned to the bar, picked up his tankard with a rather weary gesture, and drank from it. He had the air of a man who is turning over a number of things in his mind.

'The point is, isn't it,' I said, helping him, 'that the spoilt kiln gives you a heaven-sent opportunity to get away.'

'That's putting it too crudely,' he objected.

'All right, let's *be* crude. You want to get away from here and go to London and lead the artistic life. But what's waiting for you when you get there is so hellish that even *you* shrink from it. So you have to have some big colourful justification – "I can't be a burden to Ned at a time like this" – to make it seem all right and give you the motive to stifle your hesitations.'

Robert yawned. His tension seemed to have drained away, leaving him, if anything, rather bored with the discussion.

'Well, analyse it if you like, Joe,' he said flatly. 'I'm going. When I heard about the damage, it seemed to flash on me suddenly how much I wanted to get away. And this seemed the right moment, when I wouldn't seem to be doing it just out of the blue. I don't suppose anybody'll be fooled. I expect they'll all be like you and say I wanted an excuse to go and picked on the first one that came up.'

'What about your people?' I asked, meaning the seal and the walrus.

'They'll be asleep,' he said shortly.

For a moment I thought he was speaking in metaphor. It just didn't strike me that he really meant *asleep*. Then it did strike me.

'You don't mean to say', I asked, 'that you're going to sneak out in the dead of night?'

He nodded. 'What else?'

I understood then, of course. He just wasn't going to put up with all the caterwauling. All the same, it was pretty sudden.

'Dash my rags,' I said again. I took another drink out of my tankard, trying to get abreast of the situation. Then another thought struck me. 'This'll make it pretty hard for you to come back.'

'Come *back*?' Robert asked incredulously, as if I were mad.

So he was *really* going it. Putting a match to his boats and bridges right in front of my eyes. All I could think of to ask was, 'When?'

'Tonight, of course,' he said.

This time I really had to cling to the bar. It was all so rapid. Going off! For ever! Tonight! Impossible to return!

'You're what they call impulsive,' I said, watching him narrowly to see if he would rebut the charge. But he just took no notice.

'Let's have another drink, Joe,' he said. 'We might as well get a few inside us, considering all we've got to do before the night's out.'

'We?' I asked, still watching him.

'You'll come along with me, won't you?' he said, not wheedling at all, but merely in the same tone in which he would have asked, 'This is the way to the town hall, isn't it?'

In a way the parallel was quite a close one, because in his mind I represented something rather like the town hall. You know – immovable, useful, not exciting, that sort of thing. And he knew the way to me all right. I didn't even have to say Yes. I just got the beer and handed him his.

'The strategy's dead simple,' he said, setting his mug down after a long swig. 'The old folks always go to bed about ten. They don't wait up for me. So we'll stay in the pub till closing time, then walk about a bit to give them a chance to get safely off to sleep, then I'll duck in and put a few immediate necessities in a case, and off.'

'Leaving a message written in duck's blood on the mirror,'

I said. 'Just what is the special satisfaction it gives you to go about the thing in this melodramatic way? You could perfectly well give it a day or two, fix up some accommodation in London, and state your case for going like a normal sane person.'

'State my case!' Robert jeered loudly. 'Can you imagine me stating my case to the sort of people I'm surrounded by? Can you imagine me trying to talk the old folks into it, then talk Ned into it? I'd be so exhausted at the end of that lot that I'd have to talk myself into it.'

He splashed a lot of beer down his throat, then banged his mug down. 'State my case!' he cried more loudly. It seemed to be the phrase that had annoyed him, more than the suggestion itself. 'That's rich! As if my position was the sort that can be stated . . . as if . . . as if . . .' He went on maundering, dropping his voice to an undertone, then burst out in a loud hiss, 'All I want to do with my case is to pack it.'

'Yes, but what train are you going on?' I persisted, still sticking to my role of human ballast.

'Half past eleven,' he answered promptly. Evidently he'd looked up the train; it wasn't all a matter of wild impulse.

I held my head and rocked softly to and fro, freshly appalled.

'Look, Robert,' I said. 'For the love of God give it a few minutes' thought. It's a three-hour trip. That means you'll hit London at half past two, having had no sleep, and too late to – '

'Sleep!' he interrupted. 'What else have I had to do for the last nineteen years in this dump but sleep? Even when I was awake, dressed and moving about, I was asleep inside me. The core of my mind hasn't woken up once yet. It's been asleep ever since I was born, because there's never been anything worth waking it up to take part in. Well, now it's awake at last.'

'All right,' I said pacifically. I didn't want him to work himself up any more.

'Awake at last!' he shouted, banging his fist on the bar.

All the same, I was really concerned for him, and I rallied to the attack. If he had to go off to London and starve, all right, but at least one could try to persuade him to do it more steadily.

'Now look, Robert,' I said again. 'Just get a picture of the situation. You get to London. It's half past two. Probably it's raining, or foggy, or something. Anyway, it's London autumnal weather. You get off the train.'

'I get off the train,' he repeated as if hypnotized.

'And you're standing there with a suitcase in your hand.'

'I'm standing there with a suitcase in my hand.'

'Right – now what do you do?' I asked rather crossly. I was sick of his echoing me.

'Now what do I do?' he repeated in a trance. I was thankful there was nobody else in the bar, to see him behaving so strangely. 'I go over to the Left Luggage Office and I leave my case. Then I'm standing there without my suitcase in my hand. If there's an all-night refreshment bar open, I get a cup of coffee or something. If not, I do without. In either case, I walk off the station. The streets are deserted. Everybody in London is in bed, asleep. Except for the burglars robbing the houses, and the policemen looking out for the burglars, and the poets leaning out of their windows trying to read rhymes in the sky – just a few people like that. Even the whores are asleep. I'm not accosted. I'm not spoken to by anybody. Now and then a policeman looks at me a bit suspiciously, but I just walk past. When I find somewhere to live I'll be a Londoner, but just for tonight I'm nobody, not even a ghost. I'm alive, so I can't be a ghost. The houses and the cathedrals and the offices and the theatres and the all-in wrestling arenas and the pubs – they're all just waiting. The drains are waiting down underneath the streets. The birds are waiting in their nests, and the buses in their garages. And do you know what they're waiting for?'

'No,' I said. I supposed he was drunk, with having the beer on an empty stomach.

'For the dawn,' said Robert, leaning forward. 'It's their signal to start existing again. And I'm waiting for the dawn too. When it starts, I'll be standing in some back street in London. Nowhere grand, like St Paul's or Westminster Bridge or anything. And I'll see the dawn come up over London. That'll be my signal to start existing. And then I'll just wait till people are up and about and then go and get myself a room – and by the time you're having your breakfast I'll be a Londoner.'

'For Christ's sake,' I said weakly.

'And I'll deserve it too,' said Robert. 'There must be millions of people who've lived in London all their lives and haven't ever seen the dawn. I'll know something about their city that they don't know.'

'And they'll know something that you don't know,' I said. 'What to use for money.'

'Go ahead and be smart,' he said defiantly. 'You think that because I'm interested in things like seeing the dawn, because I'm equipped with the aesthetic sensibilities of a man rather than an ape, I must be an utter fool about practical things. Well, don't worry about it. I've got twenty-six pounds saved up, lying there in the bank, and another three in my pocket. I'm not jumping in without a lifebelt.'

'Twenty-nine pounds?' I said. 'Twenty-nine whole pounds between you and starvation? You'll have to be careful to choose a good address, somewhere like Park Lane or Knightsbridge. An income like that really needs living up to.'

All the same, I could see what he meant. At that time you could live – pretty miserably, but still live – on a pound a week. So he would have about six months to look around in. He had a point, though I didn't want to admit it for fear of encouraging him too much. Looking back on it now I can't see why I bothered – why I even thought I was having any influence on him at all. I suppose an utter lack of effect on another person is always a hard thing to admit to oneself.

Anyway, time passed with this and that, and as the bar slowly filled up we retreated to a corner and sat there doing nothing much except drink beer and watch the clock. It was rather like waiting to go out on a raid into enemy territory; we had our iron rations, our rope-soled shoes, pocket compasses and the rest of it, our faces were blacked and we had been given full instructions. Now all we had to do was wait. When the clock struck ten, Robert would walk out of the pub and begin the rapid process of shaking the dust off his feet. And the next morning, while I was still asleep in bed, he would be standing on some London pavement, saluting the dawn of his real life. We sat through several long silences – as ten o'clock approached it seemed to get harder and harder to think of anything to say – and I had plenty of time to realize the mixed nature of my feelings. The thing that chiefly struck me was the utter impossibility of imagining myself in Robert's position. I just couldn't think of a motive that would lead me to take any such frightening leap. Did that mean I was a coward then? From one point of view, yes, but from another (the usual one) I was merely being sensible and Robert very foolish. It all depended on how you looked at it. I tried to work along these lines, but all the time I knew it couldn't be done: I did feel myself inferior to Robert. I was the one with the common sense, but he was the one who was living on the grand scale; although he was still within the framework we had both always known, sitting there beside me in our usual pub, he had already left me behind and broken through into another dimension. All I could do was to wonder what it was like there; I knew I should never inhabit it.

'Ned's going to be livid,' I said at seven minutes to ten.

Robert had been sitting in reverie, but he answered immediately to this stimulus. 'Ned doesn't need me.'

'I didn't say he needed you. I said he was going to be livid at you ducking out. He'll just see it as another disaster on top of the spoilt kiln.'

'Let him,' said Robert, flapping his hand in dismissal. 'I did plenty of designs he hasn't got round to using yet. He'll be able to keep on issuing them for years.' (This was true.) 'He won't know I've gone except when he comes to make out the pay cheques.'

'Last orders,' the landlord droned. I stared at him, momentarily unable to believe that he could say anything so symbolic without being conscious of it. 'Shall we have another one?' I asked Robert. But as I turned to speak to him I could see that his tension had suddenly returned and gripped him; he was standing up, crazy to get out into the street, as if by beginning to pace about a few minutes before it was necessary he could somehow hurry time along, force his grandparents into bed and to sleep, speed up the train that was already hurrying towards him, clench his powerful hands round the bull's horns. 'Let's get out,' he muttered, more to himself than to me, and strode towards the door.

On his way out an old fellow sitting in a cane chair reached up as if to grab his coat. 'Young man,' he said. 'Eh, young man.'

Robert halted, and raised his eyebrows.

'Yer weark at Roper's, dunna yer?'

The eyebrows came down and the head nodded. It was like watching a marionette.

'Is it true as they 'ad a spoilt kill this mornin'?'

Some of the other men struck in to say that there was no need to ask Roper's employees – everyone knew it. But most of them kept quiet and waited to hear what extra bit of news Robert could add.

He waited for a silence and then said, as if unable to believe his ears. 'Spoilt kill?'

'Aye,' they cried.

Robert shook his head pityingly. 'I'm sorry you're all so easy to take in,' he said. 'You ought to have your heads screwed on right, with all your experience of the trade. What Roper's were doing was to produce a batch of experimental pottery – they were varying the oven temperature on purpose to produce a new set of spatial density relationships.'

I liked 'spatial density relationships'. It sounded good and for a moment it had them baffled. Then a hubbub of derision and incredulity broke out. He had managed to fool them for a couple of seconds, and they were laughing as much at themselves as at him.

'Last ORDERS!' the landlord shouted through the noise.

Robert bowed as if acknowledging applause, and we slipped out into the street. I was glad he had made an exit, even if he had had to do it by talking rubbish. I knew the difference it made to his spirits.

And he was right, certainly, to jump at anything that gave him a bit of a lift. It was pretty depressing out in the street, with a gusty wind throwing handfuls of light drizzle in your face, and half an hour's hanging about to be got through somehow. I'd have suggested taking him home with me to wait it out, but that would have involved letting a third person in on the act: my mother. With her sitting there it would have been hopeless to try and pretend that Robert had just dropped in for a cup of coffee. My father was one of the last men to be killed in 1918, and ever since then my mother has had nothing to do, in the intervals of bringing me up, except sit about and see through people's evasions. She isn't censorious – she just sees through people's evasions. I winced at the thought of confronting her with Robert, at this point.

We walked round the streets, not saying anything. For the first few minutes it was quiet, and then the pubs started emptying and the pavements were crowded with men talking, arguing and laughing. There wasn't much traffic, and they crowded the narrow streets, calling across to one another, keeping up an endless flow of sharp little fragments of repartee. These people, in the town I mustn't name, aren't dour, like

Northerners; on the other hand they aren't shut up inside themselves, like the southern English; they're volatile, friendly and sardonic. The more they like each other the faster the sharp little epigrams fly through the air, like a non-stop conversational darts match.

We shuffled along, in the procession but not of it, and once Robert broke his silence to say, 'I like these people.' I said, 'I wonder if you'll find them likeable where you're going?'

'What's the difference?' He took me up sharply. 'I'm the person I've got to like. Besides, I can only afford to like these people here because I'm already on my way out. If I had to stay bogged down here, I'd hate them. I'd think of them as so many jailers.'

After that we didn't speak. We just paced along, and as the half-hour ran out I realized that we had our faces turned towards Robert's home. Finally we were standing outside the back garden gate. The front of the house gave on to the street, and the back on to a long, narrow garden, with a gate opening on a rough sandy path; on the other side of this path lay the back gardens of a similar set of houses. Robert muttered, 'Wait here', and I was left standing in the narrow strip between two garden fences. The reason I remember the setting so well was because it was so utterly quiet. We were inside the town, but the town was away beyond the long strips of garden and the tall houses. It was as quiet as some Devonshire lane; a cat came padding along the top of the fence and I could almost hear it laying its feet down in a fastidious straight line. Last orders! I thought; it was like the moment of immobility before a swimmer dives in. A slight stirring drew my attention, and I saw for the first time that there was a pair of lovers about twenty yards away, standing well back in the shadows to get on with a quiet bit of necking. Amid this stillness, life was going on just as much as in some roaring street; the cat was hunting; the lovers were on the way to spawning a child; in the dark house in front of me Robert was walking along the diving board. All I could do was hope to God he wasn't going to find he'd gone into the shallow end.

I heard a door click, and then he was coming along the garden path, carrying one quite small suitcase. I opened the gate for him, like a servant.

'Clean as a whistle,' he said, chuckling; action always sent his spirits up.

42

'Did you leave a note?' I asked.

He shook his head. 'No time. I'll post one from London.'

'That won't get them till the day after tomorrow.'

'Too bad,' said Robert, starting off past the lovers with his suitcase.

I followed, feeling that for the present purposes I ought to have been a woman. It was a woman's part to persuade Robert to show a little more tenderness. Coming from me, it just wouldn't sound good enough. It wasn't as if I liked the seal and the walrus much. Still, I tried.

'You might spare them the anxiety,' I said to his back.

Through the gloom I heard him laugh shortly. 'Anxiety! Yes, they might be anxious in case I came back. I think I'll send them a telegram. "Swine husks delicious, cancel fatted calf." '

There was over an hour to wait, but we went straight to the station. At least we could be sitting down there, and not lugging the suitcase. In the waiting-room we sat looking about, avoiding each other's eyes, trying not to make it seem that we were searching for topics.

'London,' I said at last.

Robert's eyes brightened. I'm sorry to use such a cliché, but they actually did brighten.

'Where I ought to have been all along,' he said.

I silently agreed. At that time it seemed a reasonable proposition. I hadn't realized yet that the only reason England has any intellectual and artistic life at all is because men like Robert aren't reared in London. They take their originality with them, and London consumes it all and gives them nothing back. It's because the provinces accept dreariness that London can boast of its brilliance. But I had to live a few years yet before I could see things of that kind.

A very long silence followed. We didn't even say anything when we heard the train coming into the station. We just sat on in our chairs until it actually drew up, as if we didn't trust it to be the right train until it stopped and introduced itself.

'London Euston!' the porter shouted, as if it were all perfectly natural. Robert took hold of his bag, but in spite of his outward calm I could see that he didn't think it all perfectly natural

'So long, Joe,' he said and got on to the train.

43

'Remember me to the dawn,' I said.

He smiled and went into the compartment. I saw him putting his case on to the rack. The train stood there for a little while, but I didn't expect Robert to come back to the window to say any last words. I waited, just in case, but he didn't. Then the train pulled out.

# III

After that I didn't hear anything from, or about, Robert for some months. I was learning to be a newspaper man, and that gave me enough to think about. Still, I did have the grace to feel a bit ashamed of myself when I got a picture postcard from a Chelsea address, smudgily inscribed, 'Come and see how the other half do it.' I really ought to have thought about him more, I told myself. So the next time I ran into Ned we hatched a scheme for going to see Robert together. He suggested it, actually, and I could quite see why. It would tide them over that awkward first meeting if I was there.

The scheme fell through, at the last minute, because of some big business deal Ned had to stay and attend to. So I went up alone, with his assurance that he'd follow, either late on the same night or first thing in the morning. To this day I don't know how genuine that sudden bit of urgent business was; perhaps he just got cold feet and wanted me to go ahead and soften things up. Anyway, there I was, on a fine May evening, wandering about Chelsea trying to find this place, Chesterfield Mews.

Nobody seemed to know, even in the pubs along the King's Road, and I hadn't got a street plan or anything. There didn't seem to be any policemen about either, and by about nine o'clock I was really wondering what to do. I wandered down towards the river, making up my mind to have one more really intensive try; for half an hour I would ask *every* person who came along, even children, drunks, obvious criminals and perverts, beggars, evangelists, handbill distributors, sandwich men, parsons, Lascar stokers, deaf mutes, to tell me where Chesterfield Mews was. I wouldn't pass over *anyone*.

The first person who came along was a good specimen of the type I wouldn't have asked if it hadn't been for my resolution. She was a woman of about sixty, dressed like a young girl. She had sandals and bare legs, and her hair fell straight down across her forehead in a fringe. She had dyed this fringe blonde, but the rest of her hair was almost entirely grey. She had a pair of ear-rings on that looked as if they were made of wood, and she was carrying a big leather bag which seemed to be full of potatoes. I felt really sorry for her. One of the casualties of modern life, I thought.

When I asked her where Chesterfield Mews was, she looked at me skittishly. She'd encircled her poor baggy old eyes with stuff that looked like blacklead, and the eyes themselves were as bloodshot as hell. But her voice seemed to have kept fresher than the rest of her; it was one of those professionally modulated voices that people only get if they go on the stage.

'I'm going there myself,' she phrased. 'You can walk along with me.'

I said it was very good of her and I'd be glad to carry the potatoes.

'They're figurines, not potatoes,' she said. 'Abstract designs, in china. I'm just bringing them back from being fired.' But she was quite kind about it. I said I was short-sighted and always thought anything was a potato if it was about the size of one.

We lolloped along. She talked most of the way about what a nice neighbourhood Chesterfield Mews was in. Full of character. I just listened and wondered if everyone that lived there looked like her. She kept saying it was an oasis, and after about the third time she said it she began to shuffle like a camel. Her ear-rings swayed like temple bells and she began to raise her voice till she was chanting like a muezzin. Looking back on it, I'm surprised I wasn't more taken aback by the whole thing, but I suppose the reason was that, to a nineteen-year-old provincial, London was in any case as exotic as Baghdad; it was the place where you might find *anything*.

As we walked on I got bolder, and determined to show that I knew my way about. Man-of-the-world stuff. So I said, 'When were you on the stage?'

For a moment the old dame didn't answer, and I thought she was asking herself how I came to know so much about her. I got a smirk ready. Then she said, in an ominously quiet voice, 'May I ask why you put that in the past tense?'

That stumped me. I couldn't very well tell her the truth, which was that I naturally assumed anyone as old as her must have retired from the stage about thirty years previously. It wouldn't have surprised me to learn that her last appearance had been with Sir Henry Irving in *The Bells*.

So I gave a light laugh. 'Ha, ha,' I said. 'It's like the potatoes, isn't it? Just not thinking what I was saying. And then, of course, so many of the theatrical people you meet have left the stage now that it's been knocked all ends up. The cinema,' I babbled. 'The wireless.' In view of her age I might have added something about the gramophone and the magic lantern, but I didn't.

'The theatre is as living today as ever it was,' she said, declaiming like Medea. 'For a genuine artist there is always a place. I have as much work now as ever I did.'

I didn't ask her how much *that* was.

'In some respects the theatre is healthier now than when my mother was a girl,' she went on. 'Don't swing the bag about too much, you'll crack the figurines.'

When her mother was a girl, I thought, Shakespeare was at the height of his powers. Some people are never satisfied.

Given another few minutes I'd have smoothed the slight roughness out of the situation. After all she wasn't a bad-tempered old thing; she was just standing on her dignity as a promising young actress, a thing she was obviously prepared to go on doing as long as there was room on her birthday cake for all the candles. But before I had a chance to open my tanks and release a flood of oil over the waves, we had rounded a corner and this was Chesterfield Mews. I had just time to notice that it was gaunt and peeling and Victorianly tatty, before she halted at the foot of some crumbling grey stone steps and waved her hand towards the house. 'This is where I'm going,' she said.

I saw the number. 'Me too,' I said, trying to keep my voice neutral. I didn't want her to think I was surprised to find myself going to a house that anybody as cracked as her would live in. But inwardly I was feeling that Robert couldn't be making much of a success of things, if he was having to live in the same house as this poor old thing with her delusions and her potato figurines.

'Who was it you wanted to see?' she asked.

'Mr Lamb. Robert Lamb,' I said.

For some reason she laughed, first naturally and then, remembering that she was an actress, stagily. Long after the idea, whatever it was, had ceased to strike her as funny, she went on giving peal after peal, just for practice.

'Let me in on the joke,' I said testily.

At that moment the window at the top of the house was thrown open. It was directly above us, but it was about a thousand feet high, and in the dusk I didn't see at first whose head came thrusting out. But when I heard his voice I knew I had found Robert.

'Darling, come up, don't just stand there,' he called.

'All right,' I called.

There was a pause and then he said, 'Celia.'

'Yes,' says this old woman.

'Who is it you've got with you?'

'A friend of yours, darling,' she called, grubbing in her handbag for the key.

'I'm the potato man,' I shouted, getting irritable.

He leaned out till I thought he would fall on me and called, 'Is it Joe?'

I would have answered, but by this time the old hag had found her key and let us in. Silently I followed her up the stairs, which seemed to go on for ever. I kept telling myself that it didn't matter that Robert and the crone called each other 'darling'. She was on the stage, after all, or somewhere near it, and theatrical people always called each other 'darling'. Besides, for all I knew to the contrary, the word was a usual mode of address in London.

Finally we got to the top of the stairs. The old girl didn't seem very worn out by the climb; she was like a tough, stringy old chicken. I was blowing a bit, but of course even in those days I was carrying too much weight.

There was Robert in this awful attic place, with a cracked skylight, easels and all the rest of the stuff.

'Nice to see you, Joe,' he said, but instead of coming across to shake my hand, or anything like that, he actually put his arms round the old dame and gave her a kiss. Not the sort you give to your auntie either.

47

'Introduce me,' I said. This was another London habit I hadn't heard about.

He gave me her name. It was something like Celia Ratsrake. I didn't catch it properly and somehow I never cared to check on it.

After a minute the bag went out and I said, 'What's it like living on your own?'

'On my own?' said Robert incredulously. 'Oh, I see, you're asking it as a trap question. Well, don't worry. This isn't the provinces, you know. I'm living with Celia, as you can see perfectly well.'

'Has she reached the age of consent?' I asked.

'As a matter of fact she has,' said Robert heavily. 'As a matter of fact I find life with a mature woman a lot more pleasant. I'm not under any illusions. I know Celia will never see forty again.'

'Oh, come,' I said. 'She was exaggerating when she told you that. She was in fun. She said it with your tongue in her cheek.'

'And I'd like to know what bloody business it is of yours,' said Robert, lapsing easily into the manner we had used towards one another back home. It suited him better than this 'as a matter of fact' stuff.

'I'm just jealous,' I said. 'A mature woman. It's just what I've always wanted. Only I find it hard to click with mature women. They've got security and it makes them smug. They don't want anything else.'

'What do you mean, they've got security?'

'The Old Age Pension,' I said. 'Ten shillings a week.'

That was what it was in those days.

Heaven knows what terrific row might have blown up if Celia hadn't come back into the room. And of course I was behaving badly; it was very definitely Robert's own business whom he lived with. But on my own behalf I can plead sheer shock. It really shattered me to find that his big, bold Bohemian life didn't amount to anything more picturesque than setting up in this garret with one of the ruins that Cromwell knocked about a bit. After a time, of course, I got used to it, and in any case I never had any quarrel with Celia personally. She was rather a nice old thing. Altogether, the psychology of it all is a bit baffling. I was used enough to seeing sweet young girls becoming the wives or mistresses of paunchy wrinkled old men who looked like scabby old apes. Why the reverse should horrify me so much more, I never fathomed. But it did. I hated to think of Robert sleeping with Celia, and for that matter I hate to think about it now.

Anyway, we all settled down quite amiably. I went out and got a few bottles of beer from a pub round the corner, and we sat about and drank it and had some bread and cheese. There were paintings stacked all round the walls, and under the sky-light stood an easel with an almost completed portrait of Celia on it. It was a pretty remarkable work, archaeologically speaking. It was like Troy when Schliemann had finished with it, whereas her actual appearance was like Troy when it lay waiting for Schliemann to happen along. He had made her look much as she must have done twenty years before, only rather more attractive. No wonder she liked him. I looked at the portrait and at Robert, choosing a moment when he didn't know I was looking at him. I was trying to fathom him. The way his mind worked was a mystery to me, but I could see it in glimpses. This portrait of Celia, for instance. It was just how she imagined herself. With a startling blend of cynicism and sympathy he had captured on canvas her own conception of her appearance. And – this is the part I can't pin down in words – he had conveyed, to the right onlooker, that he knew what he was doing. Something about the quality of the lines, the slightly too flamboyant colouring, said quite unmistakably 'This is what she thinks she looks like.' Even without seeing the real Celia I think I should have guessed it. And it had another quality too. One of forgiveness. After looking at the picture you couldn't so easily go on thinking Celia a disgusting old woman because she was carrying on with a youth who might have been her youngest son. After all, if she really thought she looked like the woman in the portrait – and she did think so, obviously – it became less disgusting of her; why shouldn't a fine, handsome woman, only a little past her first youth, enjoy herself now and then? That portrait was the first thing of Robert's I had seen since his lightning sketch of the Bloater on skates; and once again I felt, callow as I was, the thrill of contact with the power of art. I nearly wrote 'great art', and damn it, I don't see why I shouldn't have. Robert was great, in those days, however unformed he still might have seemed.

They put me up for the night, as it was too late for me to go wandering about looking for an hotel. This of course was a mistake. There was really only one room to this place, and mercifully Robert hadn't gone quite so Bohemian as to suggest that he and I and Celia should sleep in it together; so I had to push the old broken sofa out on to the landing and try to get a little sleep on that. The banister rails were broken, mostly, and the few that remained looked as if the dry rot had set in so far that they would crumble if you tapped them with your finger-nail. I knew that if I rolled out of bed during the night, as I sometimes did, there would be nothing to stop me from plunging down the well of the staircase and beating my brains out on the stone floor at the bottom. I tried to turn the sofa round so that the back was towards the banisters, but there wasn't room; I should have had to take it back into the studio and turn it round there, and by this time Robert and Celia had retired. I decided I'd rather risk smashing my skull like an egg-shell than have the sight of Celia without her corsage.

In the end I took off my belt and buckled it round my ankle and passed the other end round the leg of the sofa. The idea was to wake myself up if I started to slip off the thing. Actually I needn't have worried. About waking myself up, I mean. For the first two hours the stink kept me awake, for the next two the broken springs of the sofa, and for the last four it was the caretaker's cough. I'll take them in order.

The smell came from the kitchen, which was on the floor below where I was lying. Earlier on I'd taken a quick butcher's inside and that had been enough for me. Everybody who lived in the place used the one kitchen, but it was nobody's job to clean it up – the old situation. I particularly remember that there was a kind of packing-case in one corner, which was evidently where they threw scraps of food and refuse. I think most of the smell came from this – it could hardly have been emptied for a year or two – but some of it undoubtedly came from the sink. Next I pass to the sofa springs. These had been at their best in the year Celia's mother got married, in which year they had probably been taken out and loaned to Gottfried Daimler to use in the rear axle of the first motor-car. They had suffered considerably and been replaced by someone unused to metal work. It took me a long time to realize how bad they were, because at first they gave a little bit under my weight and seemed comparatively docile; but gradually they revived and thrust their inquiring heads further and further up, like infernal periscopes. There was a kind of central Andean range of them, up in the middle of the sofa, and I finally managed to lie along the edge so that I missed most of these. My backside hung over towards the rotten banisters and the belt pulled uncomfortably at my ankle. Then the caretaker started coughing.

At first I couldn't make up my mind what it was. He was dying of tuberculosis, and the coughing of somebody in that condition isn't like ordinary coughing. I wondered whether it was some unidentifiable animal they were keeping down there; or was it an amateur engineer cutting up sheet-metal with a power-saw? When I realized what it was I sat up on the sofa and listened intently, not letting myself miss a single detail of its horribleness. I did this as a kind of penance. I thought that if he could suffer like that, it was the least I could do to share in the suffering a bit. I didn't know, until I asked Robert later, that it was the caretaker (Robert called him 'the *concierge*', to show that we were all cosmopolitans together), and when I did know, it made it all the worse. Apparently the person who owned the house, having had it carved up into flats, had put this poor old man in to carry the ash-buckets about, and so on, more out of pity than anything else, as there wasn't any real need for a caretaker, even if you called him a *concierge*. This was the thirties remember, when to give anybody a job was an act of charity. Anyway, the reason why the packing-case full of scraps had not been emptied for so long was doubtless that it was too heavy for the old consumptive to lift. I expect he went into the kitchen now and again and looked round and spat a few tubercles into the atmosphere, just to help matters along, and had a go at the packing-case to see if he could lift it, and always found he couldn't. So there it stayed.

I lay awake listening to this terrible metallic crash that he somehow produced from his ruined chest, and thought about Life. I won't burden the story with details of what I thought about it, but my thoughts were pretty tiring, because I actually lost consciousness about the time the first birds began to sing. Yes, friends, I went to *sleep*. And quite deeply, because it must have been about nine o'clock when I felt a persistent hard pressure in my ribs. The effect at first was to make me dream that I was at a bullfight in Madrid and that the excited spectators were pressing towards the barrier and crushing me against it. No doubt the picador, or whatever they call them, was just about to slaughter the bull, or get gored, or something.

I got quite excited about this, because it seemed to me a mistake to have come to the bullfight, and I wanted to get away from the barrier and go home before they did any more damage to the bull.

'Stand back there,' I said, fighting.

'Don't – don't!' said one of the crowd, urgently in English.

'Back,' I snapped. 'Leave the bull alone. Leave it alone.'

I sat up. A portly middle-aged man was standing wedged between me and the banisters. He was evidently afraid, and quite rightly, that if he put any of his weight on the banisters they would break and he would be killed. So he was keeping as close to me as possible, edging his way past to get at the door of Robert's studio. This meant that his knees exerted a steady pressure on my ribs as he inched along. He was dressed in a quiet grey suit and looked very well bred and every inch a gentleman. His face was the kind that is normally ruddy, though at the moment it was grey with panic.

My mind was still not working at all steadily, because I now had a wild idea that this was the doctor come to attend the dying man downstairs. He looked a bit like my idea of a Harley Street man.

'Wrong floor,' I said, trying to lean back out of reach of those knees.

'I want to see Mr Lamb. I know he lives here,' said the man. He had what I thought was an educated London voice.

'He's engaged,' I said. 'Engaged to be married.'

'I'll just go past, if you'll kindly – '

'He's engaged!' I said loudly.

Robert opened the door. He was in his trousers and shirt, doing up his braces.

'Mr Cartridge!' he said. He made it sound as if he were really flattered and pleased. He had not shaved.

'If your friend would just let me get past,' said this Cartridge.

'I'm not a friend,' I said. 'I just live here.' I could see that this Cartridge didn't like me and never would like me, and I didn't want Robert to have to start on handicap. For I had remembered who he was, Justin Cartridge, the big name among art critics. A connoisseur. A collector. He not only talked and wrote about pictures, he bought them. He commissioned them. He probably ate them, grew them in his garden, slept on them and mended his shoes with the ones he had finished with.

'I hadn't forgotten, of course, that you were coming round this morning,' said Robert, polite but manly and dignified. It was good stuff considering that he pretty clearly *had* forgotten, or hadn't expected him so early, or something.

'Everything's ready for you,' he added, turning to lead the way into the studio. As he spoke Celia appeared, as if in obedience to a prearranged signal. She had evidently spent the last fifteen seconds wriggling into her clothes, with such vigour that she had wriggled half out of them again She had also dashed a couple of handfuls of face-powder over her cheeks and spattered a bit of rouge about. I averted my eyes.

'Hallo, Justin,' she said breezily.

'Celia,' this Cartridge said mechanically, as if naming an object in a recognition test. I supposed they were on Christian-name terms because they had known each other better in some former epoch when they were both younger.

We all waited, but Cartridge didn't seem to be going to elaborate on his one-word speech of greeting. I wondered if he was a Quaker, committed to telling the literal truth at all times, which would at least account for his not saying he was glad to see her, or hoped she was all right, or anything like that.

'Well, I'm going to make some coffee,' said Celia, edging past my couch and thumping off down the stairs. 'Would you like some?' she asked me as she came past. I accepted and then remembered the kitchen. I wasn't fussy, but I didn't want my coffee made there. Jumping up, I began to dress, which wasn't difficult because I hadn't taken anything off except my collar, tie and shoes. I was in such a hurry to get ready and make my escape that I didn't bother to notice what Robert did with Cartridge, but as I hurried away I noticed that they had gone into the studio.

'Sorry,' I shouted as I ran past the kitchen door. 'I've got to hurry off – I've just remembered.'

'Well, surely you want some coffee? It'll be ready straight away,' she called. She was really a good-natured old haversack. That's what made me feel so awful.

'Important business,' I shouted from the floor below. 'Fleet Street. Hustle. Get there first, newspaper man's golden rule.'

I was still shouting as I opened the front door and tumbled out into the sunshine. There, just putting his hand up to ring the bell, was Ned Roper.

'In there, constable,' I said. 'But be careful. They're loaded.'

He showed no surprise. Probably he never expected other people to behave sensibly anyway. He was the one with the monopoly of common sense.

'Don't go, Joe,' he said in his calm, firm way. 'I'm just going up to see Robert.'

I saw what he meant. He wanted me to be there because, in some way, they both found me calming. Their personalities didn't clash so violently when I was there.

I hesitated. If I went back Celia would offer me a cup of coffee. It would also involve me in explaining how I had suddenly ceased to have important business. I should also get in bad with Robert for interrupting his tête-à-tête with Cartridge. I thought quickly.

'I'll come with you', I said, 'on condition you come round the corner with me and find a Lyons and have some breakfast. Then we can come back in half an hour and I'll umpire while you and Robert make it up.'

'I've had my breakfast,' he said, bringing his organizing power massively into play.

'Then watch while I have some,' I said.

Still talking, we walked down Chesterfield Mews. It was a sunny morning a long time ago, when we were all very young.


# IV

Half an hour later we were ringing Robert's bell again. I felt dirty and uncomfortable, not having washed or shaved, but at least I had absorbed some bacon and eggs and coffee. Celia put her head out and threw us the key down.

'Come into the kitchen,' she called. 'Robert's still busy with Justin.'

'Watch it,' I said to Ned as we went upstairs. 'If she gives you any coffee, pour it into your turn-ups.' I didn't need to tell him who Celia was because we had been into all that over breakfast.

Ned took Celia in his stride. He accepted some coffee and

went through a very convincing show of drinking it; I had to watch really closely to establish that, as he strolled about the room, cup in hand, he kept passing the sink and spilling a bit into it. He really made it seem as if he was drinking the stuff, and his politeness didn't stop there; he even showed an interest in the china potatoes, asking Celia for details of who made them and how they were marketed. In the middle of their chit-chat there was a clump of feet going down the stairs. Two pairs went down, the front door banged, one pair came up, and there was Robert in the kitchen doorway.

'The tight-fisted old sod,' he said. Too wrapped up in his indignation to notice that Ned was there, he simply addressed the company at large. 'He thinks he's doing something big by dangling a rope too high up for me to grab it. Mr God Almighty Cartridge will be pleased to help you stuff your paintings up a bull's bum.'

'Here, darling, here,' Celia crooned soothingly, and gave him a cup of coffee, which he took and drained without even pausing to see how many cockroaches had drowned in it.

'Bloody old scum,' he said.

'It's fresh made,' Celia protested.

'I mean Cartridge.'

'Hallo, Robert,' said Ned from his corner.

Robert stopped his pacing and stared into Ned's face. I stood by, attentive as a referee.

'So you called,' he said.

'Didn't you know I would?'

'No, I didn't.'

Ned smiled as if it were just like Robert to forget who his *real* friends were.

'You surely must have realized that I'd be dropping in to see how you were getting on.'

'I surely didn't. But now that you're here you'll do as well as anyone else to grumble to. That bastard Cartridge has just left.'

'Evidently.'

'He was snooping round the dealers' and he saw one or two of my things. Stuff they'd bought, dirt cheap, for the invest-ment. He liked them and wrote to me to go round to his place with an armful. All right. I get the treatment. The servant brings the tea-tray in. Polite chat and macaroons. The servant takes the tea-tray out. My stomach's rumbling like a train because I

55

haven't eaten enough lately. All right. Cartridge gets his glasses on and looks at my drawings and water-colours. He can see they're bloody good, though he's not going to say so of course. Vaguely indicates that he could possibly do this or that "to encourage me". *Encourage my bottom.*'

'Don't be vulgar,' I said.

'Encourage my arse,' Robert shouted. 'He knows he's on to a good thing. But what does he think?' He went on more calmly. 'He thinks it's no good letting me get recognition too fast. It might give me a swollen head. On the other hand he mustn't let me slip out of his hands, otherwise someone else might corner me, and Mr Sensitive Know-all Cartridge would look funny then, wouldn't he? So what does he do? *What does he do?*'

'We'll take three guesses,' I said.

'He comes round here this morning,' Robert continued venomously, as if this were the worst of Cartridge's offences. 'Comes right bloody round here this morning, doesn't he, Joe?'

'Yes,' I said.

'Joe knows,' said Robert. 'Joe'll tell you. Not one bleeder in the house was even awake and he's got in and starts banging on the studio door. Nine o'clock. Ask Joe.'

'Ask me, Ned,' I said. 'And I'll tell you it's true.'

'Just to tell me,' Robert went on, ' – *just – to – tell – me –* ' He paused, then bellowed, ' – a load of garbage that I'd have thanked him to keep buttoned up in his mouth!'

Ned had been leaning against the wall, listening, with his arms folded; but now he straightened up and came forward, as if the time had come for him to take over control of the situation.

'Let's just have the facts, Robert, old man,' he said briskly. 'What exactly did he – '

'*Facts!*' Robert spluttered. The word seemed to enrage him more than anything that had so far happened; for several minutes the three of us waited with bowed heads, like people listening to publicly offered prayer, while he built up a massive edifice of bad language.

'So what it came down to, in the end,' said Robert finally, 'is that he said he'd got me the offer of a show from one of the better galleries.'

He stopped to give us time to ask what was wrong with that, but we were all sufficiently used to his rhetorical devices to know that the snag would follow in its own time. So we rode the pause out.

'All right. So I'm grabbing at the rope he's dangling down. I reach up for it. It looks a good enough rope. My fingers are closing on it. So what does the old bleeder do? He whisks it up, right out of my – '

'The *facts*, Robert, the facts!' Ned cut in. There was an edge to his voice, this time, that revealed how sick of it all he was getting.

All the same, I wished he could have kept quiet and waited. I was there to prevent any sort of friction between them, and if Ned was going to needle him it wouldn't make my job any easier. Robert stopped and began glaring at Ned.

'I'm just telling you, for Christ's sake,' he said. 'What's the hurry? If you've got a train to catch, go along. We won't detain you. We – '

At this point Celia took over. I was glad she was there. It was a real lesson in the power of a woman, even one like her, to calm a man down, even one like him. She took his face between her hands, which, speaking personally, I shouldn't have cared for if I'd been him, and began to murmur and coo and generally drool over him. Ned and I stood there, sickened but too brave to faint, like strong men watching a fearsome emergency operation.

'He's so easily upset,' she said to us over her shoulder. 'He needs help in getting over these things. Life is very cruel to people like him.'

I suppose that sentence, *Life is very cruel to people like him*, was one she had read in a novel or had to speak in some trifling play. But it struck me, and I often recalled it as I watched Robert lurching blindly through the years, banging into every sharp corner.

'Well, then,' said Robert suddenly, getting his face out from between Celia's hands like a boxer discarding the services of his second, 'it was all agreed that this gallery was to put on a one-man show and give everyone a chance to see my work and talk about it and make me famous, not to mention buy it and make me rich, when he let slip one little detail. *Fifty pounds.*'

In the silence that followed I said, 'Money pounds?'

'No, pounds of lizard-shit,' Robert shouted, turning on me. 'Pounds of . . . ' and for several minutes he went on naming progressively, more unmentionable things that he needed pounds of. Even Celia winced.

'Because the gallery will only take half the risk and the whole thing is bound to cost a hundred smackers, more or less,' he finished with a burst of unexpected matter-of-factness.

'For a cocktail-party?' Ned asked in his business voice.

'For a cocktail-party, for cards to be printed and sent out, for advertising,' Robert started, and quickly began once more to give his imagination the rein, this time naming progressively more unmentionable things the money would be needed for.

When he ran out of any more things to list, and silence fell, I suddenly noticed that Ned had drawn up a chair and was sitting at the table. He had to brush aside a lot of dirty crockery and scraps of food to get a few inches of clear space, but when he had he began writing something. I craned to see. It was a cheque.

'That's yours, when the ink's dry, Robert,' he said, tearing it out of the book.

Robert went over and picked it up. Then he put it down again with a small but firm shake of his head.

'It's going to take too long for this ink to dry, boy,' he said. 'There's fifty quid's worth of it.'

'It'll dry just as soon as five bob's worth,' said Ned evenly.

Robert shook his head again, a little more vigorously this time, but to soften the effect he smiled at Ned.

'Sorry, Ned,' he said. 'I appreciate it and all that. But this is my difficulty, and I've got to get out of it myself. I can't start on the wrong foot.'

Ned sat down on the kitchen chair and tilted it back comfortably. Then he stuck his legs out and put his hands in his jacket pockets, with the thumbs showing, and looked up at Robert.

'Now, just a minute,' he began. 'You don't want to begin on the wrong foot, as you call it. Let's examine this concept.'

'Let's examine this concept' was one of Ned's favourite expressions. It was his way of saying, 'Sit back and I'll talk you out of whatever position you've decided to take up.' I suppose if the hands at his factory wanted more money for overtime, or free bus travel, or something, he'd say, 'Let's examine this concept.' And I'm quite sure that when he asked a girl if she'd like to sleep with him, and she said No, he'd say, 'Let's examine this concept.'

'Examine it yourself,' said Robert impatiently. 'Hold it up to the light and examine it.'

'Now, just a minute, just a minute, Robert,' said Ned.

'Examine your arse in a glass,' Robert went on fiercely. It was his old trick of taking one word that annoyed him and building a tirade round it. 'Examine – '

'Darling, do listen to him,' said Celia, starting forward from her station over the sink. I could see she had been filling in the last minute by thinking what a lot of problems this cheque could solve. 'Do let the man tell you what he thinks.'

I half expected Robert to fire up, but he just closed his eyes wearily. 'Celia,' he said in a faint voice, 'do something for me, would you mind? Do just one little thing for me?'

He paused for her to ask 'What?' but she didn't. So he took it as read.

'Just go upstairs and fetch me my woollen dressing-gown, will you, please, darling?' he asked, squeezing her hand.

'But you haven't got a woollen dressing-gown.'

'But difficulties were made to be overcome, darling,' said Robert with a patient smile. 'A little detail like that won't bother you. You can so easily go out and buy some wool and needles and knit me one.'

'Knit you – '

'And by the time you've finished we'll have finished our little business conversation. It'll just give you something to do.'

Without a word Celia crossed the room to the door and was gone. I didn't see her face, as I was in the corner opposite the door, but from the back I should say she was rehearsing the way Desdemona goes off after Othello has slapped her in the presence of the Venetian envoy, Lodovico.

After she had closed the door Robert said, 'All right, Ned, I'll take the loan, and many thanks.'

The silence went on a bit longer. I could see Ned trying to lower himself on to this new plane. He and I had been prepared for a long and acrimonious argument, quite possibly ending with Robert still refusing to touch the cheque. Now we had the sensation of a man who jumps off what he thinks is a twenty-foot building in the dark and finds it was only three feet.

'I'm glad you'll take it,' said Ned at last.

'I'm glad too,' said Robert, putting the cheque in his wallet along with its other contents, two bus tickets and a hairpin.

'Just a bit surprised,' Ned went on.

'Surprised?'

'I thought you were going to make a fuss about it. Then you changed your mind so quickly.'

Robert smiled. 'It's not a bad thing, to know when to change your mind,' he said.

Ned and I looked at him. This was all we were going to get, obviously. We could spin theories for the rest of our lives, but we should never know for certain whether he had wanted to take the cheque all along, and just waited to get Celia out of the way, or whether he had genuinely changed his mind in the space of a few seconds. My own guess, then as now, was that he didn't believe in letting Celia know too much about his doings, financial and otherwise; he might perfectly well have wanted her to think he had refused the money, so that he would have the advantage of holding fifty pounds she didn't know about. That would, at any rate, fit in with his general attitude towards women.

'Don't think I won't repay this, Ned, one day,' he now said briskly, as if beginning to push the interview along to its close.

Ned, however, clearly didn't want the interview pushed to its close. Not just yet. He liked to put things in order, and then take a good look at them to satisfy himself that they *were* in order. No scamping it for him. He stood up and launched into what seemed like a little prepared speech.

'Pay me back if you like, all right, but remember there's no hurry over it. The business isn't doing so badly. In fact we're weathering this depression better than a lot of firms with more money behind them.'

Robert nodded absently. Either he was bored already, or he didn't want to be told how the firm was prospering since (or because?) he had left it.

'The older firms had their set procedures and their established markets. So when the slump came they had difficulty in swinging round to meet it. They were too inflexible. That's where it wasn't such a bad thing for a new firm like mine to *start* in a bad time. At least we can start from scratch and organize so as to pick up what bits of trade *are* going.'

Robert was frankly not listening by this time. Perhaps in recognition of this, but more probably just because he had finished with the topic, Ned left off talking about the firm and got on to his next heading.

'So there isn't a lot of difficulty about finding a few pounds now and then. And I might as well tell you you're welcome to your share of what there is going, Robert.'

Robert slowly turned to face him. The cheque was in his wallet, the wallet in his pocket, and it had begun to burn through into his flesh. He was beginning – I could see it – passionately to want reassurance that he wasn't going to have to sell any part of himself for the money.

'Why am I welcome to it?' he said. His voice was very dead and without inflection.

Ned hesitated a second, then began talking in a frank, confidence-inspiring tone, as he might talk to a wavering shareholders' meeting.

'Well, if you want me to answer that question quite straight, Robert, without any evasions and without leaving anything unsaid in case it might seem sentimental, I'll put it in a nutshell. You're welcome to it because you're an artist.'

'The goose that might lay the golden eggs?' Robert sneered.

'From the point of view of the community as a whole, that's what artists are, yes. If you mean from my personal point of view, that's an undeserved and mean thing to say, Robert, old man, and if I didn't know how obstinate you are I'd suggest you took it back.'

Robert, since turning to face Ned, had stood absolutely still. Now he slowly moved round on one heel till he was at right angles to Ned, and facing me. He fixed his gaze on a point some three feet above my head, stood still for a moment and then spoke.

'I take it back,' he said.

'My attitude to artists,' Ned went on levelly, 'is that they're a necessity for the rest of us. We've got to have them about, even if the cost is pretty high. The cost may be in terms of money, or it may be in terms of bad temper and squabbling.'

I understood. This was the speech he had prepared before coming, the declaration of how he forgave Robert for leaving his firm without consulting him. I was finding it pretty embarrassing, but I understood that from Ned's point of view it had to be gone through. Ned wasn't the sort of person who could decide anything tacitly and thereafter just let it appear. If he came to a conclusion about how he was going to treat anybody, he announced that conclusion to the person concerned. And I saw why too. It was because Ned thought of himself as an organization, not a person. It was Ned Roper,

Limited, Incorporated, and Society Anonymous. The gigantic corporation. The head of a vast empire. The least he could do was to give fair warning of a change of attitude. He wasn't telling Robert all this, about how nice he was going to be to him, so that Robert could start in at once being grateful. He was merely announcing it. Ned Roper, Limited, will hereinafter pursue the undermentioned policy.

Robert didn't get any of this. The way he saw it, Ned was making him a bit of a sermon, to clear his own conscience for being a business man and making money, and had given him fifty pounds first as a way of making him listen. I know he thought this because he told me so afterwards. 'Buying himself fifty pounds' worth of attention,' he called it. I tried to straighten him out, but it was no use. Those two weren't made to understand each other.

'So this is the way I see it, in a nutshell,' said Ned, winding up. 'My métier, the thing I know how to do, brings me money in. Yours doesn't. So, granting that the two are equally necessary, there has to be a bit of a share-out.'

Robert paced a few steps up and down while he digested this, then stopped with his back towards Ned. Turning his head to an angle of ninety degrees, he spoke over his shoulder.

'I get the point one way, but not the other. I can see what you're contributing to the share-out, but what am I going to contribute?'

'Your art,' said Ned flatly.

'That's just what I'm worried about. Contribute my art? In what sense contribute it? Put it into the kitty?'

Ned leaned against the wall, relaxed. The argument, as usual, was all going his way.

'You know, your trouble is that you let words bother you, Robert, old man. You get stuck on the word contribute and you're like a shying horse; you won't be led past it without rearing. Let's examine this concept. When I say that your share of the bargain, the thing you're giving, is your art, that's all I do mean. The fact that you're a producing artist is enough. If you're suspicious that I'm trying to get something directly in return for any help I give you, you're mistaken. You're probably thinking I've got deep schemes for getting designs and things out of you. As it happens I don't even need any designs. Baxter's doing all right. He's provided me with enough designs to be going on with for quite some time.'

'Enough spineless pastiche, you mean.'

'All right, enough spineless pastiche. The sort of spineless pastiche that sells and keeps the business going so that my workpeople stay in jobs and I have enough to live on – '

'And enough to give largesse to starving painters.'

' – and enough to spare to help out men who are producing something other than Baxter's spineless pastiche. Don't you see that that's how the Baxters of this world can be used?'

Robert's manner changed in an instant. He drew himself up portentously, walked stiff-legged over to the table, and sat down on a kitchen chair, hitching up his trousers carefully, as if afraid of destroying a knife-edged crease. Putting his finger-tips together, he leaned back with closed eyes.

'Take a letter, Miss Bolsterworthy,' he said in a calm, precise voice that seemed to exude prestige and money. 'Mr Edward Baxter, Esq. Dear Mr Edward Baxter. The Lamb Artistic Corporation wishes you to know of its profound gratitude for your help in guaranteeing its continued existence with your distinguished unadulterated cowshit.'

'Oh, come off it, boy,' Ned chuckled. The chuckle was a very false one, obviously assumed as a cloak for genuine annoyance; he didn't like the act. I didn't either, but I could see that some sort of defence for his pride was very necessary for Robert just then. If it came to that, I didn't like the act either of them was doing. If Robert's work really was so important to Ned's existence he could equally well have sent him fifty pound notes with a note saying 'From a friend', and kept his manifesto to himself. But of course I had known both of them long enough to know what each of them wanted. Robert's material needs were no more pressing than Ned's emotional ones. If Robert wanted to go on indulging his belief that business men were robots whose only justification was to minister to the needs of artists, Ned equally wanted to make a dent in this egoism and at the same time buy himself a place in the creative sun. He wasn't the first person, nor yet the thousand and first, to make the wistful discovery that the next best thing to being creative yourself is to become, in one way or another, necessary to someone who is creative.

I didn't like the way the situation was going, but before I could think of anything to say to improve it Robert must have decided the same thing himself. Stripping off his magnate expression, he stood up abruptly.

'Come on, men,' he said, starting towards the door.

'Come on, where?' I asked cautiously.

'We're going out for a drink,' said Robert, all beaming and charm. 'This has got to be celebrated.'

Neither of us felt like asking him whether 'this' referred to the new *entente* or the fifty pounds, but I had my own ideas.

'Will they be open?' asked Ned, glancing at his watch.

Robert laughed. 'This is London,' he called over his shoulder as he began to go down the stairs. Ned didn't exactly wince – he was too controlled for that – but I guessed that it was exactly that sort of remark that flicked him on the raw. He didn't like being reminded that Robert, as well as being an artist, was a Londoner as well, and knew all about big city ways. In the town I mustn't name, the pubs never opened before twelve.

We went out. I noticed that Robert didn't call Celia to go with us. Either he felt an aversion to being seen in public with her, in case people took her for his grandmother, or he just didn't want her about as long as any reference might be made to the fifty pounds.

We went to a pub in the King's Road, but before we had been there five minutes Robert asked us to wait a minute and darted out. He was away a long time, and when he got back it was obvious that he was in a temper again.

'How to get blood out of a stone,' he said, breathing heavily, 'in ten easy lessons or five hard ones.'

'What is it this time?' I asked.

'The bank,' he said, glancing quickly at Ned as if wondering whether this bit was suitable for his ears.

'I should have thought you'd be quite popular with them,' Ned smiled, lifting his glass; he was drinking light ale. 'With fifty quid to deposit.'

'It was getting some cash out of them that was the trouble,' said Robert. 'Naturally after I put the cheque in I wanted a bit of cash to be going on with. They said I hadn't any money, that my balance stood at about sixpence, which I knew already. So I said I had some money now – fifty pounds. So they tried to pull the stuff about having to wait a couple of days for the cheque to be cleared.' He laughed mirthlessly. 'I soon got them out of that. I made them ring up your bank at home. That satisfied them that your cheque wouldn't bounce.'

As he was talking I could see Ned getting more and more

uncomfortable. But, to his credit, he didn't say anything. If he was wondering – and obviously he *was* wondering – how much of his fifty pounds Robert had drawn out to squander on wine, women and drugs, instead of using it to finance his exhibition, he was keeping the question to himself.

'Anyway, I brought them to heel,' said Robert gaily, tapping his inside pocket. 'I extracted some cabbage out of them, so drink up, lads.'

Ned, who had paid for the first round, drained his glass with a rather resigned air and set it down on the counter. Robert looked at it contemptuously.

'This isn't a light ale do, Ned,' he said. 'A whisky won't hurt you, eh?'

'No, it won't hurt me,' said Ned without expression.

Without protest he allowed Robert to spend on whisky one-fiftieth of the money he had given him. The stuff was cheaper in those days – a whole bottle of it only cost about twelve-and-six – so you'll understand that by the time he had spent a pound we were feeling the benefit. I suggested we had better have something solid in our stomachs, and was just rapping on the counter to get the barman's attention, with the idea of ordering some bread and cheese, when Robert cut in again.

'Bread and cheese, Joe?' he sneered. 'Where do you think you are? This isn't an occasion for bread and cheese. We're in the big time now. We're all going out to lunch. I've got the money, and I'll take you where you'll get a lunch worth calling a – '

He was going on like this, aggressively, when the barman came up, in response to my rapping.

'Some bread and cheese, please,' I said.

'For two,' Ned added.

Robert looked from one to the other of us. His face had gone a deep red, and he looked in danger of choking.

'Didn't you men hear what I said?' he demanded.

'We heard you,' I said. I thought, like Ned, that it was getting time to be firm.

Robert banged his fist on the counter. 'Then what's all this about eating mouldy beggarly stuff like bread and cheese?'

'We're not hungry,' said Ned, evidently in a genuine attempt to placate him and smooth this thing over without having to challenge him on the real issue. 'There were a lot of calories in the whisky.'

'Yes,' I rallied round eagerly, 'and it's a well-known scientific fact that if you take alcoholic drink before a meal it acts as an appetizer for a few minutes, but after those minutes are up – '

'Oh, stow it!' Robert shouted angrily. 'I've had enough of your – '

' – it turns into sugar, the alcohol does, and feeds you,' I babbled. 'So no wonder Ned and I are – '

'God damn it, SHARRAP!' Robert thundered. He pounded on the bar with both fists. 'I invited you men to come out and have a good lunch on me, and this is how you treat me – it's an insult – it's – '

The barman came up with two plates, each bearing a portion of bread and cheese. He put them down directly in front of Robert, at the same time staring directly into his face as if determined to attract his attention.

'What's this?' Robert asked, his voice only a little louder than a whisper. He pointed at the plates with the air of not trusting himself to speak further.

'Bread and cheese, same as ordered,' said the barman.

'Eat it yourself,' said Robert deliberately, leaning over the bar.

They glared at each other for a few seconds, and then the barman said, in a calm insulting voice, 'I'm not hungry.'

Robert recoiled, then bounded back at him with apoplectic fury. 'You're not hungry, eh?' he shouted. 'Well, nobody's hungry, see? These two aren't hungry. I'm not hungry. We – '

'Easy now, easy now,' said a man who seemed to be the landlord, coming over from the other end of the bar.

'Come away, Robert, old man,' said Ned, taking him by the elbow.

'I'll fight any man in this pub who says he's hungry!' Robert shouted. He waved his fists about, and the barman lifted the flap of the bar and began to come out.

'No, Jack, no,' said the landlord, holding on to him. 'Get your friend out of here,' he called to us. 'Get him out while he's safe. Jack'll kill him.'

'Leave me get at him,' Jack snarled. 'I'll bread and cheese him.'

I only vaguely remember the exact moves of the next few seconds, but broadly what happened was that a Japanese, or a man who looked like a Japanese, who was sitting by the door, jumped up and held it open, and Ned and I pushed Robert roughly across the room and out. There was a bit more blustering in the street, and I particularly remember how uncomfortable and embarrassed it made Ned, who hated to be stared at. Probably this accounted for the fact that we gave up arguing with Robert, who was still shouting that we had insulted him by refusing to go and lunch out of his, or rather Ned's, or rather the gallery's, fifty pounds. All in the space of a few minutes we had hailed a taxi, bundled into it, Robert had snarled out the address of an expensive restaurant, and we had been whirled there and deposited on the pavement.

'Well, this is it,' said Robert, beginning to go up the steps. I made a last effort.

'Oh, come on now, Robert,' I said. 'We don't need to go to a place like this.'

'What's wrong with it?' he demanded.

'I don't like the colour scheme,' I said. 'They paper the walls with five-pound notes, and it hurts my eyesight.'

I might just have managed to tip the balance, but unfortunately at that moment Ned spoke up.

'Joe's right,' he said decisively. 'There's no point in – '

That did it. It was fatal for Ned to push himself forward at this point; it reminded Robert of all the pressures that were driving him on in this lunatic way. 'No point, eh?' he snapped. 'Well, let me point out that I happen to be the only one of us three who actually *lives* in London. And when I choose a place to invite you to eat at, I choose a *good* one. And when you've finished making fool objections, perhaps you'll just come in with me and let's get some lunch inside us. I'm hungry even if you're not.' And he marched up the stairs.

After that I don't remember so much. For one thing, of course, I was pretty drunk, and Robert insisted on pouring about five pounds' worth of wine down our throats, including his own, of course. But I think the main reason why I don't remember much about the scene in the restaurant is that my Freudian censor has cut it out. He's the boy who goes over the stack of battered old recordings that I call my memory and puts in some work with a sapphire needle. Then when I play them over I keep coming to patches that consist of nothing but needle-hiss. Understandably, a lot of these gaps are associated with expensive restaurants – most people have a *few* dreadful memories of those places – and a lot are also associated with Robert. When the two come together, it's the censor's day on duty. I can only salvage one or two fragments:

67

Robert grabbing the wine list and madly ordering up and down the pages, a bottle of this and a bottle of that, and in response to the wine-waiter's cuttingly polite 'Are you going to drink them in that order, sir?' snarling, 'If they're decent vintage, which I doubt, it doesn't matter what order they're drunk in.' Or Robert suddenly breaking off his discourse to stare at me more and more searchingly, finally saying, 'You need a shave, Joe, you know that? I must say it's embarrassing to go to a decent restaurant with a man who can't even be bothered to shave his face'; his eyes, as he said it, burning out from under his tangled hair, his top shirt button missing, his tie a frenetic knot. Or Ned intervening in a last faint effort to stop Robert ordering us all portions of smoked salmon to start off a lunch that was already ruinous. (He succeeded too; with an engaging air of being ready to listen to reason, Robert cancelled the smoked salmon and switched to caviar at twice the price. After that Ned gave up.)

It was all an agony; my general impression of that is certainly clear enough. Not even Robert enjoyed it; he talked all the time, loudly, and was very overbearing with the waiters and so on, but it was clear that he hadn't much appetite for the feast he had insisted on providing; he drank almost continuously, but scarcely did more with his food than pick at it. In fact, as I glanced at him from time to time I gradually became aware of what was driving him on. It wasn't simply self-indulgence, the wish to compensate himself for the lean times he'd been having; nor was it, wholly, the desire to make a splash and assert himself in front of Ned. All that was there of course, and so was the urge to avoid seeming a humble pensioner of Ned's – to rub it in that he'd spend the money in any way he chose. But underlying it all, I could see, was his old super-stition. When Robert's behaviour seemed outwardly inexplic-able, you could often account for it by looking for a super-stitious impulse. He was, I think, intensely afraid of the hidden unaccountable Powers whose presence he felt in his life, and continually out to appease them. And – I never questioned him, but this is how I reconstruct it – one of the things that called for appeasement, as he saw it, was material success. If Ned was going to give him a handsome money present, that was all right, but something must be done to buy off the jealous gods; a substantial part of it must be squandered – simply thrown away – and quickly.

Anyway, by about three we had had the full treatment, down to coffee with two glasses of brandy each. The waiter had been round with a box of cigars, and Robert had chosen a grotesquely big one and scolded Ned and me for refusing. He told us we had no gift for enjoyment, but he scowled so gloomily as he said it that I noticed the waiter looking at him curiously as he lit the cigar for him. Anyway, once the cigar was drawing well there was nothing for it but to go; Robert couldn't think of any way of spinning it out, so he called for the bill.

When I saw it coming I ducked out. I didn't want to be there when it was presented. Not that I was afraid Robert would be unable to meet it, or protest against it, or anything; it was pure superstitious fear. I didn't want to be within six feet of such a horrible thing. It might have exploded or bitten us, or given off a poisonous vapour, or something. So I said I had to go to the lavatory, and as the waiter bore down on us, carrying the evil slip of paper on a silver tray, as if it had been the head of John the Baptist, I pushed my chair back and made a bolt for the opposite door.

Once in the lobby, I thought I might as well collect our coats from the cloak-room. The attendant handed them over and looked without expression at the half-crown I gave him. Not knowing how to take this, I decided to act the part of the eccentric millionaire who had been left his untold wealth, by an even more eccentric father or uncle, conditionally upon his swearing never to tip more than half a crown. Turning away with an eccentric half-smile, which must have made me look merely idiotic, I bumped into an even more richly liveried flunkey, who expertly grabbed the three raincoats from me, quickly selected the least tatty-looking one, which was Ned's, and began to help me on with it. Still fighting to sustain the eccentric-millionaire *persona*, I gave what I intended to be an idiosyncratic chuckle, but which unfortunately issued as a loud, brainless laugh. When the servant looped the other two coats over my outstretched right arm, I belched quietly several times, as if in acknowledgment, then hiccuped. By now thoroughly alarmed, I dived my hand into Ned's coat pocket in search of suitable largesse, and to my joy felt a small heavy coin about one inch in diameter – a shilling. Bringing it out, I pressed it rapturously into the man's hand, at the same time moving away with an awkward shuffling gait, holding the two coats over my arm like a rag-and-bone merchant. My brain was late in defining a queer sensation of uneasiness that had arisen just as the coin changed hands, and I had covered several yards of carpet before I knew for certain that what I had given the fellow was, in fact, a halfpenny .Breaking into a run as this knowledge exploded inside my skull, I gave the swing doors a powerful shove, and landed on my knees outside with two overcoats wrapped protectively round my calves. Robert and Ned followed immediately behind.

I half expected them to make some comment on my style of exit, but they were arguing among themselves.

'Here, Joe, you try and get him to see reason,' Ned called to me, quite angrily. His fatalistic calm had crumbled, leaving him obviously in a bad temper. Robert, with the cigar projecting about a yard out of his mouth, was blowing out great plumes of smoke and trying to look nonchalant.

'I'm simply suggesting', he said to me, 'that we should follow up our lunch by adjourning to a little club I know of, near here, where we can have the noggin which the justly popular licensing laws of England would otherwise deny us.' He spoke in an exaggeratedly courtly way, gesturing with his cigar, making polite little bows, and generally acting like a fool. The whites of his eyes, I remember noticing, seemed pinker than they had when we set out.

'Noggin!' Ned broke in furiously. 'If you want to go on soaking, and get the whole lot of us drunk, why don't you say so in plain language?'

'Plain language,' said Robert, waving his hand delicately in the air, 'plain language is, at certain – ah – junctures of my life – infinitely wearisome to me.'

I saw that he was in his quote exquisite unquote mood, and that for the next hour or two we should get nothing out of him but his Oscar Wilde act, full of dandysme and 'shocking' drivel. The prospect bored me so heavily that all of a sudden I felt too somnolent to move. I wanted to bundle the three raincoats up into a pillow and lie down on the pavement with my head on them for a nice long sleep, while Ned and Robert argued it out.

Perhaps it was the lack of moral support from me that made Ned give in; at any rate, the next thing was that we were in a taxi again. This must have been sheer conspicuous waste on Robert's part, because we had hardly time to get into it before

70

we were out again and going into a place that seemed no different from the private bar of an ordinary pub, only a bit more flashy. It was a long, narrow room with a little bar at one end, and leather-covered sofas and armchairs. Two men in white coats were working, one pouring out the drinks behind the bar and giving them to the other one to distribute. You weren't allowed to go up to the bar yourself, evidently.

Robert had us equipped with a brandy each, in balloon glasses, before we knew what was happening. My head was beginning to ache; I can never understand why *everybody* doesn't hate drinking in the afternoon as much as I do. It was at about this point in the day that I finally ceased caring what all this was doing to the relationship of Ned and Robert, and how much of the fifty pounds was still left, and that sort of thing. Let the sods get on with it, I thought.

I think I dozed off, at any rate fell into a coma, over my brandy, because the next thing I remember is suddenly looking up over Robert's shoulder and seeing two familiar faces.

'It's a small show,' I said. I think I meant to say, 'It shows what a small world this is.' Anyway, there stood a man called Randall, who had been one of our schoolmasters, and with him was Stocker, his soft bruiser's face more pallid than ever.

Ned and Robert looked round, following my eyes, and there was a little reunion scene. By attending to the conversation I gathered that our finding them there wasn't such a coincidence as all that, because it was Randall who had put Stocker on to this afternoon drinking club, and Stocker had put Robert on to it.

It didn't surprise me that Randall should have nosed this place out. He was well known as a drunkard. I suppose every school has at least one master who just can't take the punishment the boys dish out, and who begins fairly early to hit the bottle, ending up as a quiet soak. In Randall's case it was so well known that it had long ceased to be a sore topic; the boys used to rib him quite openly about his inflexible habit of spending every lunch-time in the Grapes, down the road. I remember when I was in his form, it was our idea of a joke to buy him a bottle of beer and put it on his desk, with a glass, on the last day of term. He drank it all right, of course. And I dare say the drink kept him happy. His temper wasn't any worse than anyone else's, and he was always able to walk straight and go about his business, during school hours, at any rate.

Here he was then, a middle-aged man with spindly legs and a beer-drinker's paunch. His eyes were as watery as a bloodhound's and you could light a stove with his breath. Just one of life's casualties, like Celia.

They joined us, and Stocker said, 'You chaps on holiday?'

'Not exactly,' said Robert grandly. 'We're celebrating. A little piece of good fortune that's . . . ah, come my way.'

'Good fortune' to Stocker could only mean something to do with a woman, and I noticed him glancing round to see if Robert did actually have a woman with him; perhaps he thought she had gone to the ladies' room and would be joining us in a minute.

'A show of my paintings has been arranged,' said Robert, revolving the butt of his cigar in his fingers, 'or at any rate . . . can be, is on the point of being, arranged.' Stocker's face went blank.

'Still up to that lark are you, Lamb?' Randall asked suddenly. He had a way of staring at you with his head slightly lowered, so that his sandy eyebrows, which were very thick, hung down over his eyes like creepers; he did it now to Robert.

'Yes,' said Robert easily. 'Just for the time being, you know.'

'Oh?'

'Just to tide me over till I can get a decent, steady job,' said Robert, all dead-pan.

'What sort of a job?' Randall demanded, peering through the creepers.

'Something steady and respectable. Say like school-teaching.'

At that point even Randall twigged that he was being baited, so with a grunt he gave up the conversation and picked up his glass. For the rest of the time he was with us we didn't get another word out of him. He didn't sulk, he just kept his mouth shut except when drinking with it.

'Well, if you're celebrating,' Stocker was saying, 'what about stringing along with me? I might put you up some snipe.'

'Snipe?' said Ned, leaning across.

'Bints,' said Stocker. 'Mice. Blimey, how do you spend your evenings in town?'

Here it goes, I thought. A solid foundation of hard liquor, some money smouldering in Robert's pocket, and we have to run into this character. That's all it took.

'Look, Stocker, old man,' I said, hitching my chair towards his so as to be able to talk confidentially, 'you'll be better off hunting snipe on your own. It's not that we don't appreciate it and all that, but, well . . .'

'Well, what?' he asked roughly.

'It's rather delicate,' I said, speaking quietly because I could see the others were listening. 'It's just that – we don't want to do anything to make trouble for Robert.' My voice was barely audible even to myself.

'Why don't you speak up?' asked Stocker in irritation, leaning towards me. 'What the hell's the – '

'It's like this,' I cut in, boosting output by a couple of decibels or so. 'Robert's – well, suited. He's got himself fixed up. And where's the sense of – '

'That true, Robert?' Stocker asked, turning to him.

'Is what true?'

'That you've got yourself fixed up with a bint?'

I tried to kick Stocker's ankle, but it was too late. Anyone as ready to take offence as Robert, as sensitive to the least intrusion on his privacy, might easily flare up at this heavy-handed questioning. But, as I saw a moment later, I had overlooked the other main ingredient of his character at this time; the desire to seem the Compleat Artist, version of S.W.3.

'My domestic wants are supplied,' he smiled, 'if that's what you mean.'

'I didn't say anything about your domestic wants. I said, is it true what Joe says that you've got yourself fitted out with a tabby?'

'My humble roof,' said Robert, still doing the quote exquisite unquote on us, 'is shared by a distinguished actress.'

'An *actress*?' Stocker half rose. 'This I've got to see.'

'She's on the roof,' I put in, quietly despairing. 'She shares it with Robert.' He took no notice.

By now, I realized with a start, it was about five o'clock. My head was aching and I would have given anything for a cup of tea instead of brandy, brandy all the time. There was only one way to fight my fatigue and drunkenness – to give way to it. I decided there and then to give up all attempt to behave responsibly, keep my attention fixed on what went on, think or talk coherently. My only chance of survival, it seemed to me, lay in releasing my hold on the lifeline and deliberately sinking like a stone, down into the roomy depths where my headache, thirst and lassitude wouldn't matter. I felt like a man who has died at sea and is being sewn into his shroud ready to be swung overboard for a marine burial. I even muttered to myself, 'His heavy-shotted hammock-shroud Drops in his vast and wandering grave.' God bless Tennyson! I smiled carelessly to myself and began to pat Randall's sleeve affectionately, not because I mistook him for Tennyson but because he happened to be sitting next to me. He took no notice. Conversational tides, full of starfish, whales, plankton and fragments of purposely dismantled ships, washed over me. I floated downwards through landscape gardens of sea-plants and rock-formations. The light grew dimmer. Soon I would be among the deep-sea fish, who die if they are brought within a mile of the surface. It was all delightfully relaxing.

From down there I could hear the voices of my companions only as rumours, much as if they came through on a faulty wireless set owned by somebody living near by who then set the news in imperfect circulation. What I finally got clear, however, was that we were going back to Chesterfield Mews. Nothing would satisfy Stocker but to take a look at Robert's actress. Celia! I had forgotten her existence, but now I remembered her I began to laugh softly to myself. They dragged me up on to my feet and the group moved off, except for Randall, who must have preferred to stay where he was and where he could go on drinking. From my diving-bell I registered that up above me, at atmosphere level, the party had reached the pavement outside and a taxi was being organized. A moment later we were all sitting on sprung leather seats, and the London scene was being drawn across the windows like a moving back-cloth. It came to me as a distant tidal motion. I was away, inhabiting a different element. I had walked off into the fourth dimension so far that I could only be made out with field-glasses, and then as no more than a diminishing speck. I was no longer down in the sea. I was sitting in an office, beautifully upholstered, somewhere on the star Sirius, reading an account of what was going on in the London taxicab. The account was coming through second by second on a ticker-tape, and I was reading it off and laughing like mad.

Stocker was questioning Robert, as the taxi moved through Knightsbridge, about Celia. He seemed to want to know *every-thing* about her; not only obvious things such as where Robert had found her, what sort of plays she acted in, and so on, but things about what she liked to eat, where she was born. Was she country bred? He got quite angry when Robert didn't know this. It seemed to make a tremendous difference to him whether Celia had been born and bred among cows and trees and grass or among houses and streets. What interested me, though, as I sat reading it off the ticker-tape in my office in Sirius, was not so much Stocker's questions as Robert's replies. He was drawing an amazing picture of Celia, using nothing but words. He kept his hands quite still, folded in his lap, so as not even to invoke the aid of gesture. At first I didn't recognize the woman he was describing as Celia, but after a few minutes it burst on me. He was describing the woman he had painted in his portrait: the archaeological reconstruction! Deftly using the most colourful and heartening words in the English tongue he threw up a mound of language that settled down slowly, like a heap of feathers, into a perfect likeness of the picture in his studio. I listened in rapture. The ticker-tape stopped working and the actual words came through interstellar space and registered on my ear-drums. Before the taxi had got to the King's Road I was having serious doubts about my own perceptions. How could I be certain that my view of Celia was correct and Robert's an illusion? He knew her better than I did, and besides, what is perceived depends a good deal on the perceiver; people whose minds are small and ugly generally find everything small and ugly that they look at. Not that I thought Celia was small – just slightly shrunken with age – but I certainly found her ugly. And yet, here was Robert, holding Stocker spellbound with a description of the fascinating woman he had painted. I stole a glance at Ned. His face was entirely without expression.

The taxi seemed to be stopping and starting a good deal. One time it would be a traffic jam, another time it would be Robert wanting to call in and buy a few bottles of brandy for us to go on drinking when we got back. (From far out on Sirius I watched, aghast, as the bright clinking weapons were taken on board.) During one of these pauses, with the driver sitting carelessly smoking, the engine purring, the meter ticking, the near-side door open and Robert and Stocker in a shop, loading up with bottles, I made a brief descent from my alien constellation for the purpose of exchanging a few words with Ned. I saw his blank face, as if through a radio-telescope, and immediately I was down there beside him, holding on

75

with one hand to the earth's crust, talking gently to him and trying to bring him a little comfort.

He didn't seem to need it though. He had lent, or more precisely given, Robert a fairly big sum of money for him to put to a specific use, and there was Robert simply showering it about; but the spectacle didn't seem to have made Ned angry, or even sad. He just took it impassively, as if he had sunk a lot of capital in a business that had turned out to be a loss. As I watched him, and heard him explain his attitude, I understood what it is that makes industrialists tick. They are gamblers whose one joy in life is to pick a number and put some money on it. It has to be a large enough sum of money to make them feel excited over the result, but the number doesn't have to come up. It can fail them and they're still happy as long as they have any money left to put on the next number.

'I shall simply alter my strategy,' he said calmly. 'In future if Robert needs funds to arrange for an exhibition I shall find out the name of the gallery and go round and pay the money direct to them.'

'Robert would murder you if he got to hear of it,' I said.

'He wouldn't get to hear of it,' said Ned. 'I wouldn't even allow the gallery to tell him that a well-wisher had put up the money, or anything like that. I'd just tell them to make out that they were taking a risk themselves.'

'Would that be good for Robert?' I asked. 'It would encourage him to live in a world of illusion.'

Ned pointed through the open door of the taxi. Robert was coming out of the shop doorway with what looked like a dozen bottles in his arms. His face was flushed and he stumbled heavily over the doorstep, only regaining his balance with an effort. Behind him Stocker's face showed momentarily like the silver-grey profile of a badger.

'Is this good for him?' he asked.

I gave up. As Robert and Stocker rejoined us I relinquished my hold on the earth's crust and flew back to Sirius, closing my eyes to protect them from being congealed in the frozen darkness between the constellations.

And what Stocker actually did think of Celia I never found out. Or, if I did, it's slipped my mind. Not surprisingly, what with one thing and another and the many years that have gone by since then.

# V

All that was in 1934. And I might as well pass pretty quickly over the next part of the story. After all, what were any of us doing between '34 and '39? We were waiting for the war to happen and that was all. There wasn't for people of my age much drama in this waiting, because there had never been any choice to be made. By the time we came on the scene it was all arranged. Long before we were of an age even to think of influencing the course of events, Hitler was safely in power and the mobilization of the Germans had begun. All we knew was that it was only a matter of time, and not much time, before the balloon went up.

In my memory the last few pre-war years are all rolled into one rather long one; I can't keep the summer of '37 apart from that of '38, and so on. School-days were over, but the main business of life, being an adult, couldn't get started properly until we knew whether we were going to survive or not. I suppose all three of us, Robert, Ned and I, revealed our characters in the different ways we rode these years out. Robert was the one it made least difference to. He lived so utterly in the present, and in such a self-contained world, that outside events never touched him. He struggled through those years, living partly on hope and partly on the support of people who were prepared to risk a little money on his ultimately having a name. A dealer would now and then buy a picture, dirt cheap, to keep in an attic until it could be trotted out as 'an early Robert Lamb'. Or some connoisseur, like Cartridge, would ask him down somewhere for a week-end, and he would stoke up with food and drink for thirty-six hours and lard his ribs against the next week or two of bread and margarine. But most important was the help he got from Ned. Not once in those years did Ned visit London – and he went pretty often – without looking up Robert and taking him out for a good square meal. For countless hours he must have sat in Soho restaurants, watching pounds' worth of food disappearing into Robert's inside, chased by gallons of wine. Fuel, everything was fuel, to be taken in and emerge later in the form of oil-paintings, water-colours, tempera, gouache, pastel, pen-and-ink, the lot. For Robert was going at it bald-headed. His technical advances were enormous. When he got an idea for a painting he would tear into the job of making anything up to fifty or sixty preliminary studies, in every possible medium, even clay modelling. Looking back, I'm surprised that he never knew what was going on in the world at large, because one of his biggest expenses must have been the number of newspapers he had to buy. He put varnish on them and tacked them on to stretchers to make a cheap sub-stitute for canvas. I'd go in and find him surrounded by thirty or forty of these dramatic, staring colour-sketches of his, all done on newspaper. Afterwards he'd burn them in the stove. If I protested he'd brush me aside; it was a quirk of his that he didn't want any of his preliminary unfinished work to survive. 'Inchoate' was a favourite word with him at this time, and he always brought it out to describe these intermediate stages of his pictures. 'All inchoate stuff,' he would say, gathering up an armful of varnished newspaper sheets. He would also toss the word about in condemning other painters (he never men-tioned any other painter except in dismissal). 'Him?' he would say, if you brought up a name. 'Hopeless. All that work he puts in, trying to give his work a finished look – and all the time it's pathetically obvious, underneath that gloss, that the stuff's fatally inchoate.' I don't think there was one artist practising in the thirties whose work Robert didn't describe, at some time or other, as 'fatally inchoate'.

Ned, meanwhile, went on examining this concept and that concept. He had effortlessly put himself at the head of his frightened rabble of relatives and got to the stage where he didn't even consult them; he didn't see why he should try to fool them into thinking that he cared anything for their opinions on how a factory should be run. It was like his queer trick of referring to his firm as a new one, as if unwilling to recognize the years before he took it over. He had complete control by the time he was twenty-one, and he had his own characteristic way of getting ready for the war. Although the factory was doing well, he didn't try to expand it at all. No new buildings, no extra workpeople. Instead, he bought *sites* for new buildings, and acquired the lease of garages and ware-houses and one thing and another. In other words, he *prepared* for expansion; he laid the foundations for that sudden jump into prominence that the firm was to make after the war. One day, when I happened to be round at the works, he even showed me the designs for a whole range of household stuff, to be called 'Blue Seal Ware'. It looked the goods. Some of the designs were Robert's, by the way, tidied up a bit.

'You'll need a London showroom for this lot,' I said.

He looked at me pityingly. 'Think I don't know that?' he said. 'I'm negotiating for a place now. But the lease doesn't run out for a bit and that suits me fine. I shan't be fitting up a showroom in town and opening it till the war's come and gone. As soon as it is I'll get busy and push Blue Seal ware till it's the rage of the post-war fashion world.'

'What if we don't win the war?'

'I don't know,' he said seriously. 'I haven't got alternative plans for that.'

After that there was nothing for it but for Ned to join up, as soon as the war started, and rise to the highest rank possible in order to make sure we didn't lose the war. Because if we had, his plans for expansion would have been held up indefinitely.

Oddly enough, both he and Robert joined up a full year before they need have done; just after Munich, to be precise. There again, I suppose, their characters come out pretty clearly.

One evening that autumn, just after Mr Chamberlain had got back from Munich, I had a telephone call from Ned inviting me to dinner.

'House-warming?' I asked. He had just bought a biggish house, outside the town, where he reigned over a bunch of downtrodden female relatives, including his old mum.

'Partly,' he said, 'and partly picture-warming. Robert's here. I'm storing his canvases for him. Come any time you like. It might be the last get-together we shall have for some time.'

I hurried over. I had a motor-cycle in those days, and I remember how the headlamp cut a white segment out of the darkness and played on the high banks lining the steep, narrow lane up to Ned's new house. If only we could all see ahead, I thought; if only it were this easy to throw a beam through the blankness of time. I got so engrossed in this vein of thought that when the road suddenly tilted upwards – Ned's house was up on a knob – I didn't change down quickly enough and stalled the motor. I had to turn round and run downhill to start it again, which struck me as more emblematic than ever.

Anyway, I got there, and as I went up the drive I saw the house blazing out like a factory. Every light was on. When I got inside I saw why. Robert was stalking about, throwing doors open, examining the rooms to assess their fitness as store-rooms for his paintings. I saw no sign of the gaggle of female dependants; probably they were down in the coal-cellar with the door bolted behind them, waiting for the terror to pass.

'Hallo, Joe,' he said when he saw me. 'Just give me a hand taking these upstairs.'

I got hold of a couple of canvases and followed him. Ned, who had just opened the door to me, brought up the rear with a portfolio of drawings. Upstairs we wandered from room to room. Every time Robert pushed open a door I winced, expecting to see some bedridden old aunt cowering down among the sheets; but the rooms were empty, as if the whole house had waited for this moment to fulfil its destiny. I can only remember one room that we didn't go into; one of the upstairs rooms, in a rather inaccessible part of the house, which was locked; on purpose, evidently, because I heard Robert suggest, 'What about this one?' and Ned say, 'Full up'. What it was full of I couldn't guess, though it amused me to invent a number of disreputable possibilities. I kept my inventions to myself, naturally. And we wandered about, with canvases under our arms, all through the rest of the house.

This, evidently, was the view favoured by Robert. He seemed to be interviewing the rooms as they came before him, one by one, in the capacity of humble applicants for the job of looking after the pictures.

'Basically, there's only one problem,' he was saying as he led us about. 'Damp. Give them a really dry atmosphere and they'll be all right, provided − *provided*' − he turned admonishingly to Ned − 'that they're stored with plenty of space. They mustn't be stacked touching one another.'

'They'll be left exactly as you put them this evening,' said Ned equably. He seemed remarkably good-tempered about Robert's dictatorial requisitioning of his house.

'What's the idea?' I kept saying, patiently, trying to get abreast of the situation but quite willing to wait till it suited them. Finally, during a lull in the more urgent business, Ned explained.

'We're joining up,' he said.

'Already?' I asked. 'Why not wait for it?'

Then they both started to tell me at once. They had all sorts of reasons. Joining up was like anything else – it was a matter of first come, first served. Quite soon, when the war actually started, everyone would be conscripted; but by that time, they, Robert and Ned, would be comfortably settled, well ahead with their training, and in a position to get a better share of what was going.

This reasoning, I saw immediately, was Ned's. Robert didn't see things in that way. Ned was the one who had foresight, who prided himself on being one jump ahead, who cared about things like getting commissions. All the same, I could see, just as easily, that Ned had no sooner voiced these ideas than Robert had been forced, by the nature of their relationship, to adopt them. If Ned was going to join up and get organized before the war started, so was he. Moreover, it was important for Robert to enlist while there was still comparative freedom of choice as to which arm you went into. Otherwise he might find himself in the same one as Ned; and, since Ned was bound to be promoted much more rapidly, this might mean that he would find himself having to obey him as an officer. The idea! I could perfectly well understand that it was worth an extra few months in uniform, to Robert, to make sure that this didn't happen.

So they roughed it out. Ned was going into the army and Robert into the navy. I noticed that they didn't bother to ask me what I was going to do. It was all too obvious that I would stay quietly at home until I was actually *made* to join up. I'm the stuff of which the rank and file of every British army is made.

After dinner – the female contingent emerged for long enough to dish it out – we went to it again, carting paintings and easels about. But by now I was getting the picture a little clearer. No wonder Ned was pleased with himself. He was right in on the act, this time, in a way that nobody would ever be able to ignore. Future historians might fail to notice, or to establish, the amount of financial help that he had given Robert over the last three years; but the question was bound to come up, 'What happened to his earlier work while he was in the navy?' and then the answer would have to be, 'It was carefully stored by the eminent Maecenas, his lifelong supporter, Sir Edward Roper, KCB, OBE, knight, bart., OM, LSD, GWR, OHMS.' It was the surest method of getting right into the centre of the picture and staying there.

(Afterwards, as I rode home, I thought of something else. During all the years Ned had never actually *bought* a picture from Robert. And it now flashed on me that I knew the reason for this. He wanted to involve Robert in the kind of indebtedness that you feel to people who are utterly disinterested. To buy even a single canvas would have been to enable Robert, later, to say that he did the whole thing as a business speculation. Oh, Ned was clever about getting what he wanted.)

Anyway, we went on half the night. This set here and this here and these somewhere else. There was one huge painting, an abstract which I had watched growing over the last six months, that really gave us a headache.

'There's nothing for it but to hang this on a wall,' Robert said firmly. 'Out of any possibility of dust.'

'There's no dust here, Robert,' said Ned kindly, as if reassuring a child.

'You don't understand,' said Robert impatiently. 'This is a knife-palette job. It's finished all right, but there are some parts of it that I was still going over up to a few days ago. That paint's *thick*. It won't dry in five minutes – it may take *months*. And during that time it must be protected from dust.'

He looked round at Ned and me to see if we had understood what he was saying. He was probably wondering whether he ought to go right back to the beginning and explain what dust was.

'Now, which of the rooms gets dusted most frequently?' he demanded.

'For Christ's sake,' said Ned, spreading his hands. 'Every room gets dusted equally often. There's an army of women in this house and none of them have got anything to do with their lives except dust. If you like I'll get them to wear gauze masks whenever they approach this picture, in case they cough and deposit particles of phlegm and lung tissue on it.'

'That wouldn't matter,' said Robert seriously. 'It would show up in patches and it could probably be cleaned off. Whereas dust . . .' he went on maundering and we took less and less notice.

We had a final whisky before I left. Robert was sleeping at Ned's; he had come up that day from London in the firm's van, which Ned had sent down specially, complete with driver, to bring his stuff up. Ned explained this to me with his 'Where-would-he-be-without-me?' look firmly in place. He had scored and he knew it.

What was more, Robert knew it. He made, in those last few minutes that I was with them, a clumsy attempt to buy off some of this moral obligation.

'By the way, Ned, old man,' he said, trying to seem nonchalant, 'Joe here's my witness that you can choose any picture you like and keep it, when the time comes to hand the stuff back. Sort of commission for keeping them.'

It was just like seeing a boxer go in with his guard open. All Ned had to do was to smile, a little sadly, and shake his head, and Robert was down with the referee counting him out.

'I'm glad the pictures are safe, and that you won't be having to worry about them,' he said, enjoying himself thoroughly. 'That's all the commission I'm interested in.'

'Except the one the army's keeping warm for you,' I put in to break the thing up. I felt like someone throwing a bucket of water over two dogs to stop them fighting.

When I was sure the subject had been safely changed, I finished my drink and left, cutting the same segment out of the darkness as I went down the narrow lane. There was nothing else I could do. It was six years before the three of us came together again. Meanwhile the pictures stayed there in Ned's house. I assume they were all right. At least, I never heard that the knife-palette job got any dust on it.

Well, as I say, we'll skip the war. Let it be enough that we all three survived; I was the only one to get anything describable as a 'war wound', when I broke my wrist falling out of a lorry on Salisbury Plain. In short, by the New Year of 1946 we were all back in roughly the same positions as we had been in 1938. We were a bit more chipped and shop-soiled, of course, and we all fancied ourselves vastly more mature, though in fact life had its most important lessons still in store for us. Not that six years of war service had left no mark on any of us: that wouldn't be possible. Ned had reached the rank of major, and one of the things it had given him was a high social gloss; he had effortlessly shed any trace of our local accent — a thing neither Robert nor I ever tried hard enough to do — and could come the old Buckingham Palace quite faultlessly. But underneath it there wasn't any great change, nothing that altered the structure of his character. He had simply become more like himself; shed the last remnants of provincial *gaucherie*, which didn't, in any case, essentially belong to his character, and acquired a deeper skill in getting what he wanted. And, as I found out in the first conversation I had with him after we were demobbed, army life hadn't remedied any of his real weaknesses. He was still putting his trust in material efficiency, in 'getting on'; the lesson of his school-days, that life must be seen in competitive terms, had sunk in too deeply, and into too receptive a soil, for anything to root it out now. We talked about Robert, and I could see at once that whatever deficiency it was in Ned that made him fear Robert as a rival — fear him deeply, right down in the core of his being — was still unhealed. And the fact that he had risen to be a major, and Robert had got no further than being a medical orderly, didn't seem to help him. In fact he was rather sensitive about it, as if he felt it made him vulnerable; the competence he had shown was so much the kind of thing Robert would be satirical about. He also had the penetration to see that it was clever of Robert to have become a medical orderly; Robert didn't want to be changed, and that was about the only job he could have fitted into that wouldn't have changed him. But there we were, once again; Ned at the head of his business, me back on the paper, and Robert face to face with the old eternal struggle to make a living at his painting.

Ned was off the mark at once, of course. Blue Seal Pottery seemed to become a vogue overnight, like the Vespa, or Swedish furniture, or any of those things. One minute it was just a cloud of sales talk, the next — wham! It was everywhere. He had the showroom opened in town by the autumn of 1946, and during the next year or two nothing could stop him; neither fuel shortages, labour difficulties nor official restrictions could frustrate his drive towards really big-time expansion — the sort of thing he had always dreamed of, but had been too canny to launch in the thirties, with the war hanging over us. It was just like watching a rocket going up — except that it never burst and fell back to earth. Or rather, it did burst, repeatedly, but each new explosion seemed to provide the motive force for a fresh lunge towards the stratosphere.

In the town I mustn't name he was the white-haired boy. Every time he pulled off a big deal it made a paragraph in the Sentry. I particularly liked this because I was generally in charge of getting the story, and all I had to do was to ring him up and he would put me on to his private secretary (he called her

'My P.S.', and after a while I just asked for 'Puss') and she would read out a specially prepared 'release'. Ned was always thinking in big terms; his methods were those of an industrialist dealing in untold millions, controlling the economic destinies of entire continents, even when he was in fact only on the fringe of the big stuff. It was all part of the job of making people feel confidence in him; getting them, in short, to accept him at his own valuation of himself, as he had done all along.

His London showroom was one of these things you dream about after getting drunk on champagne. It had a real princess in it. I never found out where she was a princess of, and I never actually heard anyone say she was a princess, but I knew she was. She had dark-blue eyelids that she must have put on with a stove brush. Her finger-nails practically reached across the room. She was terrific.

As for me, I went back on the paper and before long I was principal assistant to the News Editor. The News Editor was a pretty old man, and it was understood that when he retired I was to have his job. Just to get in practice I started straight-away to do all the work. Also there was one perk I managed to corner; when there were any trips to London to be done I was the one to go. It used to work out at about one trip to town per fortnight, depending on how much I could invent in the way of pointless reasons why it was important for me to go. They were pretty good about it, I must say.

As for Robert, he started off badly. Not only did he have to start from scratch, for the bit of reputation he had begun to acquire had not survived the war years, and younger people were already beginning to come along; he even had to back down a few paces. He was in a worse position, strategically, than in 1938, largely through the impossibility of finding a studio in London. Immediately on being demobbed he went the rounds, full of hope, but before a single day was out he had seen the uselessness of trying to find anything in town. The coldest, darkest and least practical studio was fetching far more than the most palatial ones had when he first went there. I was only sketchily in touch with him, and for a few months I couldn't have said where he was, but finally it came through, by the ordinary channels of gossip, that he had been lent, or given, a tumbledown little place in some Northamptonshire village. I shook my head over this news; it didn't sound like Robert at all. Quite apart from anything else the countryside was no use for his art; he never looked at it except out of train windows, and then only with distaste. Those of his pictures that weren't abstract were always of people and buildings. I wrote and asked him if he objected to visitors; if not, I said, I would come and see him when I got a day off. He wasn't exactly crazy about being visited, evidently, because nearly three weeks had gone by before I got a postcard, unstamped; I had to pay the postman fourpence before being rewarded with the scrawled message, 'Come if you like.'

So on a warm spring day, just after that gruesome winter of 1946–7, I took off. I had no car, as yet, and my motor-cycle had long since been exchanged for two empty milk bottles and a cigarette card, so it meant spending half a day on country stations, waiting for trains full of yokels carrying trussed chickens and bundles of wood, or in village squares waiting for buses. Finally I caught the last of a long chain of buses, and when I climbed down from it at the indicated place, Robert's cottage was before me and he was staring moodily down out of the upstairs window.

'Come straight up,' he said grimly, by way of greeting.

I opened the front door – it had a string latch – and began to push my way through the living-room or whatever the chief downstairs room was called. 'Push' is the word. There was so much junk piled about that you really had to work hard to get through it. There was a stoutly made table in the middle of the room, and most of the lighter stuff, like canvases, dirty crockery and clothes, and cardboard boxes of rotting fruit and vegetables, had been heaped on to this in a kind of unsteady mound; the heavier things, like buckets of ashes, logs, water-butts, zinc baths, and clay flowerpots with toads hibernating in them, were grouped underneath and around it. I found the stairs and went up to Robert's floor. He was at work, with his back to the tiny window; he had made the bed into a work-bench, by laying a board across it, and he had his lino-cutter and ink roller busy.

'I can't paint,' he said, plunging straight into the subject of his difficulties. 'There's no skylight, and the window's no bigger than a greyhound's arse. So I'm doing lino-cuts. Adaptable, that's me.'

'Why not wood engravings?' I asked. He had done some of these before and made a small but definite success out of them.

'Ask yourself,' said Robert wearily. 'The right kind of wood costs money. Not much money but more than linoleum. So I work with linoleum. When a cheaper material comes out I'll work with that. I'm trying to think of a way of painting watercolours that uses nothing but water. It's all I can afford to drink, so I might as well paint with it.'

There didn't seem to be much to say to this. I looked round, a bit helplessly. The room was very messy though less cluttered than the one downstairs. I supposed he had been driven upstairs by the rising tide of chaos, but it didn't seem right to ask if this were so. It would only have depressed him still more.

Robert went on paring away at the square of linoleum, to the accompaniment of a lot of snarling; it was rather like the old days in the 'design department' at Ned's, but much grimmer. He really had something to complain about now.

'I wouldn't ask a convicted criminal to live in a hovel like this,' he said. 'It's bad enough now the weather's cleared, but you just can't picture what it was like in the winter. I was snowed up till it was impossible to get the front door open. Not that I cared. I was in bed. I tell you I didn't care in the slightest whether I survived or not. I stayed in bed for twenty-three days. Look at them marked on the wall.'

I followed his finger. Near the head of the bed, roughly scribbled in charcoal on the whitewash, was a calendar for January and February, with every date methodically crossed out. It gave me a quick appalling vision of the length of Robert's solitary winter.

'What did you live on?' I asked.

'Bovril, I think. I can't remember too well. And milk, when the milkman could get to the door. He'd stopped deliveries because I fell behind with the bill, but he started again at the height of the cold spell without my asking. He used to come past and leave a pint every day on the window-sill downstairs. Some days it was all I had. Not that I minded. I'd got plenty of fuel, and with the fire going and my clothes on in bed I just lay there thinking it was nice to be warm. And thinking what I'd do if ever I got out from under all this.'

As he said 'all this' his hand flipped outwards to indicate the cottage and its pitiful furnishings. I understood. 'All this' meant poverty, neglect and dirt; it meant accepting charity from the milkman, and having no one to talk to, and lying in bed scratching off each day as it slowly wormed past.

'I didn't have any artificial light,' he said, talking faster as the thing crowded back on him. 'There's an oil lamp but I hadn't any oil.' He laid down his lino-cutter and gave his whole attention to the narrative. 'I was going to bed at three and four o'clock, and just lying there till midnight, sometimes as late as two in the morning, without even trying to go to sleep. The snow always threw a kind of glare up, even on the darkest night; it used to shine upwards on to the ceiling. That's when I did some really deep thinking. About how good it would be to get out of all this. How I was going to enjoy the feeling of a bit of money in my pocket, and my work being talked about, and my name in the papers and people going into galleries to see the things I'd done and telling one another about them. And the food! I made up a separate menu every day. And the girls I was going to get to bed with. I thought about that more than food, at first, but as I got weaker I thought about food more, and girls hardly at all.'

His face caught the light from the window, and I saw how pale he was. I hadn't realized, when I got my first glimpse of him, that he looked much different from his usual self; but now I saw it. It wasn't that his face was thin; on the contrary, it was unhealthily bloated, as if he had lived on bread and potatoes for months. This sudden clear view of his face, coupled with his fast, wild talking, suddenly made me realize that he was half crazed. So this was what he had come to! He had made a goddess of Art and kneeled before her, willing to ignore everything else, and she had kicked him in the face for his trouble. *Why do people do it?* I asked myself. In my uncontrollable impulse to do something, to make some kind of constructive suggestion, I blurted out, 'What about Ned?'

Robert halted in his pacing about and turned to stare at me. His face was grim, heavy, threatening even.

'What about him?'

I knew I was on slippery ground, but I went on, like a skater who drives forward faster and faster to avoid falling. 'If Ned had known you were in this kind of state he'd have made it his business to help you.'

'His business!' Robert shouted. 'Yes, he'd have made it his business! That's just about what it amounted to! I was just one of the concerns he had a controlling share in! Well, let me tell you that I'm not at home to Ned. He ferreted out my address from somewhere and wrote to ask how I was doing.

*And I threw the letter in the fire.* If I can't keep going without Ned, I'll starve. I'd be happier starving than eating crumbs out of his hand.'

I stood there, silenced. Of course there were lots of common-sense arguments I could have brought up, but common sense itself told me that it would be a waste of time. What could I do then? Obviously, feed him.

'How far is the village?' I asked. 'Is there a pub there where they can cook a decent meal?'

'I've never tried them, but I believe there's food laid on, of a kind, at the Coach and Horses,' he said. 'Why? Are you going to take over Ned's role and stand me a square meal?'

Instead of bothering to fend off the sneer, I just said simply, 'Yes. Get your coat on.'

We walked down to the village and got a meal. This in itself was a feat that I would never have attempted on my own behalf; at that time you had to go down on your knees for a ham sandwich, and for a hot meal you had practically to sign an undertaking that the landlord could be named as your sole legatee, requisition your house and garden, sleep with your wife and/or sister, and wipe his boots on your waistcoat. It took me about forty minutes' solid arguing, during which time Robert sat contentedly in the bar drinking stout from pint glasses, before they even agreed to *start* cooking anything. I was roused, however, by the urgency of Robert's need, and I battered down obstacle after obstacle. So in the end there we were, facing each other across a table, and with something to get our teeth into that was at any rate hot and plentiful.

Robert gorged like a man driven insane by hunger. I was afraid he'd throw it all up over the table-cloth before he even got to the end of it, but he didn't. He managed the whole lot, plus a wedge of cheese and another pint of stout. Then we walked, very slowly, back to the cottage. A mild sunshine had struggled through the veil of cloud, and the scene was relatively cheerful. Robert, the top button of his trousers undone in deference to his full belly, the sun playing benignly on his pallid, stubbly face, looked happier; he even recovered enough buoyancy to start railing against the world. His particular theme, I remember, was the damage done to genuine artists by pseudo ones.

'It was the greatest misfortune in the history of the arts', he pontificated, 'when the decay of religious belief left them isolated as the only thing that could be believed in. In a world where nobody else believed in what he was doing, the artist was the only person who still felt absolutely certain that he wasn't wasting his life. So what happened? Everybody tried to get into the act. I suppose it was about 1920 that the rot started. In they poured, like a horde of sick rats, buying up studios, living like artists, dressing like artists, doing everything except produce art like artists. Result – the rents of studios went up beyond the reach of the only people who were entitled to have them. Look at me. Stuck out here like a stray mongrel in a cave. All the things I need absolutely unobtainable. If I were in London I could at least go to galleries and look things up in the British Museum and all that. But here I am, and there *they* are, cluttering up Chelsea and doing nothing but chatter about painting . . . no, by God, some of them actually do paint – those are the ones I hate worst. They actually dare insult good canvas by dabbing at it with their expensive new brushes. Women, mostly. Amateur tarts who keep up the pose of being artistic because they think it marks them off from the professionals. Well, so it does, but give me the professionals. At least they're cleaner – they know what they want and go straight for it.' Etc. etc. On he rambled, stabbing wildly with his hands as if lopping off the heads of the people he was denouncing. I liked that; it piped off his desperation into a harmless channel, and if he could be encouraged in that direction I had some hopes of his sanity.

But it seemed imperative, all the same, to get him out of this hole. Still careless of how many bricks I dropped, as long as I could be of some use, I asked him why he didn't come back home; at least he had friends there who could keep an eye on him. (What I meant, in plain English, was that it would be easier to stand him a meal if he was on the spot: but I didn't put it that way; there would be no sense in making my English *too* plain.)

But at the mention of the town I mustn't name, he suddenly fell silent. 'It's impossible,' he said, and when I tried to get him to explain he just shook his head. Looking back on it now, I think he had a sense of guilt, whether or not he admitted it to himself. He had never been back to visit the seal and the walrus, after that night when I had accompanied him to the station, and they had died during the war; first the walrus, then, only about a year later, the seal; although Robert had been in England at the time, and could easily have got leave to attend both funerals, he hadn't. Couldn't face it, I suppose. Anyway, he seemed to be psychologically committed to the policy of giving the place a miss. I saw, soon enough, that we'd never get him back there.

By now it was the middle of the afternoon. I had to think about getting back, if I wasn't going to be stuck here for the night. Robert had the time-table, and it seemed that the next bus to the station was more or less due. All we had to do was to listen for its approach.

I sat on the bit of Robert's bed that wasn't covered by the board. It was a bad moment. I didn't want to go, but I couldn't see how I could help him if I stayed. I made him accept the 'loan' of the few shillings I had left over – the lunch hadn't been cheap – but that brought me to the end of my resources. I looked at him. He had picked up his lino-cutter and was paring away again, as if I had already left. It wasn't rudeness; he wanted to use the daylight. I didn't know what to do. I swear I felt like crying. It was like leaving a man on a raft in mid Atlantic.

And there was something worse – something I haven't mentioned yet, which had haunted me increasingly all the time I had been with him. He had stopped being superstitious. The old sense of being subservient to those mysterious Powers, which had to be appeased and humoured, but from whose bounty all his real strength was desired – it was gone. Perhaps it had ebbed away during those lonely nights in bed, with the glimmer from the snow striking upwards on to the ceiling, and making a hard, analytical, faith-killing kind of light. But whatever was the reason it had gone. He had found 'real' life so hard that he had no fear left over to give to the creating Furies. And the release from fear could only mean, in his case, the release from love and awe. The circuit was broken. Whether he knew it or not, I knew it, and I felt as if it were his death bed I was sitting on the end of.

The chugging of the bus came through the afternoon air. Through the window I saw it coming round the bend in the road, a quarter of a mile away.

'Well, here it is,' I said.

Robert looked up from his work. 'It'll take you right to the station,' he said. 'Have a good trip back.'

He smiled. I smiled back. Why had we suddenly become

polite, almost distant? We were like the vicar and the doctor going our separate ways after the squire's tea-party.

'I'll try and get over and see you again,' I said.

'Do,' he said, nodding graciously as if reminding me to help myself to a peach from his hot-house on my way down the drive.

The bus was nearly there. I had to say something. 'Robert,' I said.

'Yes?' He was courteous, attentive.

I waved my hand as he had done when he spoke of 'all this'. I indicated his poverty, his semi-starvation, the dirt and inconvenience.

'I — I'm sure it won't be for ever,' I said. And without looking at him I turned and went down the stairs and out.

What I didn't know, and neither did he, was that I was right.

# VI

The first wave of Robert's success, when it did come, rolled in out of a calm sea and knocked us all off our feet. It was in the autumn after I visited him in the spring, that the thing broke. I'd felt worried about him all through the summer, but — like most people — I'd somehow accepted my worrying as a valid substitute for *doing* anything; and, being pretty busy with one thing and another, I never got down into Northamptonshire to see him. I felt all the more of a cad about this because I had, since that awful visit, ceased to feel the sort of confidence in Robert's powers that I'd always felt before; the sense I had always had of his resilience, and his inexorable surge towards due recognition, had been badly eroded, and in its place I had the haunting vision (when I let it haunt me, which was pretty shamefully seldom) of his isolation, his being ground down by the sheer weight of odds against him. It was rugged. But beyond admitting its ruggedness, I did nothing, largely because there wasn't anything I *could* do. Unless you happen to be an art critic or a gallery director, there isn't much you can do for an artist, short of giving him money, and I hadn't any of that; not any that I didn't need, anyway.

Summer narrowed down into autumn, and suddenly, one foggy morning in October, it happened. I had just got to the office and was leafing through a pile of dailies that had been dumped on my desk — we get most of them in, of course, and keep an eye on them. This particular morning I was half heartedly wondering whether there would be anything about Robert in one or two of them; he was having a show, nothing very promising, and not in a West End gallery, but still a show was a show. We had run a few lines about it the night before, and, partly because of my nagging conscience, I was hoping there might be a chance to scrape together enough dope for another few lines later in the week, about how the show had gone, and so forth.

I looked at the papers, lying neat and prim on my desk. There's something about the way newspapers are folded that makes one half yearn and half dread to open them out — it's one of those irrevocable things, like breaking ice. I lifted my hand several times to the stack, and several times contented myself with merely shuffling them, so as to get the smallest on top, or something equally fatuous. Once I unfold these, I thought, they'll be so much waste paper; at present they're triumphs of industrialism. I remember this queer little struggle very clearly, because it was so unusual for me to have this sort of whim — I generally deflower dozens of newspapers in a day with no more hesitation than if they had been Circassian slave girls. It must have been one of those odd little kinks in the time corridor, or something of the kind, bringing it home to me that the apparently trivial action I was about to perform was actually one of the most significant of my life.

Fanciful? Possibly, but it certainly worked out like that. Once I had got that stack of papers open and looked at them, I was living in a new epoch. I mean it — I was no longer an uncouth provincial boor, remarkable only for his fatness and idleness; I was the boyhood friend and associate of Robert Lamb, the painter whose personality became a legend and whose art affected the entire sensibility of his time. Et cetera and so on. And why not? Every great name that has rocketed up into the skies, for everyone to wonder at, has dragged up with it a cluster of obscure names — people who get into the act, whose names are household words, just because they knew these prodigies. If you don't happen to be in that position, though, don't bother to envy those of us who are. It's cold up here on the stick of the rocket.

I opened the first paper, and began slowly leafing through it, holding my red pencil in case there was anything I wanted to encircle for the boss's consideration. But I never used the red pencil that morning. That very first paper told me that everything else was crowded out. It was one of the kind that don't recognize the existence of any of the arts, until someone gets involved in a scandal, or goes bankrupt, or commits suicide. So they had tried to classify Robert under the heading of scandal. They ran a headline on one of the gossip-and-feature pages – 'THIS PAINTER GIVES IT TO 'EM STRAIGHT', or something like that. The usual drool followed; Robert's show had been crowded, his pictures were considered shocking ('merciless', I remember, came in a couple of times), and his personal remarks about people, especially about fellow artists, had topped up the mixture. There was a picture of him scowling; it was the expression he wore when delivering his grating monologues about art and life in general, and how well I knew it. I could guess, from his expression, just the sort of thing he must have been saying at the moment the shutter clicked. Saying that somebody or other was 'fatally inchoate', I shouldn't wonder. Well, from now on a lot of people beside myself were going to be familiar with that expression. I opened the next paper, and the next. They all had something about Robert's show, and most of them had garnished it with one or two of his truculent remarks. The man was a natural, of course, and they had woken up to it. It had been a grim summer and the press was only too glad to have something to print that would make a change from the international situation. Robert came in absolutely pat. Being an artist, he could provide a focus for the vague and rootless culture snobbery that was part of the air of post-war England; being rough and aggressive he fitted into the role of professional brick-dropper and stone-thrower, another character dear to the downtrodden modern Englishman; and the people who really had a genuine interest in art couldn't scoff and hold aloof, because his pictures really were the freshest and strongest thing we had to boast of.

All that day I was on the telephone, to the news agencies, to the gallery where the show had been held, to people like

Justin Cartridge (who, of course, was bragging at the top of his voice about having recognized Robert from the start); I put together the story and we ran it in the early edition; odds and ends of detail still kept coming in, all through the afternoon, and for the late edition we bumped it up a bit – made it a column longer. I even got the boss to agree to a short item, with a headline, on the front page, drawing attention to the fuller story inside. He didn't feel too happy about making a fuss over someone who had done nothing but paint a few rotten old pictures, and didn't even live in the district, but I carried the point; it wasn't a day when there was much football to report. So Robert had made the front page, twenty-four hours after his first emergence into the limelight – and all thanks to his well-known, well-loved, well-creased, well-thumbed and well-spat-on friend, a name known to all students of English painting, Joe S. Shaw, S. for soap.

After that it was left-right-left, too quick to follow, till we were all genuinely punch-drunk. He was in the illustrated pages, talking to Sir Mortimer Plombières, enjoying a joke with Lady Bidet on the staircase. He was in the Sunday papers. He was in the dailies and the weeklies and the monthlies. The rest of us began to forget about him; he no longer concerned us. That autumn and winter went by, and then the spring, and then half the summer. It was a very hot summer, for the first two months at any rate, and heat makes human beings incapable of thinking about anything except their own bodies; human beings who aren't accustomed to it, anyway. I was sitting inertly in the office late one afternoon thinking about my own body, and thinking at a slightly more superficial level that it was getting time to go home, when a telephone call from London came through. A personal one, for me.

'Joe?' It was Robert's voice. 'Good, I've caught you. Come to a party next Saturday night.'

'Where?' I asked, stalling. Saturday night was my night off and I didn't want to waste it.

'What does it matter where?' he asked angrily. 'If you want to know, it's at my house. Where else would I give a party?'

I asked him where that was, and he named a pretty ritzy part of Hampstead, near the Heath. As if I couldn't have guessed!

'Well, what time can I expect you?' he asked, as the pips sounded.

I played for time a bit more, but finally he got me to admit that I could come, and that I didn't have to return till the next day. Then he progressed to the thing he had *really* rung up to ask me.

'Listen, bring Ned along, will you?'

'I don't know if he's free,' I said. 'Why don't you ring him up?'

'Damn it,' he said, getting into a very unconvincing imitation of a temper, 'have I got to spend my entire life on the telephone, just to ask a few people to a party? Why can't you ring him? You've got the office phone. Yes,' he went on, not waiting to hear anything I might have to say, 'you whip up old Ned and the two of you come along here any time you like on Saturday. The party'll be under way about nine.'

It was on the tip of my tongue to say that I didn't want to act as a buffer state between him and Ned, but I didn't say it. After all, why didn't I want to? Why shouldn't I act up to the only role I seemed likely to be cast for?

'Come not between the fell opposed points Of mighty opposites,' I said, frowning into the telephone.

'Right,' said Robert vaguely. 'See you Saturday.'

He rang off and I sat trying to think. But it was too hot.

Ned and I travelled first class on the Euston express. I had never taken a first-class ticket in my life before, though I had, of course, sometimes been driven into a first-class compartment by shortage of seats elsewhere, and paid the difference when the man came round. But Ned, who was ahead of me at the ticket-office window, slammed his money down with such a brusque 'Euston, first return,' that I had to follow his lead and make the best of it. I could see that he was in no mood to have his importance diminished by mixing with the rabble. He was Ned Roper, captain of industry, off to London to grace with his presence a party given by his old friend, Mr Robert Lamb, the well-known artist. His old and indebted friend, Mr Robert Lamb, who so readily acknowledged that without his timely and oft-repeated aid, etc. I could see I was in for a sticky journey.

We got into a compartment on our own. It was a non-smoker; Ned didn't smoke and he didn't see why he should breathe the fumes of people who did. People like me, for instance. The train pulled out, and he sat in silence for some time, looking through some papers he had brought with him.

When we made our first stop at Rugby a clergyman tried to enter the compartment. He looked like a very important clergyman, perhaps a bishop, though now I come to think of it he didn't seem to be wearing gaiters. Perhaps he was a bishop who had no horse. Anyway, he had silver hair, golden pince-nez, and a Very Reverend face. But it all availed him nothing with Ned. He had got no further than putting his apostolic hand on the door-handle when Ned gave him a look that dared him to open it and come in. He stood still for a moment and then moved down the train. Probably he went and sat in the guard's van with the parcels.

Peace for a bit, I thought. But no: Ned's eye was suddenly caught by a bell marked 'Attendant'. With a sinking heart I saw him lean forward and press the button. For God's sake, I thought. Even I could have told him that the bell had been installed thirty years ago, when the carriage had been made; back in the days when express trains carried attendants who ministered to the wishes of first-class passengers. It was all safely on record in the history books; the days when English trains were safe and punctual and clean, and covered seventy miles within the hour, the days when a pound was worth a pound. And here was Ned, in the year of grace 1948, ringing the bell for the attendant.

I said nothing. After a moment he rang again. I mean pressed the bell again: obviously it wasn't connected to any sound-producing mechanism.

'They're a damned long time coming,' he remarked to no one special.

'You don't actually think there's anybody at the other end of that bell, do you?' I couldn't help asking.

As I might have expected, he flared up. 'It says "Attendant", doesn't it?' he demanded. 'What's the point of – ' At that moment he caught sight of something that caused him to break off and grab for the door-handle. It was a man in the short buff jacket of a dining-car steward, moving down the corridor.

Ned had the door open before the man could sidle past.

'Yes, in here,' he called.

The man put his head into the compartment and asked shortly, 'What d'you mean, in here?'

'It was me ringing,' Ned explained.

'Ringing?' the man echoed incredulously. 'You mean ringing the bell?'

Ned, I was glad to see, had sufficient sanity left to give him that point. He had the man there now, whether the bell had summoned him or not.

'I'd like a whisky and soda,' he said. 'You'll have one, won't you, Joe? Two,' he added, turning back to the attendant.

The man continued to stare at him unblinkingly, like a reptile.

'That's all,' said Ned, pretending to turn back to the papers on his lap. But it was a poor performance. His opponent had got him rattled, and he showed it badly.

There was a short silence while the steward stared down at the top of Ned's head, then he closed the door silently and walked off down the corridor. We never saw him again; it was woundingly obvious that he simply dismissed Ned from his mind, as some poor crazed wretch who had heard that the licensing laws permitted him to drink whisky on a train at five o'clock in the afternoon, and thought this entitled him to ask for some.

We crept off the train at Euston, and went out into the misty evening in search of something to eat. In a taxi, of course; Ned had us in one even before we had decided where we were going. First he told the driver to make for Park Lane, then he rapped on the glass and redirected him, then finally he had a brainwave and remembered the name of some extra special superb restaurant, where we could do ourselves really proud, and redirected the driver again. This third time the man showed no signs of having heard; he just snatched at the wheel in a silent fit of temper, without slowing down, and flung the cab round in about twice its own length, nearly dragging the tyres off. Ned was thrown into the corner and I came bouncing down on him and crushed the breath from his body. Crimson, he banged on the glass.

'Watch what you're doing!' he called.

For answer, the driver crammed on his brakes, so that we were both jerked down from the seat a second time and fell with our knees on the floor. Then he turned and smiled at us through the glass, sliding the panel to one side so that we could speak to him.

'Beg pardon, sir?' he asked silkily.

'I said watch what you're doing,' said Ned, heaving himself back on to the seat.

'You put your trust in the police, sir, that's my advice,' said the driver. He shut the panel and we moved on. Perhaps he meant that Ned could leave it to the police to run him in if he did anything irregular. I was glad when we got out.

At the restaurant it was the same. Nobody could run about fast enough for Ned. The food wasn't good enough and it wasn't well enough cooked. He wanted a table at the side of the room, preferably in a corner, and they could only give us one in the middle. I really believe we'd have been thrown out of any ordinary restaurant; the only thing that saved us was that this was extremely expensive, the sort of place where they make a living by allowing rich people to behave badly. The unexpressed bargain is, 'You pay us ten times what everything's worth, and in return we'll provide you with a little pocket of territory where you can play at being as important as you used to be.' And Ned played. He needed that particular drug and he simply wallowed in it. I felt terrible about being with him, but on the other hand I couldn't leave him to it. I wasn't in a very forgiving mood, but at least I could understand what was the matter. The bad times had started. The one really big shot among us was the one big shot no longer.

Finally, when Ned had rung every ounce of solace out of behaving intolerably at the restaurant, we moved on to the party. I had been dreading the taxi ride, but fortunately this particular driver was fairly docile, and we had no accidents.

We drew up in a quiet street which looked at first sight as if it had been converted to a municipal car-park. One house was blazing with light, and its front door was ajar. Welcome to Liberality Hall. Come and join the brilliant throng of thronging brilliance. I wondered why I had not had the sense to stay at home, but Ned was already thronging up the garden path, so I thronged after him and we thronged in.

A thickset woman peeled the coats off our backs and gave us the once-over. She looked like a woman police sergeant (professional) and cross-Channel swimmer (amateur). When she had got our coats firmly over her arm, she seemed to feel better, and pointed with her free hand to the room where the party was obviously going on.

'In there to the ghosts,' she said. Being very quick-witted, Ned and I realized that she was a foreigner and given to little mistakes in English, like saying 'ghosts' for 'guests'. Looking back on it now, I realize that there is also the possiblity that she meant, 'In there for the *coats*', and was really pointing to the small room they were using for the vestibule. Anyway, we smiled stiffly and went to join the other ghosts.

The room was very full. It was full of the sort of people who go to parties given by celebrities. That is, it divided into three layers. First, a sprinkling of people equal in stature to the celebrity himself; people who had genuine gifts, whose names meant something, whose acquaintance could be counted as one of the solid advantages of success – or its only one. Then a much thicker layer of people who were not gifted, not particularly interesting, had nothing to contribute, but nevertheless seemed quite at home, as if it were a matter of course that any new-made celebrity should devote a fair slice of his time to hobnobbing with them. Human furniture, I said to myself, feeling grimmer every second. Then there was the third layer, much smaller again – in fact nearly as small as the top layer. These were the people who hadn't got anything to contribute and knew it. The surprise they were feeling, at finding themselves in Robert's house at all, kept showing in their faces in spite of all their efforts to hide it. I felt some kinship with this group, which was just as well considering I was one of them.

And there was Robert. He turned and saw us at once, though he was pretty thickly surrounded with people who seemed to be hanging on his words. And he stopped in mid sentence. We had not advanced five steps into the room before he was with us, shaking our hands.

'Nice to see you, boys,' he said quite quietly.

Ned and I murmured the usual formula, and the ice was just breaking up nicely when Ned, the fool, couldn't resist adding, 'Haven't seen much of you lately.'

'You could have done,' Robert came back at him, very sharply. 'I've been in this house for months. You must have been in London quite often.'

Ned realized, I suppose, that he had been a fool to start provoking Robert by insinuating that he had no time for his old friends, and he made a lame effort to back out. 'Didn't know where you lived,' he muttered.

'Don't give me that,' Robert grated. 'An administrative wizard like you couldn't be baffled by a simple problem like finding my address. If every reporter from every third-rate paper knew it, it can't have been so hard to find.'

The reference to reporters was unfortunate, not because I was there – I had the sense not to mind it – but because it seemed to Ned like a veiled boast about his fame. So instead of spreading a little butter, he reared up more aggressively than ever, and snarled something about reporters that neither Robert nor I caught, but we understood its tone.

*Quick*, I thought. *Get them out of this deadlock.* So far the whole scene had only lasted about thirty seconds. Nobody else had noticed that the two of them were on the brink of a quarrel. Conversation was still buzzing away as loudly as ever. But in a moment, if Robert didn't rejoin his group, or make some other host-like move, one of those nasty silences would begin to spread through the room. And I hadn't come all the way to London to listen to that.

So I threw back my head and bawled with laughter. It sounded idiotically false; a child in arms could have told that I was faking it. But I kept on, peal after peal. The impression was, or at any rate I hoped the impression was, that Robert and Ned had been putting their faces close together and muttering because they had been telling one another the latest joke about the commercial traveller and the landlady's daughter.

Ned and Robert glared at me. I bowed double, whacking my thigh, then straightened up and gave Ned a heavy blow in the ribs. He reeled, and I swung round on Robert and beat viciously on his back. The three of us tottered like drunken giraffes. Through my squalling burst of laughter I heard that dreaded silence, but only for a moment. Then the ghosts all turned to one another and began talking harder than ever. In this way they expressed their tact and sympathy. Robert was momentarily in an awkward position – that was how they saw it. Two louts had come in, up in town for the evening. Old pals of his boyhood days, who had doubtless presumed on that fact to excuse their gate-crashing. What a wretched early life Robert must have had, if he had been forced to choose his friends from among people like these. (But then these artists *suffer* so much.) They certainly were a horrible pair. The tall, fair one looked reasonably gentlemanly, but the fat one was really scruffy and, besides, he was quite obviously drunk. That horrible *laugh*. Really, it was too much.

It was too much for me too, but I went on laughing until I was sure the moment of crisis was past. By the time I allowed it to die away, neither Robert nor Ned had any thought in their minds except to break up our little *totentanz* and start behaving as normally as they knew how.

Robert's version of behaving normally of course was to go back to the group that had been hanging on his words and set up some more words for them to hang on. He took care to have Ned along with him, and to bring him into the conversation a good deal. But here he ran into another problem: Ned didn't need to be taken under anybody's wing. His appearance, his clothes, and his bearing (a rather relaxed version of his board-room manner) had already made the ghosts realize that they'd misjudged him; and when they heard that he was Blue Seal Pottery, he was immediately marked up as Somebody, and went into the top class with the four or five other Somebodies who were there. Like all parties this one was made up of a few suns and lots of planets; within ten minutes Ned was a sun, and had his own satellites revolving happily round him. He split off from Robert's group, but not abruptly, and the two of them were obviously on easy terms. I breathed again.

As for me, I was just a moon: I'd have been the satellite of a planet, if one had asked me. I got a glass in my hand and joined the mob surrounding Robert. Or rather, I went and stood on its outer periphery and listened. I didn't need to follow very attentively what he was saying. I knew it all from long ago. He was giving one of his snarling monologues, the sort I had heard him give so many times down through the years. I had only to close my eyes, which I felt like doing anyway, and I was back in the Genius Room listening to him giving tongue about Baxter, or sitting in the pub near his grandparents' home, hearing his views on provincial life, or the public, or what not. Nothing had changed, except that where he had once had no more impressive audience than old Joe Shaw, he now had a well-dressed, moneyed bunch like this to hammer at. I drained my glass, and got another from a tray. Was it only last winter that I had visited him in the cottage? I saw his haggard face, his powerful frame wasting away amid that sea of chaos and dirt, his mad, fixed look when he talked about food or women, his remorseless drive onwards, paring and paring at that slab of linoleum in the last hour of natural light. *Good luck to you, boy,* I thought; *get what you can while it's there.* The tray came past again, and this time I took a couple, vaguely hoping the flunkey would think I was getting one for a lady. In rapid succession I tossed them back. This party needed softening at the edges, and as I couldn't work on the ghosts I might as well work on myself. I turned my attention back to Robert's harangue. He had got on to the subject of sham artists; the very subject he had chosen to hold forth on as we walked back to his cottage that spring day, after I had stood him a meal at the village inn. Stood him a meal! It struck me, now, as wildly funny that Robert should ever have needed *me* to stake him to a plate of meat-and-potato pie. And only a few months ago! That's how powerful success is; its magic can make even the recent past seem incredible. 'These are the people', Robert was saying impressively, 'who've con-stituted the greatest menace that the serious artist has known in our time.' I felt like calling out to him to be careful. After all, at least half this bunch were exactly the type he was talking about. The women, in particular; they were mainly the sort who are too well heeled and too idle to take up any sort of work on reaching adult years, and, at a loss how to fill in the five or six years between leaving school and getting married, move to town and find a 'studio' – so much more interesting than 'lodgings' or 'a flat' – where they daub a bit to keep up appearances and impress the eligible Philistine. It was all written across them so plainly – and here was Robert lashing them and all their works with his tongue. And what was more, I realized, they were *loving* it. I took another couple of drinks, this time not even perfunctorily pretending that the second was destined for someone else, and settled down to listen care-fully for a clue to this enigma. 'If only they could be sent back where they belong,' Robert was roaring, 'and leave the Latin Quarter to the people who originally brought it into being. And it isn't only a question of rents. Look at all the privately financed one-man shows. The galleries are booked up half the time, showing worthless pictures done by people who can afford to pay to have them shown.' I looked across at the ring of faces round him: they were all rapt with attention and pleasure. Suddenly the truth slammed into me, and I wanted to sit down and bury my face in my hands. To them it was all a new game. The more Robert raved and grumbled the more they appreciated the act. They didn't know, in any real sense, what he was talking about; how could they, when the words he was using were, to them, nothing but words? The word 'rheumatism' doesn't mean much to you until you've *had* rheumatism; neither do the words 'poverty' and 'loneliness'. If Robert told them that people like themselves were responsible for the high rents of studios, they nodded rapturously, never having had the experience of walking around Chelsea on a rainy afternoon, in leaking shoes and with their entire worldly possessions under one arm, knocking at one door after another and finding all the rents too high. I didn't blame these people, and in any case I had no more experience of that kind of thing than they had; it just so happened that I wasn't quite so cushioned off from reality as they were, quite so unable to imagine what being down on your luck could mean.

I was standing there, thinking gloomily along these sort of lines, when Ned came up to me; or, rather, halted at my side on his way across the room.

'Going well,' he said bluffly.

'Going well who for?' I asked.

'Well, for Robert, primarily,' he said. Something in his manner made me look at him closely for a moment. His expression was certainly a curious one. I'd have expected it to be registering either generous pleasure at Robert's success, which he obviously would have liked to register, or, alternatively, envy, which you'd have thought he was feeling underneath. But what I saw – only for an instant, but very plainly – was something quite different from either: it was *triumph*. A kind of Mephistophelean *schadenfreude*.

But what had he got to be triumphant about?

'It's good to see Robert on top at last,' I said, to test him.

'Isn't it!' he said enthusiastically – a shade too enthusiastically, I thought. 'You know I've waited a long time for this to happen, Joe.'

And again that queer look came into his eyes as he glanced over at Robert. I glanced over too. Robert was still holding forth, in the middle of a knot of satellites; what with braying and gesturing and generally parodying himself, he seemed less real, more like an unskilful imitation, than he had a short while ago, when we came in. It was as if his reality was leaking away from him in the poisonous atmosphere of the party. Was it the party, or was it just the general atmosphere of his life? I thought of the concentration of Robert-ness, so to speak, that I remembered in that hellish cottage; the way, depressed as he was, he had generated so much of the essence of his identity that the place had been saturated with it. The new atmosphere was different; a dilution, and in a way something worse than a dilution; an adulteration perhaps. I looked at Ned again.

'Of course, he'll have to be careful,' I said.

'Careful? Why?'

'Well . . . not to let it spoil him,' I said lamely.

Ned gave one of those easy, genial laughs. 'It'll take more than this to spoil old Robert,' he said. 'Why, if poverty couldn't get him down all those years, why should a bit of prosperity?'

*You know why*, I thought. *You know the danger he's in – and aren't you glad.*

I turned away, to get a drink. So that pattern was possible. Robert could become a fashionable money-making artist, just another version of Ned, only more repulsive because of his greater pretensions. That ought to set Ned's mind at ease. *Damn them both!* I thought.

I was beginning to feel a trifle unsteady on my legs, and in any case I felt the need to keep some hold on my sense of proportion – after all, Robert's whole life wasn't going to be spent giving parties like this one. So I did the sensible thing; I moved slowly towards the door and out. Originally I only meant to stand in the hall for a minute or two, out of the smoke and chatter; but when I got there the front door was still ajar and I could see that it was a fine, moonlit, crisp autumnal night. It was too tempting. The garden was the place for me, and I started off towards it.

The thickset foreign woman jumped out on me, but I was ready for her and dodged aside.

'Your goat?' she suggested hoarsely.

'No, just my calf,' I countered with an airy laugh. Silently she handed me my scarf, and I put it round my neck, keeping an alert eye on her in case she should dart forward and drag at the two ends. But she did no more than watch me narrowly as I went out.

The garden was well tended; the moonlight didn't enable one to see colours, but even in monochrome I could tell that the effect was tasteful. I couldn't see Robert doing any gardening; however much his success might alter the structure of his character, there was one thing I was reasonably confident of never seeing, and that was Robert doing any unnecessary manual work. So this garden probably represented a pretty fair outlay of money. So did the house. I walked round the side and peeped into the garage. Nosey Parker. Inside was a new-looking car. It was a Bristol 2-litre. I thought of the cottage and the milkman leaving a bottle or two when he was passing, out of charity.

In fact, I thought of this, and thought of that, and altogether I came over quite absent-minded. Perhaps the fresh air, coming on top of what I had drunk, was a bit strong too. Anyway, I found myself walking down the garden path, away from the house, with my head down and my hands clasped behind my back, like some old don out for his constitutional.

So it happened that I got to the gate at exactly the moment when a taxi drew up there and a girl got out. Nothing very unusual about that. It was the girl who was unusual. I didn't think I was seeing right, at first. Surely no girl could be as elegantly built as that? Ordinary blonde human hair couldn't, surely, have that silvery effect, even in moonlight?

I had seen photographs of women that streamlined their shapes and made them look so alluring that you knew it was all a trick, that once the spell was broken and they moved, you would see that they were just ordinary, if pretty, women. But this one moved and was still like that.

She paid the taxi-man, whose mind seemed to be moving in much the same grooves as mine, to judge from the fact that he put the money down on the floor under his seat and tried to move off in top gear. Then she came straight up to me. I thought she was about to ask me a question, and I got ready to answer it to the very, very best of my ability.

But she just halted and looked at me, and I realized that she had come up to me so directly because I was standing in the gateway blocking her way.

'Sorry,' I said, trying to step aside. But the gatepost was terribly in the way and I bounced back into her path. 'You must have come to the aid of the party,' I said, babbling.

'This way,' I said, turning and going up the path at a canter. When I reached the house I turned back and looked at her. She was still standing at the gate, as if afraid to come any nearer. I suppose she thought I was a lunatic. I waved my arms about. 'Don't let me detain you!' I called. 'I mean come along!' I was wondering, all the time, what the hell I thought I was playing at.

Then the thickset woman appeared from her den again and was obviously coming to see what the fuss was about. Oh,

NO! I thought. *Not you!* *Anything but you!* I blocked her path. 'Robert!' I shouted. 'Robert!'

'What is the mat?' the woman asked. I panicked. If she said anything like that to the girl, it would be the finish; she would get into another taxi (there were probably a dozen, permanently following her) and never be seen again.

'Robert!' I called again. The woman walked towards me, stiff-legged and menacing, like a mastiff.

Robert appeared at the door of the room where the party was. He was scowling, and the scene that met his eyes didn't alter his expression.

'What the blazes are you fooling about at, Joe?' he demanded.

'Look in the garden,' I hissed, still trying to head the woman off.

'Don't let this man worry you, Mrs Sienkiewicz,' he said, and I felt a shudder of pure dread at the thought that the woman bore the same name as the author of *Quo Vadis?*. 'Look in the garden!' I shouted in a high, quavering voice. The woman seemed about to throw herself on me.

Robert pushed past me, grim-faced. I suppose he expected to find a man-eating sheep in the garden. I didn't dare turn my head, or Mrs Sienkiewicz would have been at my throat, but I heard his footsteps begin abruptly and then stop dead. *He had seen her.*

We were all statues. Mrs Sienkiewicz glared at me; I watched her hands, ready to beat off any sudden rain of blows. Outside in the moonlight Robert and the girl stood like figures of hammered metal.

# VII

After that it was all over except for rubbing one's bruises. Robert was in love and he didn't care who knew it. Or rather, he did care; he wanted the entire world to be fully informed about the state of his feelings. And they were, of course; it all made admirable news fodder. Because the girl, as I might have known the instant I set eyes on her, wasn't unknown in her own right. As I realized when we got back into the room and I saw her by electric light, I had seen her photograph often enough. She was Myra Chetwynd, the fashion model. At that time if you wanted to sell a garment to the women of England, the *sine qua non* was to take a picture of Myra wearing it. Or rather, to take a picture of Myra wearing a specially tailored version of it that enabled her to make it look about five times as elegant as it was. Or, most often of all, to take a picture of Myra wearing an ordinary version of it that was rigged with about a dozen pegs and fifty pins, round the back where you couldn't see.

Whatever the mixture was, it *worked*, and the result was that Myra had become an important symbol, not without realizing it either. A symbol of possession, of achievement, of ease, of having it good: what the ad. man, in his sickening dialect, calls 'gracious living'. In the post-war scramble for comforts and diversions, Myra was the publicly accepted emblem of success.

The interesting thing is that Robert always swore he had never heard of her, and didn't remember seeing her photograph. According to him Myra impinged on his consciousness for the first time when they confronted each other in his garden on the evening of his party. And for all I know it may be true. Considering the kind of life he had led since coming back from the war it wouldn't be surprising if he had never lifted his head high enough to look at a poster. But of course the real reason may be something subtler; it may be that the rest of us notice a face like Myra's, that we see staring at us from every hoarding, because it stands out from the sea of faces we just don't notice. We don't use our eyes, so it sticks in our minds when we're *forced* to notice something. This wouldn't apply to an artist. On the other hand, it's always possible that Robert was simply not telling the truth – that he was half aware of something suspect in his own motive and wanted to get in first with his denial.

Anyway, there it was. The booming fashionable artist and the blooming artistic fashionable were headed for domestic bliss. Or domestic something, at any rate. It was coming and there was nothing the rest of us could do but take cover.

The papers splashed Robert again, but this time as an appendage; Myra was the real news. I don't know how he took this, because I was keeping out of his way. After the party I went back to the town I mustn't name and stayed there, out of harm's way. I had enough to put up with as it was. From Stocker, for instance. He had two motives for being in and out of the Sentry office. One was to sit on the corner of my desk and outline what he'd do if he had Robert's opportunities. I kept telling him I didn't want to hear about it, but he didn't seem to understand me. The other was because he was getting his hooks on a girl called June who worked for us. He always referred to her as 'Joe's secretary', though in fact she did secretarial work for two or three of us. I think it gave him a malicious pleasure to imply that he not only wasted my time whenever he felt like it, but also got off with my secretary, a thing he no doubt imagined I was secretly burning to do myself. I often wondered why I liked him, till I remembered that I didn't like him.

But I'm going too fast. We didn't know for certain that Robert was actually going to marry Myra during those early weeks. All we knew was that he had asked her to sit for him. We knew that before the party broke up, on that crucial first evening. It was all satisfyingly dramatic; rumours were flying about, even reaching us in our Midland fastness, about how the tide of Robert's infatuation mounted week by week, how after finishing one portrait he began immediately on another, then another, declaring that Myra's beauty was inexpressible, and all the rest of it; and how, one afternoon, he finally exploded, seized his engagement book, tore it up, and declared his intention of accepting no engagements, professional or social, until he had managed a portrait of Myra which satisfied him. Reading between the lines, I should say that if he really did do anything of the kind, Myra would have reacted immediately by asking him what, in that event, he expected her to do with her engagement book. And I expect he proposed to her there and then, pointing out that if their two engagement books became one, it wouldn't matter if they both got torn up. Not that it will ever be known, and not that it matters. By the New Year the wedding was imminent. The date was fixed, the invitations arrived, we all noted without surprise that the breakfast was to be in an hotel in Park Lane; and once more I was on the old platform, waiting for the Euston express.

It was morning, about half past ten. There was a bit of raw

winter sunshine, making the scene look rather Turneresque. I remember thinking that it was an appropriate day for an artist's wedding; happy the bride the sun shines on, and happy the painter for whose wedding Nature gives a really convincing imitation of art. I didn't have time to work this thought up into a beautiful aphorism, on the lines of, 'Not to discriminate every moment some passionate attitude in those about us, and in the brilliance of their gifts some tragic dividing of forces on their ways, is, on this short day of frost and sun, to sleep before evening', because I began to be aware of the identity of some of the heavily muffled figures who, like me, were pacing the platform. One was Stocker. Another was Randall. The one at the far end, standing consciously apart, was Ned.

I didn't say anything. I supposed they had already seen me and one another, but didn't feel like facing the stern fact that we were all travelling together. We went on not speaking even after the train had rolled in and we had all boarded the buffet car. It was one of those stand-up buffets, and we put our bags down on the floor, ordered drinks and raised them to our lips, still ignoring each other. Randall and Stocker were on beer, I had a stout because I felt I needed strengthening, and Ned's was a whisky; a double, I noticed.

We drank, then looked at each other, then drank again. Nobody else was in the buffet car. We could have a little agony session all to ourselves. Outside, streaking past, were the miles of waterlogged, frozen, hibernating England; inside were the drinks and the rhythmically shifting bar-fittings; further inside still, inside our heads, was our knowledge of ourselves and one another.

This knowledge was the trouble. We all knew too much. We all knew that Randall was going to the wedding to get a skinful of free champagne. That Stocker was going to get an eyeful of non-free Myra. That I was going because I couldn't find any motive for not going. That Ned was going because if he stayed away we should know he felt the jealousy that we knew he felt anyway.

It was Randall who broke the silence. Ducking his head, with that characteristic gesture of his, so that he was looking up at us through fronds of sandy eyebrow, he flicked his eyes over each of our faces in turn; as if we were all back in class and he was searching for a boy who looked likely not to know the answer to his next question.

'Married,' he said. 'Lamb's getting married. Never thought of him as a steady type. But now, marriage. Steady him down.' He picked up his glass, gulped, and ducked his head again. 'You lot,' he barked. 'When *you* going to get married?'

Stocker laughed contemptuously. It was all so easy from his point of view. Marriage meant letting a woman tie you up. And once you were tied up, where was the supply of fresh meat to come from? He turned to Randall, sneering.

'When *you* do,' he said.

I could see that this rejoinder made Ned as uncomfortable as it made me. It was perilously close to making fun of a dwarf or hunchback. If Randall got married his salary wouldn't stretch to so much booze. He'd made his choice long ago, and it seemed unfair of Stocker to remind him of it. I wanted to speak, to break the silence that had come down on us again. But I couldn't think of anything, and I was glad when Ned, who was standing slightly apart from the rest of us, staring abstractedly into his glass, suddenly spoke up.

'Marriage,' he said musingly. 'The trouble is that it means so many different things to different people.' He paused, and I thought this was all we were going to get, but he went on, 'What it all hinges on, as I see it, is the degree of success one has in life.' As he said *success* he seemed to grow taller and more insubstantial. 'Take a man whose one aim is to settle down in a safe job. By the time he's twenty-five he can usually see the whole of his future life ahead – barring accidents, of course. He knows what kind of work he'll be doing, what kind of house he'll be living in, what kind of people he'll have for his neighbours. Comfort – that's what he wants. So, naturally, he marries the first girl who'll give it him. And he knows he's not going to run into any trouble later, because everything's going to keep on as it is, except that they'll get fatter and cosier.'

Comfort! As he talked it flashed in on me how little of it he could ever expect in his life. Hardly even as much as Robert. Ned's life was one unresting march forward, always following the spoor of Success. In the end, when he had traced the brute to its lair, he would be so weakened by the long trek that it would kill him easily.

'And one of the difficulties about being successful', Ned was going on, 'is that you can't get married, however much you want to, until you see what kind of wife you're going to need,

Of course there are lots of these great men who've got timid, mousy little wives behind the scenes, but in a case like that what happens? He just goes everywhere by himself and leaves her alone. And when she *has* to make a public appearance, it's embarrassing for both of them.'

'Why should it be?' Randall asked. 'You mean she drops her aitches or something?'

'No, of course not. I don't mean anything as crude as that. But put it this way. Marriage is like any other business deal. A man gets the best bargain he can, and so does a woman. Now, take a man who marries in early life. His position in the world isn't consolidated. He hasn't arrived. So – to put it in business terms – he enters the market, and makes his bid, when he's in a weak position, instead of holding off till he's in a strong one.'

I couldn't let him get away with this. I knew it was a waste of breath, but I also knew that if he went on with his business terms and his bids and his markets the top of my head was going to come off.

'Ever heard of something called love, Ned?' I asked him. 'Ell, oh, vee, ee. Pronounced quietly.'

'Yes,' said Ned straightaway. He had his answer to that worked out. 'Love – in the sense you're using the word – is the emotion you feel for someone of the opposite sex who's within your reach, or you think could be brought within your reach.'

'What about the people who fall in love with film stars and what not?' Stocker put in.

'A completely separate emotion,' said Ned decisively. At any moment I expected him to say, 'Let's examine this concept.' 'Ultimately, human beings are realistic. An adolescent girl falls in love with a film actor. She has his picture over her bed, she goes to see all his films half a dozen times each, she can repeat the scraps of gossip about him that are current in bars and night clubs thousands of miles away. But this is an end in itself. She doesn't even consider the idea of getting any closer to the man. He's there for day-dreams. I'm not saying the emotions she feels about him aren't real emotions. They are. But she keeps them apart from her actual life.'

'Not quite apart,' I said. 'If she meets a man who reminds her of the idol she's likely to fall for him.'

'Yes, but who else can see the resemblance?' Ned demanded. 'If she meets a man who suits her, she'll soon cook up a resemblance to her dream-mate if that's what she needs to flavour the dish a bit. An aunt of mine married a man who reminded her of Rudolph Valentino. And it's a fact that the man had dark hair, like Valentino, and was undersized like Valentino. But the resemblance had never struck anybody but her. It was just the old principle at work. She projected her image of Valentino on to her husband in order to get that extra two-penn'orth of fun out of him. It made her happy and it didn't hurt anyone. That's what people like Valentino are for.'

We digested this while glasses were refilled. I glanced out of the window at the flat, sodden fields, the frozen ponds, the cold, heavy sky. Then we were back at our posts again and Ned was taking up the thread. Even Randall was listening.

'Now, take that same girl when she *really* falls in love,' he said, stabbing the air with his forefinger. 'When she meets a youth who comes from the next village and really goes for him. She'll find out, then, if she didn't know before, that her emotions about the film star were quite different. This time *she wants him* – that's the difference. Not his picture, not the idea of him, but him. And she's prepared to fight and scheme and generally go all out to get him: and when she accepts that she accepts the possibility of suffering if she fails. She doesn't suffer over her dream-lover. He's there, like a hot-water bottle.'

'What's this got to do with a man marrying?' Stocker asked.

'This,' said Ned. 'That the distinction between the emotion that doesn't want to go any further, and the emotion that ends either in possession or in suffering, is what I mean about love. If you know you can't have a woman you don't really suffer over her: if you know it from the start, that is. You may think it's a damned shame that you've never been introduced to Rita Hayworth, but the fact remains that you haven't and you won't be. But if she lived in the next street, and moved in your circle, you'd really suffer over her.'

Stocker mechanically put in a few words that weren't strictly to the point but Ned ignored him and ploughed on.

'So take marriage. Go back to the man with his steady job and lack of ambition. He's protected against falling for a really attractive woman – protected by this principle I've been talking about.'

'It sounds as if this principle was a pretty merciful one,' I said.

'So it is. It's an argument for a beneficent Creator. If you

113

automatically fell in love with the most attractive woman you saw, in the first place your life would be hell, and in the second the plain women would never get husbands.'

'I see what you're getting at,' I said. 'A man who's on the way up is continually raising the standard of the women he can fall for. There's something inside me that prevents me from falling in love with Rita Hayworth, but that something wouldn't work if I were a prince or a millionaire.'

I paused for Ned to take this up, but Stocker cut in. He had been growing more and more restive at our refusal to put the matter in his terms, and now he wanted to put the whole argument on a different footing.

'You're overlooking the biggest factor of all,' he said, 'and that is that women don't last. They depreciate more quickly than any other type of machine. Not that they aren't durable — a good one has an effective life of twenty years, pretty well — but they only function really efficiently during the first four weeks; after that they need a change of ownership. If you gave me a choice of either having Rita Hayworth for ten years, or a succession of much plainer women that I could change as often as I wanted to, I'd choose the plain ones. Because after a year or so there wouldn't be any fun in it. It's variety that keeps the thing going — like food.'

'Do you really need that much variety with your food?' I asked. 'I wouldn't complain if I were given bacon and egg for breakfast half a dozen times running. And that beer you're drinking looks pretty much the same as the beer you have every day about this time, but you seem to be enjoying it all right.'

'No, no, Joe,' he said, shaking his pale bruiser's face from side to side, 'you won't catch me like that. My food may be basically monotonous, but meal times come round so often that it looks like variety. The reason I don't mind bacon and egg for breakfast every day is because I've got lunch and tea and dinner in between. And I wouldn't mind having the same woman every twenty-four hours provided I could guarantee to have three others in between. Always assuming I could stand it, of course,' he added seriously.

I began to see where I was. It was useless, plainly, to argue with either of them, because they were both committed to what was, fundamentally, the same position. They both saw women not as people but as instruments. Stocker saw them as instruments of pleasure, Ned as instruments of prestige. Stocker's argument was crude, Ned's – on the surface – more subtle. But in either case there was only one way of bringing them round, and that was to get them to see a woman as a person. But what was the good? If I were to tell Ned that an unsuccessful, obscure and unambitious man might find himself a wife who, *as a human being*, was as good as anyone available for the most famous and powerful – what good would that do? Again, imagine trying to tell Stocker that if he would take to exploring women in depth, rather than brushing over each one on his way to the next, he might find some pretty surprising things. He couldn't believe any such thing even if he wanted to.

All right, I had them taped. I was free to go ahead and feel sorry for them. Only one thing wasn't clear to me: from precisely what position of superiority was I looking down on them? I knew they were thinking much the same, and it didn't surprise me when Ned asked, after a short, reflective silence, 'What about you, Joe?'

'What about me and marriage, you mean?' I stalled feebly.

'What else?' he said brusquely. 'And don't tell us it's because you're still waiting to meet Miss Right. A man meets a girl he'd like to marry just as soon as he wants to and not before.'

I was stumped. As a matter of fact that stuff about not having met Miss Right was about the only thing I *could* tell them; that they would have understood, anyway. I had a genuine difficulty, but I couldn't have explained it to either Stocker or Ned. The trouble was that once I took a wife I should have to put down roots and settle for a definite way of life. In their eyes, of course, I'd already done this. Surely nobody, they thought, could have been more settled than old Joe! They thought of me as having definitely chosen a life of cosy provincial mediocrity, rooted in the town I was born and bred in. And, outwardly, I had. But I knew all the time that there was an element of fake in it. I had fitted myself out with an exterior that proclaimed a set of loyalties at first sight and sound; anybody meeting me would put me down immediately as a man who accepted the values of midland provincial life – honest, sturdy, a bit rough round the edges, making a style out of the refusal to *have* any style. And no one knew of the rebellious feelings at the heart of all this, no one but myself. In reality I was poised in mid air between two attitudes, and couldn't have come down on either side. I needed the thick, warm stew of provincial cosiness: I was a dab hand at the 'Now-lad-you-must-take-us-as-you-find-us' stuff, and it saved me a lot of trouble when dealing with day-to-day routine. On the other hand I should have gone mad if my bluff had been called and I'd been asked to settle into that position for good. Without frequent escapes to London and the Continent, I'd have been lost. But of course when I *was* in London I felt dissatisfied there too. I couldn't really believe that any good could come out of a place so swollen, monstrous, dropsical and unhealthy. I hated the pallid, scurrying crowds, the hideous vulgarity of the advertisements, the scores of miles of dingy brick, town laid end to end against town — Barnet, Edgware, Morden, Streatham, Tooting, Fulham: vanished places, swallowed up in the vortex of London. And the tiny centre with its cosmopolitanism and its pretensions, a mere cavity emptying and filling every twenty-four hours as the ocean of humanity flooded in and out. I had never, even for a second, seen myself in the role of a Londoner. Compared with the inhabitants of the town I mustn't name, they seemed like robots.

But how could I take a wife, and presumably bring up a family, without committing myself to one or the other? How could I even *choose* a wife without choosing from one or the other? I was sickened when I thought of the hordes of identical girls walking about Hampstead and Chelsea, each one with the same pony-tail and the same tight trousers as the next one, all looking for husbands and perfectly ready to settle in the provinces and devote the rest of their lives to being brave about it. But my nausea didn't get any better when I thought of the prospect of marrying a local girl, buying a local house in a local street, and filling it with local children to be educated at local schools. *Well, why not?* I was one myself, wasn't I? But I could never quite say Yes to that; Nature had intended to make me one but something had gone wrong.

I didn't go over all this ground at the time, of course; not even inwardly. I had been over it all too many times. I just stared out of the train window and tried to think of something to say. But I never did; it just got lost. More drinks came along, the buffet car filled up with nondescript passengers, and as the train rolled through the dreary desert of North London, our conversation petered out. It depressed me a lot, that train ride. Here we were, I remember thinking, Ned and I and Stocker,

brought up in the same town, educated at the same school —
and we couldn't talk to each other. So who the hell could?

I haven't really got the heart to describe Robert's wedding. It
was just about what you might expect. I hated it all so much
that from that day to this I've never gone down Park Lane
except in a taxi with my eyes shut. In fact, my Freudian censor
has cut it out so thoroughly that I can't really remember anything except how I tortured Justin Cartridge. He was there, of
course, all benignity and pince-nez and eager to explain how
his protégés never failed to rise in the world. No doubt he'd
been looking forward to the wedding ever since it was
announced, as an invaluable chance to cut a figure and do
some good public relations work. Anyway, I was standing at
the side of the room, within easy reach of the drinks, when he
came past me, went on for a few steps, and then came back for
a second look.

'I'm sure I've seen you somewhere before, haven't I?' he said,
all gracious.

'That's for you to decide,' I said. 'I've only been out two
months.'

'Out?'

I drew myself up and held my head proud and high. 'I think
you know what I mean,' I said. 'Any of us might make a
mistake. We're all human. Society decreed that I should pay
the price, and I've paid it. But there was nothing in my sentence
that said anything about hiding my face from my fellow men
after it was all over. Society didn't say to me, "When we lock
you up . . ."'

Cartridge began to retreat backwards, glancing nervously
about for help. I followed him remorselessly. I told him I
recognized him well, that he had been one of the most popular
and appreciated of the Prison Visitors. 'Those rough chaps
respected you, Mr Cartridge,' I assured him, holding him by
the shoulder. 'I know it couldn't have been easy for you, sir.
We could see there were times when you were asking yourself,
"What's the use?" But we always knew you'd stick it. Next
visiting day you'd be there again!'

'I can only think', he managed to break in, 'that you're
confusing me with someone else. I've never been a Prison
Visitor.'

I released his shoulder, letting my hand fall helplessly to my side as if his words had knocked all the spirit out of me. Stricken, I looked into his face. I put so much heart into the act that I even felt myself turning pale.

'All right, sir,' I said. 'I'll say nothing more about it. You've got your own motives for denying it, and I can respect them, even though I can't imagine what they are. But I've just one thing to say. I'm glad those chaps you did so much to help, those poor convicts you weren't too proud to comfort and talk to by the hour – I'm glad they're not here to hear you deny all knowledge of them. As I say, they're only rough chaps, and each and every one of them has gone wrong, somewhere along the journey, or they wouldn't be there. But they've got hearts, human hearts, Mr Cartridge, and I'm glad they can't hear you, that's all.'

'What the hell's going on here?' said Robert, appearing at my elbow. He had finished his task of welcoming all the guests as they came in and had begun to circulate. People were beginning to steer clear of me and Cartridge, and he must have wanted to investigate.

'Going on?' I said grimly. 'Nothing. Oh, nothing. Nothing's at stake except the feelings of a lot of poor rough chaps that don't count.'

'He keeps saying he saw me in prison,' Cartridge said in a high voice; he was terribly angry.

'In prison?' Robert squawked. A crowd began to gather.

'Yes, in prison,' I said quietly. 'And I'm not ashamed of being grateful. If I kept my sanity during those years on the Moor it's entirely owing to – '

'He's joking, Justin,' said Robert brusquely. 'He's an old friend of mine called Joe Shaw. He's never been in prison. I've often wondered whether he was right in the head.'

Then Myra came over to us. When we saw her coming from the other side of the room, my silly joke was forgotten at once, and with every step that brought her nearer, it was driven further and further out of any possible foreground. By the time she was with us, Robert's face was radiant with the pride of possession, and Cartridge and myself were just two poor rough chaps whose feelings didn't matter.

She came up to us and halted, with her feet turning outwards at the prescribed angle. Involuntarily I waited for the flash-bulbs; when they didn't go off, I felt angry. That poised halt, that rehearsed position which long training made her adopt without thinking, that devastating eye angle. It called for a camera, and – with the exception of Cartridge – we were men, not cameras. *An occupational disease*, I sneered inwardly: only to catch myself up short with the question, *Whose disease? Hers or mine?*

'You know Justin, of course, darling,' Robert was saying. 'And this is Joe Shaw, an old friend of my youth.' He made it sound as if our friendship had been an episode of boyhood, over and done with long ago. But I didn't blame him. If I'd been marrying a girl like that and I'd had to introduce her to a back number like me, I'd have pretended I'd dropped myself years ago, if you see what I mean.

'An old friend?' she said, tilting upwards at me. (Voice low-pitched, but not husky.) 'From . . . ?' and she mentioned the town I mustn't name.

'Yes, from there,' I said.

'Oh, I do want to see it,' said Myra, putting a pretty little grain of mock-petulance into her voice, but not overdoing it. 'It sounds such a strange place from what Robert's told me. But he won't take me.' She shot me a brief glance that told me it was my cue to come in on the act, to play up the queer-fish-from-the-backwoods stuff, to say Robert was a brute not to take her anywhere she wanted to go.

I saw the cue, but something went wrong with my reactions and I fluffed it. I looked at Cartridge. He was watching Myra as if she were a mobile that threatened to come to pieces.

'You're better off in civilization,' I said, swivelling my gaze back to Myra. I spoke without thinking, but – it interested me to notice – she coloured slightly, as if feeling a rebuff in my words. So she had been quick enough to notice my glance at Cartridge and to interpret it. My half-conscious thought had been, 'It's fat white grubs like him that crawl about at the so-called "centre of things" – and you're no more real than he is.' But she *was* more real; I saw that now. Cartridge would never have picked up a nuance like that.

'Yes, Myra,' Cartridge put in, 'you stay where you're appreciated, my dear.' He wagged his big, smooth face about, beaming like an insincere lighthouse.

'I'd like to see the place where they *wouldn't* appreciate her,' said Robert pugnaciously, scowling to mask the pride that warmed him to the core. Cartridge made a slight puffing sound, as if in dismissal of the absurd idea that anyone, any-where, could fail to appreciate Myra.

'Don't let them change the subject, Joe,' she said, for some reason still being nice to me, though I had expected her never to acknowledge my existence again after the floater I started out with. 'I want to see the place Robert comes from.'

'Surely it's the places he's going to that count, as far as you're concerned,' I said. 'Once a man marries a girl like you, I find it impossible to think of him as a fellow citizen. He's set the seal on his success, today. If he comes back now it can only be as a sightseer. Or perhaps a missionary.'

I couldn't have said anything that pleased Robert more, and I knew it. To talk in that strain, in front of (a) Myra and (b) Cartridge, was my wedding-present to him, and it was worth all the toast-racks in Selfridge's.

As I talked I analysed Myra. High cheek-bones and light-blue eyes with a barely perceptible slant to them. Stocker, who knew everything about her that had ever appeared in print, had told me that there was some Scandinavian blood, and I saw it in the bones of her face.

It was pretty ironic, actually, that my little speech should have closed on the word 'missionary', because at that moment Ned, urbane as ever, appeared in our midst with the parson in tow. I call him 'the parson', but of course the marriage had been at some stylish church or other, and naturally this wasn't the sort of knot that could be tied by just any old vicar. The chap Ned was towing along was one of these distinguished, silver-haired octogenarians in gold-rimmed glasses. I think he was a Canon or something. Anyway, he was a big man, metaphorically; literally he was a small one, and his shoulders were stooped by a combination of erudition, sanctity and lumbago so that his saintly old gaze swept the carpet. Dress him in rags and he'd have had the perfect stance for one of those old wrecks who glide about picking up cigarette-ends off the pavement and stowing them away in rusty tins.

Whether Ned was conscious of it or not, he had achieved a masterly piece of stagecraft. To bob up like that on the word 'missionary', handing us the Canon on a plate, as if understanding that we needed the consolations of religion, had the effect of simply picking up the accusation of provincialism and tossing it back. And to underline it there was the *physical* difference between himself and the Canon. The old man's stoop, and the smallness of his bones, emphasized Ned's height and the springiness of his bearing, just as his rather doddering brand of other-worldliness brought out the up-to-the-minute, on-the-spot air that Ned always had; you knew he was ready for anything. He looked far more metropolitan, in that kind of Mayfair and Westminster sense, than Robert ever would in a thousand years.

And something told me that I wasn't the only person standing there who felt the contrast. Ned was fighting pretty hard to get back the ascendancy – the *worldly* ascendancy – that Robert had suddenly snatched from him. They were using slightly different weapons, but that didn't prevent the contest from being a battle of giants. I felt about three inches high.

Fortunately, in every tense situation that takes place in public, there are always one or two people about who don't see what is happening under their noses, and in this case it wasn't long before the Canon provided some relief by slamming his foot into it. Ned was asking Robert, in a rather challenging way, if he minded telling us anything about his plans for the honeymoon.

'We're not going anywhere immediately,' said Robert, playing it offhand. 'We want a few days quietly at home first. In my place out at Hampstead. Then, when we feel settled in we shall feel more like taking a fairly long trip: preferably in about six weeks, when the southern European winter's beginning to lift. I imagine we'll go over to Rome.'

That was the Canon's cue. He bobbed his head up so as to bring Robert's face into gold-rimmed focus, and said, 'That's an odd thing to hear from you, Mr Lamb.' His voice was surprisingly deep and resonant; it hadn't yet followed the lead of the rest of him and gone quavery.

'Odd?' said Robert, not catching up. 'It seems perfectly natural to me.' He gave a loud, stagy laugh, no doubt to cover up his bewilderment.

'It's the first time I've ever joined a couple in Holy Matrimony according to the rites of the Anglican Church,' the Canon persisted, 'and heard the bridegroom say, barely an hour later, that he's thinking of going over to Rome. It's hardly likely to be a sudden whim of the moment, I suppose – '

'Oh, I *see* what you're – '

'– if you've been turning the idea over in your mind for some time, it's hard to see why you should have –'

'– misunderstood me. My friend here was asking me . . .'

As they burbled on the group seemed to disintegrate. Cartridge began to look round the room to see if there was anyone important he hadn't spoken to yet. I just stood there like a tethered calf. Myra and Ned smiled across at each other; he was obviously just about to address her.

Then Stocker came round behind Cartridge and planted himself right next to Myra. I had been waiting for him to do this all along, but obviously he had been fended off pretty efficiently up to now. He must have been watching like a hawk for just such a moment of confusion that would give him his chance.

Before any of us could overbear him, he had asked Myra if she intended to go on modelling now she was married. Taken by surprise, and perhaps thinking for a moment that he represented the press, she told him she didn't.

'Pity,' he said, leaning towards her and brushing her body upwards and downwards with his eyes. 'I'll miss that regular supply of photographs of you. That was a very nice twin-set you were modelling in *Harper's* this month. I always – '

Before he had got half-way through his sentence she had taken his number and was giving him the Siberian freeze-off, a routine she must have known all about. Not that it shook him. I stood by and let it all happen. The whole thing was tiring enough without letting myself get drawn in; all these strong personalities would just have ground me to powder. The Canon was still beating down Robert's attempt to explain away that slip of the tongue; at first Robert had been laughing lightly, keeping a determined grip on his good humour, but now his face had gone red and stubborn and he was doggedly trying to find a chink in the close-knit band of words that his adversary was spooling off. It was beginning to break him down, I could see that, particularly as the Canon's voice was effortlessly pitched to be audible at fifty yards. Cartridge was slowly edging away, without appearing to move his legs, as if he had trained a patch of the carpet to become mobile and shuffle across the room to safety, carrying him with it. Stocker, making a lifetime's supply of hay while the sun shone, was asking Myra why it was that he'd never seen any photographs of her modelling lingerie.

But Ned, of course, was made of stronger stuff than I was. It took him about five seconds to get back into control. Then he took hold of Stocker's elbow.

'There you are, old man,' he said easily. 'Been looking all over for you. You must have been out of the room, weren't you?'

Stocker looked sulky and tried to jerk his elbow free, but Ned had him fast. He only paused for a second before going on in the same easy tone, '... or you'd have seen the sergeant.'

'The sergeant?'

'Yes, that police sergeant who came in just now, looking for you. He said your car was on fire.'

'I haven't got a — '

'Don't worry, they managed to put it out before too much damage was done. But they want you to go out and see to it.'

Stocker opened his mouth and got as far as, 'Don't be a — ' but Ned must have tightened that grip on his elbow, because he winced, and I put in, 'You heard what the man said: go out and see to it.'

Stocker moved a few yards away; probably he meant to do no more than *reculer pour mieux sauter*, but it was enough. At that moment a loud braying and arm-waving assault by Robert broke down the Chinese wall of the Canon's incomprehension, and the central knot of the group was free to re-form. The two-way electric trajectory between Ned and Myra was snapped, the Canon went back to his apparent search for cigarette-ends, I swivelled my trunk so as to face each person in turn, and Robert gathered Myra to him in preparation for taking her off on a farewell tour of the room. Three yards away Cartridge began to move briskly forward, as if released from hypnosis. The wedding was over. We were free to go home.

Ned stayed on in London, and so, for their own purposes, did Stocker and Randall. But as it happened Stocker did come with me as far as Leicester Square on the underground. It was an uncomfortable journey, because he spent the whole time with his mouth to my ear, grumbling, above the noise of the train, about Ned's interference. I remember him saying, 'Not even his own wife, damn it. Anybody'd think he was acting out of bloody chivalry.' I thought that rather well put. That was one thing about Ned. You had to admit that he had a lot of bloody chivalry.

# VIII

Then for a time there was another blank in the record. I was going through another of those periods of simply not thinking about Robert or Ned or any of them. I had such a struggle to keep from thinking about my own worries that I found it best to keep the mind a complete blank. This is a very difficult thing to do, but it's easier for newspaper men than for most, because if you handle news you find that your mind gets like the bed of a river – it's never empty, but the contents never stand still. The last of what has gone, the first of what is coming along, as Leonardo da Vinci said, only putting it more elegantly, of course. And in case I seem to be evading my responsibilities by not saying anything about these worries of my own that I had, let me explain at once that there's nothing to say about them. Just being me was enough of a worry. It is with most people.

About the only positive thing I did, for nearly two years, was to avoid going anywhere where I might meet Ned. I was sick of his bad temper. He had weathered Robert's rise to celebrity, and even the marriage business, but Robert had at last managed to get in a dig that hurt. He had sent him a postcard from some Mediterranean paradise, I forget where, calmly informing him that he, Robert, had 'bought a little place' and that Ned would be a welcome guest if he cared to 'forget his business worries for a bit'. For some reason it was that bit about forgetting his business worries that needled Ned. I couldn't quite understand why, because most business men are only too willing to admit that their businesses do worry them, but looking back I'd guess that he felt it as a dig at his way of life. Here was this business flair of his, which had enabled him to make money and play the part of benefactor and patron to Robert for so long; and now – poof! Robert's feckless way of life had suddenly proved to be a winner, even in the material sphere, and Ned's brand of magic had shrunk to nothing – had become, in fact, nothing but a bundle of 'worries' that he was invited to go and 'forget' at Robert's expense. He didn't trouble to conceal his anger, when he told me about it in the bar of the hotel. He even said, as he crumpled the card up and tossed it into the grate, that it had given him indigestion. I thought this over in silence. Poor old Ned. His business had never succeeded in giving him an ulcer, but Robert would do it yet.

As a matter of fact I was glad enough to avoid him, for a bit, because it meant keeping out of places which were mainly frequented by business men; and, with all due respect to this fraternity, I can get too much of them. Business men? I used to think. What right have they to hog the term 'business' to themselves? Isn't anyone else busy except them? And in this mood I would point out, nastily, to anyone who would listen, that a more accurate term would be 'money-men'. A business man is distinguished from other people, not by his being busy while they are idle, but because he is in it for the money rather than for the sake of whatever it is he's doing. If a man opens a factory to make insulators (I used to say, heavily) that isn't because he's got a passion for insulators but because he can make money out of them; if he finds he can make better money by selling copper wire or aluminium legs, he'll switch to them. A money-man estimates his success in terms of the money he makes, then tries to gloss over the fact by pretending to estimate it in terms of how busy he is. I used to keep on with this routine till I even bored myself.

This anti-business mood didn't necessarily have the effect of making me affectionate to everyone who wasn't a business man. I didn't specially admire Robert, for instance. His attitude these days, as far as (a) I ever gave him a thought, and (b) I could judge, from that distance what his attitude was, seemed to me not much better than that of a successful gambler. I used to see examples of his work from time to time, both in reproduction and in the occasional show, and I liked it much less than I used to. Some of Myra's Mayfairishness had rubbed off on to him. Or perhaps that's hard on Myra. It may not have been her doing. Anyway, there was a hard, lacquered quality about his new work that seemed to prevent it from breathing or moving. It was clever, but it was dead. I had to admit, of course, that it was very much 'of our time'. Espresso bar time. Slap-happy days are here again. If I caught sight of anything of Robert's, I gave it a quick look and passed on. And if I ever thought about Robert himself, it was to wonder whether he would ever again make one of his appearances in my life.

Of course you know he did, because you can see there are still a lot of pages of this book left, so I won't pause to rub in how surprised I was to find a note on my desk, one cold winter morning, 'Mr Lamb has tried four times to ring you up from London.'

'What's the idea of writing this down?' I asked June.

'I wanted to make absolutely sure I didn't forget it,' she said. 'It must be something terribly important. He sounded – well, absolutely, I don't know. Absolutely . . .'

'Say no more,' I said. I had been dialling the exchange number while she struggled with language. Within seconds I was speaking to him.

'When the hell are you going to be on the telephone at your place?' was the first thing he asked me. I relaxed. If it had been real trouble, not just something that annoyed him, I thought, he would have begun by telling me what it was. Actually, I was wrong.

'Never, as long as I know you,' I said. 'What's the matter this time?'

'I must see you. I must see you straight away. How soon can you be up here?'

We North Midlanders always speak of going 'down' to London, not up; I suppose because a journey southwards is a journey down the map. For some petty reason it annoyed me slightly to hear him say 'up'.

'I'm not coming down at all,' I said.

'But what about your fortnightly trip?'

'That's not for three days yet.'

There was a pause, as if Robert didn't know whether to start screaming insults or to adopt a more placatory tone. In the end he did neither, but just spoke in his normal voice, harsh and rapid.

'But I must talk to you. You're the only person I can possibly talk to.'

'Too bad,' I said.

I made as if to hang up, and it was almost as if he saw me; his next words tumbled out of the earpiece very quickly and urgently. I thought it was queer that I could hear them as soon as a person in the same room with him, although I was a hundred and forty miles away. I can never get over the wonders of modern science.

'It's something terrible, Joe. Please, you must come, Joe.'

He had never called me by my Christian name twice in two seconds, and it had a softening effect on me.

'You sound in a bad way,' I said cautiously, but I was already working out how to take my fortnightly trip to town three days earlier than usual.

'I'll be all right, if you come,' he said, reverting to his normal manner, 'but I'll bloody well not be if you don't.' He sounded like a naughty child threatening to be sick on the best carpet.

'How's Myra?' I asked, testing for weak spots.

'Never mind asking fool questions, Joe, for God's sake tell me what time to pick you up at Euston!' Robert shouted. Even across a hundred and forty miles of wire, his voice struck my ear-drum fairly hard.

'Keep your shirt on,' I said. 'Seven-thirty. And I shan't have had my dinner.'

'Damn your dinner,' I heard him howl as I rang off.

When the train got to Euston he was there, and on the right platform too. I knew it must be something serious.

'Well, what is it?' I asked.

Without answering he took me by the arm and dragged me swiftly along to where he had parked the Bristol. I was hardly in my seat before he had thrown the thing into gear and ripped off. He drove with curious concentration and used everything the car could give him; we must have averaged seven or eight miles an hour through the London traffic. I felt he ought to be given a silver cup to put on the sideboard.

The dicing took all Robert's energy, and in any case he obviously didn't want to start talking until he had got me home, where we could be uninterrupted. So I sat quiet; the train journey had left me tired and dirty and hungry and thirsty, and I didn't mind his putting off whatever frightful revelations he had to make until I felt a bit more human.

We were still some way from Hampstead, however, when he suddenly dropped the anchors and we stopped. I didn't go through the windscreen, though I forget why not.

'I can't do it,' he said. 'I must tell you now, Joe. I can't hold it in. The –'

'You've stopped outside a pub,' I said. 'Save it till we get our fists round a pint, that's all I ask.'

Without arguing he got out of the car.

We went into the pub and Robert bought a pint for me and a double Scotch for himself. I drank half mine and said, 'Well?'

'Myra's gone off with Ned.'

127

'Judas Priest,' I said. It didn't help, but I felt I had to say something.

'She's going to marry him,' said Robert.

I studied his face, trying to guess what his feelings really were. He had been, and was, suffering; that was genuine. His face was drawn. It seemed to have got thinner all at once, and somehow it looked more terrifying than it had ever done when he was half starved. I thought about this for a moment.

'That's if I'll divorce her, of course,' said Robert. He turned and rapped on the counter with his empty glass.

'You mean you might decide not to?'

'I haven't thought about it yet,' he said.

I drank the rest of my pint, looking at him carefully over the rim of the mug. 'Well, what *have* you been thinking about since you found out about it?'

'I've been thinking what a bitch she is and what a bloody swine Ned is.'

'That won't help.'

Robert looked at me with hatred. 'Go on, sermonize. Trot out your bloody little gobbets of *bourgeois* wisdom. You make me want to be sick.'

'Then *be* sick,' I said.

He could see he was wasting his breath. Whatever he said wouldn't provoke me, and it was no relief to his feelings to lash out at someone who didn't hit back. Instead, he glared at the landlord and pointed to his whisky glass.

'This horse is unfit for service,' he said bitterly.

'I'll have to get a new one then,' said the landlord calmly, stroking the ash off his cigarette with his little finger.

Robert strode angrily towards the door, calling to me over his shoulder. 'Oh, come on – don't be all night!'

'Friend of yours?' the landlord asked.

'Siamese twin,' I said. 'Separated at birth. The manners came away with me.'

I put my coat on. I could hear Robert racing the Bristol's engine already.

'Get grafted again,' the landlord called after me as I went out. 'It'd be better all round.'

Robert really wanted to get back to Hampstead. We flew past Keats's house and left enough rubber on the road to make Fanny Brawne a waterproof bonnet. Five minutes later we were in his studio.

'Look at this,' he said shortly, handing me a sheet of paper from the table. It was full of tiny creases, as if it had been crumpled into a ball and then straightened out again.

'My dear one, for you are still my dear one,' it began. 'Ned and I –'

The handwriting could only have been Myra's. I handed it back without reading any more.

'Well, read it,' he sneered. 'Go on, read it.'

'It isn't addressed to me.'

'No, it's addressed to *me*, damn you,' he shouted. 'And I'm giving it to you and you're damned well going to read it, curse you!'

I crumpled the letter up and threw it in his face. Even fat old Joe Shaw can be pushed too far.

Robert stood quite still for a moment, then collapsed into a chair and buried his face in his hands. He made no sound, but after a moment I could see that he was crying. I lit a cigarette and sat with my back to him, looking through a copy of a Swiss art magazine called *Du*. I remember thinking what a high standard of colour reproduction it showed.

Then I heard Robert get up and walk over to the other side of the room. I heard clinking and splashing, and the next thing was that he was at my elbow with a whisky for himself in his right hand and one for me in his left.

'Let's be lucky,' I said, and we drank. I hadn't had anything to eat since lunch, but I wasn't hungry.

'Does she say she loves Ned?' I asked.

He nodded. 'Not that I know how much that means, coming from her.'

'Yes, you do,' I said. 'You know quite well what love means for Myra. It means allegiance to power. Where she recognizes power, she gravitates towards it. The most powerful man in sight is always *her* man, and she's quite genuine about it. When she says she loves the man in question, she means it all right. She worships power and she's ready to love anyone who embodies it.'

This was quite a long speech to make at such a time, and it showed that subconsciously I must have been thinking about Myra a good deal. At any rate I seemed to have got her number all right.

'Bullshit, as usual,' said Robert derisively. 'If that was what made her tick, she'd stay with me rather than let herself be snapped up by a lousy provincial potter.'

'Don't fool yourself. Ned isn't a lousy provincial potter any more than Nuffield's a lousy provincial mechanic. He's the head of Blue Seal Ware, and that could mean something.'

'Provincial,' he said aimlessly.

'It depends,' I said. 'Where he lives isn't the provinces as far as ceramics are concerned, it's the metropolis. You used to know that sort of thing all right until you taught yourself to forget it.'

Robert looked at me queerly. It seemed to be dawning on him that he did not necessarily hold a monopoly in chic and glamour.

'You're not trying to tell me,' he said slowly, 'that a girl like Myra would want to go and live in a hole like that?'

'Who said anything about living there?' I said. 'He might develop the London end of the business and live mainly down here. He could buy her a house in the home counties.'

This seemed to enrage Robert. 'The home bloody counties!' he shouted. 'I'll home bloody county him! And as for Myra . . . I'll – I'll Windsor her Maidenhead! The home counties you say! I'll . . .'

Mrs Sienkiewicz came in and said, 'Meister Court Wretch to pray a visit.' Without waiting for any further ceremony, Justin Cartridge, who had come upstairs at her heels, goloshed into the room.

'Ah, Robert,' he said affably. He didn't seem to notice that I was there.

'How's it going?' he asked when Robert said nothing. I remembered having heard that Robert had been given a commission for some whacking great mural, and that Cartridge had acted as go-between and landed it for him; or claimed to have landed it, more likely.

Robert turned his back on him and answered over his shoulder: 'It's not going.'

'Not going? What d'you mean?'

'Whatever you want me to mean,' snapped Robert.

Cartridge flushed. This was too unexpected for him to be able to cope with it. Robert had never before received him without turning the charm full on, and now suddenly he had withdrawn it and substituted his black side.

'Is something the matter with you?' Cartridge asked, the

fool. I was so terrified of the explosion I knew would come if he persisted that I tried to draw him aside, muttering, by way of explanation, the first words that came into my head. 'Robert's just a bit irritable.'

'D'you hear that? I'm irritable!' Robert said menacingly, staring at Cartridge. 'I've given up biting my nails for Lent and it's made me irritable.'

Cartridge utterly ignored me. He shook off my hand from his arm as if it were an insect. He was staring at Robert, and the flush had faded, leaving his face rather pale.

'My finger-nails *and* my toe-nails,' said Robert.

'It wouldn't do for you and me to quarrel, you know, Robert,' Cartridge began ponderously.

'No, you'd look a fool, wouldn't you? You'd fly into a temper and tell me the contract for the murals was off, and then you'd have to go and explain to the directors that you hadn't been able to handle your side of the business properly and lost them an artist.'

'Oh no, I shouldn't,' said Cartridge quietly. A stubborn look had stiffened his fat face. 'I should simply tell them that I had found a better artist who was going to provide them with an altogether superior set of murals.'

'Wouldn't they ask you why you didn't get the better one in the first place?' I cut in. I was disliking Cartridge more every minute, and beginning to feel that if he was going to make trouble he might as well make it with the two of us.

Cartridge didn't exactly tell me to keep my mouth shut, but he gave me a look that conveyed something of the sort. He was evidently intent on saying something more to Robert, but he was forestalled; Robert walked across the room towards him, halted about nine inches away, and began to speak quietly. I knew this was a very bad sign. When Robert was going to throw a really violent rage he always took a run, so to speak, before delivering the ball. The more calmly he started the more loudly he would end by shouting.

'So you'll tell them you've found a better artist, will you, Cartridge?' he asked almost pleasantly. 'And when will you do that? Before you've scraped the gutters of Chelsea and found some hack who's prepared to daub paint on plaster, or after? What's going to be the sequence of events?'

'You surely don't imagine you're the only man who can do the job, do you?' said Cartridge petulantly.

'No, I don't imagine I'm the only man who can do the job,' Robert said quietly and reasonably. 'In fact I don't even imagine that I'm having anything to do with the job. I've had second thoughts about the job. Ever since you put your degenerate ape's face round the door of my studio, three minutes ago, and walked in as if you'd bought the place – as if you'd had it thrown in with a few months of my time. Ever since you committed the indiscretion of opening your nasty little mouth. You've got an unpleasantly small mouth, Cartridge, did you know that? And unpleasantly small eyes. I'm not sure that I want those nasty piggy little eyes staring at anything I've painted.'

'You'll – ' Cartridge began.

'Nor that nasty little mouth opened in my presence,' Robert shouted.

'Steady, Robert,' I said. Cartridge was a smug boor, but he had hardly deserved this.

'Steady your Aunt Fanny,' said Robert loudly. 'I want a few questions answered by this bald-headed degenerate before I send for the police and have him arrested for trespassing.' He turned to Cartridge and rapped out, 'Who asked you to come here?'

'You must be mad, Lamb. You've never objected before when I've looked in to see how you're getting on.'

'The overseer, eh? Well, let me tell you something, Cartridge. You come here when I invite you, and when I don't invite you you stay away – get that?'

Cartridge choked. To talk to him in this vein was the equivalent of throwing a fat wad of treasury notes into the fire, and nobody had done it for years.

'I shall certainly – certainly stay away in future,' he gulped, moving towards the door.

'Is that a promise?' Robert asked.

I could see the commission for the murals going up in smoke. What would a real friend do? I asked myself; stand by and watch, or make an attempt, however futile, to tell Cartridge that Robert wasn't quite himself and persuade him not to take it to heart?

'Let me have a word with you outside,' I said to Cartridge's back. I started to follow him, but Robert grabbed me and said flatly, 'Stay where you are, Joe.' I couldn't tell whether he was threatening me or not.

Cartridge, of course, had ignored my request. We heard him going down the stairs. I broke away from Robert and ran on to the landing. 'Mr Cartridge!' I called urgently. 'There's something you ought to know.'

He looked up at me from the foot of the stairs. I've seen this man before, you could feel him thinking, with his crumpled suit and fat face, and his provincial accent. His shoes aren't even clean. His tie isn't even straight. He isn't dressed with any regard for appearances, just so as to get by and not be noticed. He isn't rich and he doesn't know anybody. And he's not clever. Definitely not clever.

He turned and opened the front door and walked out. How could I possibly know anything that he ought to stay and listen to?

'You pig-headed old bugaroo!' I shouted after him. It was silly, but I hoped he heard me. Then I went back into the studio.

The exchange seemed to have done Robert good, and he was more cheerful for a few minutes; but I knew it wouldn't last. His real feelings had not been involved any more than they had been involved in his comic rage about the home counties. What exactly was the nature of these real feelings, and when they would come to the surface, I had no idea. My function was just to be there and wait.

Robert got out a packet of Gauloises, put it where we could both reach it, and began smoking as if we had agreed to have a race. It took him about four minutes to smoke the first one down to his fingers, leaving just enough stub to light the second one with. He got through the second in about the same time. Just to make a change he lit the third one with a match.

As he didn't seem to have anything in mind for us to do, I thought I might as well carry on as usual until the next emotional breaker rolled over us. So I said I was hungry.

'Mrs Sienkiewicz!' he shouted, without moving from his chair.

'Does she know Myra's gone?' I asked, to fill in the pause while we waited for her.

'I wish you wouldn't ask fool questions,' Robert sighed. His face, during this lull between bouts of artificial animation, was really ghastly; the colour of putty, with violet rings round his eyes. He looked like a consumptive bloodhound.

Mrs Sienkiewicz came in and was dispatched for coffee and sandwiches. As she put the tray down in front of me she jerked her head towards the food and said, 'It is the boast we have with the magazines close.' I nodded. I think she meant that this was the best she could provide since I had arrived unexpectedly after the shops were shut. At least she was prepared to be fairly friendly, and that was one relief.

By the time I had eaten Robert was on his twelfth Gauloise, more or less. Suddenly he burst out, 'What did you say you had instead of a heart, Joe? A beer tankard?'

I was waiting for this. My diagnosis of Myra's feelings had certainly not left much room for 'love' and that sort of thing.

'The heart business you can handle for yourself,' I said. 'All I wanted to do was to fill in the sort of thing I can probably see more clearly from where I'm standing.'

'Yes, spectators see more of the game than players, don't they?' he sneered. Somehow he managed to make it sound like the most offensive remark anyone had ever made to me. As if he had caught me looking through a keyhole at a honeymoon couple.

'You telephoned me, remember?' I said, keeping my voice quiet.

'How do you mean, I can handle the heart side of it for myself?' he asked, ignoring my question and going back to the last remark but one. 'It seems pretty clear from what's been happening that I *can't* handle it.'

'What do you want me to do? Lend you a book of instructions?'

'I want you to explain *properly* why Myra should have done a thing like that. I *must* get it straight, Joe, I *must*. I feel I could stand it if I could get it straight. If I could only see what I'd done that had driven her to prefer Ned . . . of all people! Ned!'

'What's wrong with Ned?' I asked.

'Nothing's wrong with Ned; we both know that – but damn it, Joe, you know as well as I do that he's not . . . he's not . . .'

'As attractive to women as you are?'

He hesitated, then nodded.

I said, 'All that tells me is that you don't understand much about women.'

There was a long pause. Robert took the last of the Gauloises from the packet, but instead of lighting it he began to pick it to pieces. 'Well, tell me what I did wrong,' he began again. 'I bet you can't. I just didn't do *anything* wrong. I gave her just the kind of life she liked. I tell you, Joe, I gave her everything!'

'I believe you,' I said. 'Everything that either of you could imagine. It was the things you couldn't imagine that made the difference in the end.'

'Oh, for God's sake stop talking in riddles,' he snapped.

'All right, how's this for simplicity? Ambition is the strongest thing in your character. It's the strongest thing in Ned's character. I won't say it's the strongest thing in Myra's character because she hasn't got any character. She sees it as her role in life to be the symbol of success, the reward for getting on in the world. She's like the ball in a game of rugger; the one that's got it is the important man for the time being. Till someone else takes it off him. The ball doesn't have any feelings one way or the other.'

'What the hell do you mean?' Robert interrupted.

'Oh, use your loaf, for Christ's sake!' I shouted. His incomprehension was beginning to get me down. 'Make some effort to follow me or I'll save my breath. Let me put it this way. Why did you marry Myra?'

'Why does any man marry any girl?' he countered.

'It depends,' I said. 'Sometimes it's because he's lonely and tired of living in digs and wants a home. Sometimes it's because he envies people who have children. Sometimes it's because he's sick of sleeping by himself and the girl won't oblige without a licence. More often it's because he finds a girl who gives him a sense of security by supplying elements that he hasn't got. Most often of all he just drifts into it.'

'And which did I do?'

'That's for you to say. But you understood perfectly well what I meant about the rugger ball. Myra was the symbol; as long as you had her you didn't have to keep proving that you were a big shot. She proved it for you. You knew that wherever you went people would say to themselves, "This must be one hell of a world-beater to have a wife like that." She was the talisman you carried about with you. Well, now Ned's got her.'

'And is that the best you can do', said Robert with his voice full of pained righteousness, 'in the way of imputing motives?'

'Your motives don't interest me. I can see what's in front of my nose, that's all.'

Robert had finished pulling the cigarettes to pieces and now he seemed bored. He stood up and said, 'Let's go to bed.'

'But it's only half past nine.'

'There you go again, being methodical and habit-ridden,' he

said with a kind of triumph, as if I had been tricked into saying something I wanted to keep secret. 'If you'd just learn to relax and live naturally, as artists do, you'd go to bed when you were tired, whatever time it was.'

'But I'm not tired,' I said.

Robert smiled in a pained way, as if he had to put up with my determination to be jarringly silly, and without answering went out on to the landing. I heard him telling Mrs Sienkiewicz which room I was to have, then some more bumping and banging and taps running; finally he put his head in at the door and said, 'You can go to bed when you like.'

'Thanks a frightful lot,' I said.

He went away, and I sat smoking and hitting the bottle. It was rather a relief to have him out of the way; I wanted to think about this business a bit more. Just *why* I wanted to think about it, to concern myself with it in any way, I wasn't clear about, except that there I was, dragged in whether I wanted to be or not, and I had to have *some* reaction. Giving this as my reason to myself, I leaned over and picked up Myra's letter, which was still lying where it had fallen when I threw it back in Robert's face. I unfolded it and smoothed it out; not without difficulty, as this was at least the second time it had been crumpled up. But I knew I had to read it.

After the stuff about his being her dear one, it went on:

'I feel I must give you some reason for my decision to go out of your life – for that's what I *have* decided to do – and with Ned – yes, darling Robert, I must tell you at once that it's Ned I'm going to, Ned who has offered me the haven I've been seeking so far and wide – '

First I knew about it, I thought. I hadn't noticed her seeking any haven. Still, I supposed she knew best.

' – I don't know how to give my reasons without saying things that will hurt you, my dear – and yet I don't want to hurt you, not the slightest shadow of a hurt – but I'm afraid I must have given you some pain by my decision, and it seems better to explain a little – even if it seems for the moment to make the pain worse – because in the end it's the only thing that can heal it – '

All right, I thought, explain! Go ahead and explain!

' – You see, darling, Ned offers a refuge – a place where I can be safe – with you, it was always exciting and dizzy-making – but I began to see, and after meeting Ned I could see more plainly, that I needed the kind of solidity he can give – it's not only temperament, darling, it's the whole question of environment – you see Ned works with such *solid* things, definite things like factories and clay and lorries and men – you have to spin everything out of your own personality, and it's frightening - this blaze of personality all the time – so naked – it's not that you weren't kind to me, only – '

'Ned put that idea into your head,' I said aloud. The immediacy of the thing impelled me into speech, audible speech. It was all so clear! There I stood, with the paper in my hand – thick, purple paper, with deckle edges, just the kind Myra would write on – and looked down at her large, flowing handwriting with its dashes where full stops and semicolons ought to have been. I could just see her writing it, and I could see even more clearly the events that had led up to her writing it. Ned had probably begun by adopting a tacitly sympathetic attitude towards her; the poor fragile beautiful creature, tied to this human dynamo and liable to get shaken to pieces with the sheer vibration. Without ever saying anything, simply by means of the way he looked at her and the tone of his voice, he could get all that established – drop the seed into her mind, in fact, where it could flourish. And when it had grown up into a fully developed attitude, then and not till then, it would be time for him to speak, to tell her openly that he would see what she was going through and he was prepared to rescue her. *Solid!* I had to laugh as I saw the word on the page. Ned had played that card cleverly. But then, I reflected, he may have been perfectly sincere – perfectly self-deluded, that is. The poor sod may really think of himself as solid in comparison with Robert. Personally I wouldn't put down a threepenny bit to buy the difference between them. But I could see how well that stuff would go down with Myra. For her, as much as for Ned, it represented something she *wanted* to believe. He wanted to think himself solid, and she wanted her motive to be as sensible and clear-cut as that. Simple self-preservation! Well, why not? It has, like all the basic instincts, some bedrock dignity in it. If only her mind worked as simply as that it would be plain sailing. But I could see the streak of self-deception as clearly in her case as I could in Ned's. It didn't take any penetration. It wasn't security she was after, it was power, and she was transferring herself from one power-machine to another as a result of being smooth-talked into it.

And now she was transmitting the same smooth talk as a justification for herself.

Ned's round. Oh yes, definitely. For what it was worth. But what I couldn't really understand was what they were fighting over. All that was clear was that it *was* a fight; it had taken Myra to reveal, beyond any doubt, that the two of them were in direct competition, but what was the nature of the struggle? I sat back and allowed my mind to go on from there. Presumably Ned and Robert both wanted to be happy, though it seemed a strange word to use in connection with men of their stamp: how ought they *really* to be going about it?

I wondered, principally, whether Robert couldn't bring himself to get attached to a *real* woman, someone he could see as a person and not just a symbol. And if he did, whether it would do him any good, or enough good, or the right kind of good. Perhaps he ought really to live alone; at all events, it was no use going on the assumption that he was just a case of retarded sexual development like Stocker.

And Ned? What about him? Was he feeling glad at having snatched the talisman that would prove *he* was really the big noise, or did he feel any misgivings? Then I looked at my watch. It was nearly eleven. That being so, the chances were that he would be in bed with Myra, in which case any misgivings he might be feeling would probably be overlaid fairly effectively, for the time being. I tried not to let myself think about it.

And yet Myra's attractiveness was not, I knew, the real centre of the thing. In both Robert's case and Ned's, the real driving force was ambition, with sex entering relatively little into the picture; far less than it would have done with me, for instance. If I had married Myra, which God forbid, and which wasn't very likely under any circumstances, I should have done so because that would have been my only chance of getting to bed with her. Did that make me more human than Ned and Robert, or merely more animal?

More human, I decided firmly. At least it would have been a straight issue between Myra and me, with no mirages coming between us.

I sat on, taking my whisky with less and less soda. I had finished all my cigarettes, and I couldn't find any of Robert's Gauloises lying about so I was driven back on my pipe, which I only kept for times like this. I hated it really. It confirmed me in all sorts of ways of thinking that I'd rather have broken away from. With a pipe in my mouth, I felt like fat old Uncle Joe Shaw, his shoulder ready dusted for people to cry on, his bottom nicely placed for a kick, and his jacket handy for wiping your shoes.

Anyway, I lit the thing, and was puffing away and thinking how I hated it, and how I wished there were some cigarettes about, when suddenly there was a tremendous crash. I bounded up out of my chair.

'Who's that?' I called, a bit thickly, I dare say, after the whisky.

'Rodents!' I heard Mrs Sienkiewicz shouting. I went out on to the landing. At the same instant Robert's bedroom door flew open, and he lurched out, looking terrible.

'Take me home, Joe,' he said.

He had been drinking, but he seemed fairly steady on his feet. He had his pyjamas and dressing-gown on. Mrs Sienkiewicz came running up the stairs, squalling out 'Rodents! Buglers!' but I pacified her and sent her down again. Looking past Robert's head I could see a star-shaped hole in the window-pane.

'What did you throw out?' I asked.

'The bottle. It was empty.'

I looked at him. Not even in his worst days, Chesterfield Mews or anywhere else, had he ever looked a quarter as bad as this. His face was dead white, with dark red blotches. His eyes glittered like a parrot's.

'Take me home,' he said again.

I knew then what he meant. Some instinct was driving him back to the scenes of his boyhood, among the people he had grown up with. This body blow had taken all his breath away; to muster any new confidence he had to get in among the old familiar things and start again.

Or was it just a silly whim? Ought I simply to treat him as an ordinary drunk, and push him into bed and tell him he'd be all right in the morning? Was there really any point in setting off, at almost midnight, for a journey of a hundred and forty miles?

I looked at his face again. If ever I saw a man on the point of breaking up, I saw one then. If he had an instinct to make tracks for what he called 'home' I had an instinct that he was right.

'Get your clothes on,' I said.

Robert obeyed like a child. I backed the Bristol out of the garage while he was dressing. When he came down he got in beside me without a word, not even saying he wanted to drive. I got into gear and we moved off.

The traffic had thinned out by then, of course, and we were out of London and through High Wycombe before I had time to reflect on what I'd undertaken. When I did, the mental reaction was instantaneous; fatigue seemed to hit me like a boxer's fist. I thought of the scores of miles of dark road we had to cover, of the villages and towns full of people sleeping comfortably in bed, where I ought to be. And here I was, having dashed down to London in an express train, faced with driving this thing all the way back. Joe Soap, I thought. I glanced at Robert; his eyes were open but it was impossible to tell whether he was seeing anything. He was probably in a coma. Whatever he was registering it wasn't gratitude towards me. Why should it be, indeed? Who ever did feel gratitude towards me? It was my function in life to be there and to be reliable. Pipe-smoking Uncle Joe Shaw. The first-aid station and convalescent home combined. You never think about him until you get injured.

'That's what you think,' I said out loud. We were on a quiet stretch of road; I wound the window down and got my pipe out. 'Good-bye, old pal,' I said, and threw it out into the night. It might have helped to keep me awake during the drive, but I didn't care. I was too angry with myself for having been jockeyed into this position vis-à-vis all my friends. Even Stocker seemed to think it natural that I should want to hear the confessions of a small-town Don Juan. I was the man with the collapsible psychiatrist's couch in his pocket.

And then, suddenly, the mood passed. I looked at Robert again, and saw clearly, as if for the first time, the marks of pain across his face. He was so obviously in a worse state than I was that I felt shamed into benevolence again.

I drove on, musing about how impossible it was for anyone to divine the precise nature of Robert's suffering. Wounded pride; sense of loss; all that, yes. But my own guess was that the real injury was in a different spot. If it had been possible to unscrew the top of his head and look inside, I'd have laid out seven to five that the chief disturbance was being caused not by Myra at all, but by the Furies. The ones he had ceased to believe in. In the worst days of his failure and penury, his faith in them had died; he had gone ahead, using what remained of the gift they had endowed him with, and not giving them a thought. The old habit of deliberately disregarding or wasting a certain proportion of every material gain – pouring out a libation, as it were – he had abandoned. And now they had retaliated by suddenly snatching the most glittering of his prizes; and using Ned, what was more, as the means of doing it.

As I say, that's how I imagined he saw it. It's not how I saw it myself; but I knew enough about Robert's mental processes to feel a strong suspicion that he saw the whole thing as a punishment – the whip laid across his back from above.

I looked at him again. He had started shivering. I stopped the car and looked in the back and found a rug. He didn't seem to notice when I put it over him.

'Joe Soap,' I said, and started the car again.

The funny thing was that I didn't feel any bitterness against Ned. From one point of view, of course, Ned had sinned against Robert, and yet I could see it wasn't as simple as that. If Robert had treated Myra as a woman instead of a talisman she would have stayed with him. But then if he had wanted a woman instead of a talisman he would never have married Myra. And if Ned had wanted a woman and not a talisman he would never have thought Myra worth the trouble of pinching from Robert.

In fact none of them would be in this situation if they had been able, at any time in their lives, to see other human beings as human beings, or to see life was anything more than a game of snakes and ladders.

Robert's landed on a snake, I thought, as I looked at him again. Poor old sod. He must have landed on that one they usually have on about number ninety-eight that takes you all the way down to about number five.

It made me glad I wasn't playing.

The early morning traffic had got well into its stride when we entered the town I mustn't name. It was a typical winter morning in that part of the world, with a nasty drizzle falling and everybody in a bad temper, which they would be venting by making more than the usual number of sharp jokes about one another. I imagined the thousands of nasty wisecracks rising up into the foggy air, from the bus conductors and the people streaming in at the gates of the pot-banks and the miners going down in the cages. I imagined them all grumbling loudly and humorously at one another.

I could hardly see out of my eyes by this time and I drove the Bristol the wrong way down a one-way street which I had known to be a one-one street for at least twenty years. A policeman stopped me.

'Let me see you do that once more', he said, 'and you'll be making a trip to Stafford.'

'Sorry, sir,' I said.

'Have you been drinking?' he asked.

'No, but it's a good idea,' I said politely. I was past caring.

The policeman looked at Robert, who was staring ahead of him as he'd been doing all the way up.

'What's the matter with him?'

'His wife's gone off with his best friend,' I said. The policeman must have thought it was just another flippant answer, because all he said was, 'I wish mine would. Now reverse all the way back where you've come, and watch your step or else you'll be making a trip to Stafford.'

My mother was in the kitchen having a cup of tea when I brought Robert in. He stared at her as if he hadn't seen her before, but managed to get out a 'How d'you do'.

'Back again then,' my mother said, moving stiffly towards the stove. I could see she was bent on keeping up her character as the woman nothing could surprise.

I couldn't be bothered to do any arch stuff about 'I've got a visitor for you'. I just said, 'Robert might be staying a day or two if that's all right with you, mother.'

She nodded, but Robert suddenly said, 'I shan't be staying. Thank you very much, Mrs Shaw, but I shan't be staying.'

'What will you be doing then?' she asked drily. Robert addressed his answer to me.

'I'm going round to Ned's, of course. At once. We've got to have this thing out.'

I laughed. It was no use arguing with him, so I just said, 'You'll stay for a cup of tea, anyway, won't you?'

With his tea I gave him one of the knock-out pills I had wangled out of the doctor for when my neuralgia came on. They were guaranteed to give you eight hours of unconsciousness—I can't call it sleep. My mother watched me incuriously as I crushed it and stirred it into his tea.

Robert drained his cup; he was impatient to get on the move.

'Notice anything funny about the taste?' I couldn't help asking.

'A bit strong,' he said. He drummed his fingers on the table a few times, then said, 'I think I'll rest for five minutes. Ned won't be at the works yet and I shan't bother to go out to the house.'

He sat back in an armchair and went to sleep. Even being hauled upstairs and dumped on my bed with two overcoats over him didn't seem to wake him.

'What is it this time?' my mother asked me when we were downstairs again.

'Tell you later,' I said. I felt quite wakeful again, and it seemed a waste of time, now that I was back, not to go to work. I drove there in the Bristol, and when they all asked me where I'd got hold of a car like that, I just laughed.

# IX

By the time Robert woke up, his ideas about immediately confronting Ned seemed to have got lost. When I got back that evening he had still not come down, but we heard him bumping about upstairs, having a bath and shaving. When he joined us for a meal I kept a wary eye on him at first, but it was soon clear that he had decided to behave as if nothing unusual had happened. He talked a little but never mentioned Ned or Myra.

In any case I couldn't go on sleuthing after him for ever. My fatigue had come back in the course of the afternoon, and by this time I had only one thought – bed.

'Any plans for this evening, Robert?' I asked with my hand on the door-knob.

'Nothing special. I shall just go out and walk about a bit.'

He sounded evasive, and I took it for granted that he was lying. Ought I to telephone Ned and warn him that Robert was almost certain to call and see him? But then, why the hell should I, if Ned hadn't the sense to be prepared for it in any case? After all, I argued, if you take over someone else's wife, the chances are that he won't lose much time in coming round to chew the fat a bit.

These marvellously luminous and original thoughts had taken me as far as the top of the stairs, and before I could carry them any further I was in my bed and spinning steeply down into a whirlpool of sleep.

The funny thing was that, as it turned out, Robert wasn't lying. He really did just go out and walk about. What's more, he spent the next couple of days in exactly the same way. He'd go out in the morning and stay out till nightfall, which at that time of the year was about five o'clock. He never came in for a midday meal, either to avoid bothering my mother or because it fitted in better with his plans to get something to eat as he went along.

After a while I realized what he was doing. He was taking on a special kind of fuel. So much of his inner strength came from this purely local source, and could not be derived from anything or anywhere else. These were the streets and houses, these were the people, among whom he had grown from seedling to sapling. For too long he had been trying to get away from them, to deny them, to look for fresh sources; and he might have gone on doing so, had it not been for the terrific punch in the wind that life had just dealt him. It had shaken him out of his cocksureness and made him look round for something that he could really count on to see him through. That was why he had said to me, 'Take me home'. The shock had made him realize, at last, just what it was that he was hungry and thirsty for; and the appetite with which he consumed it, during these next few days, really took my breath away. He didn't just want to take on supplies, he wanted a surfeit. He really rolled in it. The weather was piercingly cold, but he was out in it as long as there was any daylight, walking up and down the streets, going in and out of shops and pubs, riding in the buses. He'd strike up conversations with people just to hear them say something in the local accent, which for the moment so fascinated him that even to be insulted in it gave him the sensation of listening to a heavenly choir. He didn't say any of this, of course; I just twigged it, and so, I think, did my mother. Certainly I got tired of having people come up to me with, 'Guess who I've just seen in the street!' At first I used to say 'Robert Lamb?' but the disappointment written on their faces was too much for me after a time, so I used to utter just any name that came into my head. 'Anthony Eden?' I used to ask. 'Zsa Zsa Gabor? F. R. Leavis?' Then they'd have the fun of telling me it was Robert. I think what excited them was the fact that he should be wandering about among us, unheralded, after having given the place such a wide berth for so long. If he'd come down to open some exhibition or something, and the fact had been duly announced in the Sentry, no one would have cared a damn; in fact they'd have made a point of letting him see that they didn't care whether he came or stayed away. But to have him come along without any fuss, and just browse about, seemed to touch them.

The boss wanted us to run something about him in the paper, of course, but I managed to block it. I said it wasn't worth annoying Robert just to tell people something they knew already. 'They'll think we've missed it,' he objected. But I countered by saying that if we got Robert well and truly on our side, by not pestering him, he'd reward us one day by letting us in on a real scoop, something we'd get before Fleet Street. I didn't believe anything of the kind, but I wanted to see that Robert was left alone.

I should have managed it, too, if it hadn't been for an over-enthusiastic young fool of a reporter, Parsons by name. He got to know, of course, that Robert was about, and without a word to anyone he took his camera and started shadowing him. I think he had some idea of getting one of those classic photographs, the sort that win competitions and get framed in galleries. You know – Robert looking up at the sky by the side of the canal. Robert standing in the lee of a slag-heap making water while two nuns look the other way. Robert framed in the rotting wood of a slum doorway, looking with angry pity at the smoke-dyed bricks, etc. Anyway, the fool must have spent hours tracking Robert and waiting for him to get into some striking setting and assume the real right pose. Naturally Robert didn't do anything of the kind. He mooched about the streets, where Parsons couldn't point a camera at him without attracting a crowd, and where he was usually surrounded by other people anyway, nonentities who would have cluttered up the picture.

All went well until Robert decided to do some sketching. (I could understand this; it would bring his hands in as well, to share the feast.) So he went along to Watley's, the principal shop in the town for that kind of equipment. By a stroke of bad luck old Watley was in the shop himself at the time; if it had been some feather-brained girl who wouldn't have known a famous painter from a bull's foot, all would have been well. But old Watley had sold artists' materials to Robert back in the days when for all he knew Robert was buying them to paint his little sister's doll's-house. He felt, for some reason, that this put him in the picture; that in a kind of mystical way he had launched Robert on his career by taking his one-and-six for a bottle of linseed oil. (As a matter of fact Robert had often remarked, in those days, that he would be glad to be notified when old Watley decided to give away the dirt from under his finger-nails.) Anyway, this old ass came forward at Robert's request for some sketching materials, shook hands with him, and spread the whole range of the shop out on the counter. When Robert bent his head to examine the stuff, old Watley bent his head too, and the pair of them stood there looking like Rembrandt and Michelangelo as played by Abbott and Costello. It was all too much for Parsons (I wasn't there, of course, but this is how I reconstruct it): hastily fixing the flash gadget on his camera, for the light was poor, he flung the shop door open, rushed in and, so to speak, fired off a couple of rounds.

A few seconds later he was flat on his back in the middle of the shop, and his camera was out in the street. Robert's artistic temperament had broken out again.

Neither Parsons nor old Watley could – perhaps I should say would – give anything like a precise account of what Robert had said in the speech he then proceeded to make to Parsons. At all events it must have been quite an oration; something like the one he had treated Cartridge to, only more so. He held on to Parson's shoulder to make sure that Parsons stood still and attended properly, and I gathered he had started by asking him who had given him permission to take his, Robert's, photograph, and gone on from there. Half-way through, the door swung open and a Boy Scout came in with Parsons's camera. His good deed for the day, I suppose. Robert made a grab for it, no doubt intending to throw it out again, when Parsons intervened, protesting that a press camera worth a couple of hundred quid oughtn't to be sacrificed to a fit of temper. They wrestled for a minute, watched through the plate glass by a gathering crowd, and then Robert's patience snapped and he hit Parsons again. Parsons said he saw the blow coming, and knew it would hurt, but he didn't want to let go of the camera. So he did nothing to defend himself, and took Robert's fist clean on the cheek-bone. I saw him about twenty-four hours later and he certainly had a nasty contusion there. The Boy Scout wanted to run for a policeman, but old Watley restrained him; he was still hoping to cling on to the last remaining fragments of the myth he had been trying to build up about himself and Robert, and of course it would be clean out of character for him to give Robert in charge. He held the Boy Scout tightly by the arm until Parsons had got a firm grip on his camera, which was battered but not beyond repair, and scampered down the street in the direction of the *Sentry* office.

When he got there he took the films out of the camera before he would even have anything done for his bruises. He found the two negatives intact, and had them printed off straight away. When they came out he was so taken with one of them that he insisted on having it printed in that night's edition. It showed Robert looking intently at a few sketching-blocks and crayons and suchlike, and old Watley standing back a yard or so and looking benignly down at them too, as if ready to give Robert the benefit of all his years of experience, while at the same time ready to defer to his instinctive wisdom as an artist. For sheer falsity it was one of the most horrible photographs I have ever seen. Parsons said it was 'a honey'.

I tried to dissuade him, but he rounded on me and accused me of trying to hinder his career because I was conscious of being a mediocrity myself, and said that if the picture didn't appear he would sue Robert for assault, with old Watley and the Boy Scout as witnesses, and that his price for not suing him was that we should carry the picture.

We carried the picture. It was in both our daily and our weekly editions. It must have given a lot of people a good laugh.

Robert did quite a number of sketches during his last couple of days with us, using pencil, charcoal, pastel, and even an ordinary fountain-pen when the mood took him. Most of them he threw away at the end, as if the act of using his wrist and eyes had been enough in itself, without keeping the result by him. But he hung on to the five or six he liked best, and on his last evening with us he spread them out on the kitchen table and invited my mother to choose one for herself.

I looked over her shoulder as she deliberated, and I must say the sketches were magnificent. The over-cleverness which had begun to weaken Robert's work had gone, and in its place was a new force and a new freshness. He had seen this town with eyes that loved and needed what they were seeing, and if there is a better recipe for art I don't want to hear about it. The dark, narrow streets, the crowded squares, the factories dotted about at random among the houses, so that you might look down any street and suddenly see a couple of kilns, looking like giant Burgundy bottles, sending out streamers of smoke only a few feet above the huddled roofs; the railway bridges, the canals, the black churches; and everywhere people scurrying about. No one *saunters*, where I come from; it's a mode of progression that they have simply never heard of, partly because the place doesn't exactly encourage you to saunter – you keep your head down and walk smartly to avoid seeing the ugliness all round you – and partly because there's hardly such a thing as a level street in the place; you're always either toiling up a hill or scampering down one; they say it's something to do with the ending of the Pennine Chain, which peters out roundabout here in a kind of gooseflesh of little hills. All this Robert had put on paper; quickly, vividly, without a wasted stroke or a falsification anywhere. As I looked at his drawings I saw the whole nature of the town, and what those who tried to live in it would find themselves up against: yes, and the people were there too, reacting to it, making the best of it, scurrying and barging about like satirical ants, just as I had known them. Robert had drawn me, though I didn't figure in any of his sketches. He had drawn my life.

Altogether Robert had learnt a valuable lesson, if he had the sense to hold on to it. He had seen the right way for him to go, which was away from all the success-scramble and the fashionable rat-race. These drawings had been done without a thought in his head except 'Here's something I want to draw – where's a bit of paper?' There was no bunk about forming an individual manner, interpreting this and interpreting that, the whole thing coming through the head instead of straight out from his inside. He had struggled clear, for a moment, of the tendencies that were rotting him; and I knew that if he could go on in that way he would not only be among the great English artists, but all right as a man as well.

'Go this way, Robert,' I said, nodding down at the drawings on the table. 'Go this way and I know it'll come out right.'

He knew what I was thinking; he didn't have to accuse me

of talking in riddles, as a third person standing by might have done. He looked at me and nodded, without expression, but confidently.

'I'd like this one,' said my mother. We both looked to see which one she had chosen. When I saw, I realized that after all these years I still didn't know the old girl. I had expected her to choose a 'view' she could recognize; something that showed the street where she usually did her shopping, or a row of houses where she went visiting, or something of that sort. But she had gone unerringly to what I thought was the best one simply as a drawing, and I could see Robert thought so too. It was a pastel showing two old men under the arch of a railway bridge, while the wintry branches of a blackened tree leaned over as if to hear what they were saying. It had absolutely no local reference that one could point to; no kilns, no slag-heaps, to demonstrate what kind of industry goes on here; but it was an industrial scene if ever I saw one. Without putting it into words one knew at once that these two old men, now drawing their old-age pensions and with nothing to do but gossip, had lived out their lives as industrial labourers; that they had been conditioned by the same forces that had produced the railway arch and blackened the tree with smoke. Don't ask me how Robert made that clear, but he did.

And my mother had twigged that this was the best when I should never have credited her with the ability to tell a good drawing from a hole in the ground.

'That's the one I think best too, Mrs Shaw,' said Robert, quite turning on the charm. 'Congratulations. You've got taste.'

' "Taste" means thinking the same as you, does it, then?' she asked.

'Of course,' Robert smiled. She had punctured his compliment pretty neatly, but there was no need for him to admit it.

The next day Robert went back to London, without having done anything towards getting hold of Ned. He had telephoned the house, rather with the air of being afraid of looking a fool if he did not, and had seemed relieved, if anything, to be told that Ned was away and they didn't know when he'd be coming back. (This was just what I expected, of course.) At any rate, he had done the only sensible thing he could in the circumstances; he had got his balance back.

He drove down in the Bristol, and I went with him, having put things right at the office, as far as they ever are right, and got permission to put my fortnightly trip back to its usual date. Robert drove tensely fast, as always, so that I wondered why I had chosen to go down with him, but I told myself that anyway it couldn't be more dangerous than British Railways, who were killing people like flies just about that time.

When we got into London I had only one thought – to ditch Robert as soon as possible. I had done all I could do for him, and now I wanted to get hold of Ned. I didn't want Robert hanging about to complicate matters.

Fortunately Robert seemed to have only one thought – to ditch me as soon as possible. No doubt he wanted to get hold of Ned, and didn't want me hanging about to complicate matters.

'You're sure this'll be all right?' he asked over-solicitously, as I got out somewhere near Baker Street tube station.

'Fine,' I said reassuringly. 'Now you get along home.'

'See you about,' he said.

'You know where to get me.'

He had the window wound down, and he looked up at me from where he sat. I knew he wanted to thank me and couldn't think how to do it without embarrassing me or admitting that he had needed help.

In the end he just said, 'Thanks, Joe.'

'All right,' I said.

'I found that little holiday very helpful, you know.'

'Get off.'

He drove away and I walked into the tube station as quickly as my suitcase, and my fat, would let me. I was in a hurry to get round to the Blue Seal showrooms and begin the hunt for Ned, before Robert had a chance to do anything to bitch it up.

A few minutes later I was there. Realizing that I would have to stand up to the scrutiny of the princess, I knew I ought really to have found a wash-room and tidied myself up, perhaps even had a shave and a shampoo, not to mention a manicure, before going in, but I was in too much of a hurry. I decided that my hands were strong enough to manipulate the revolving doors even though they were slightly grubby, and that they could hardly have me thrown out because my suit wasn't pressed. Before this buoyant mood had passed off, I was there.

Keeping my spirits up by humming lightly, I leaned one finger-tip against the door, and at once it began to swish round. I got into step with it and it whispered me round a few degrees of the circle and then gently pushed me inside on to the ankle-sucking carpet (drove-grey). Just before I got quite inside the room I saw the princess looking across at me from behind her black glass desk, and I'm not ashamed to say that I nearly let the door carry me on towards the street.

Still, there I was, and I tried to hold my back straight and keep my head up to minimize my double chin as I walked towards her across the dove-grey marsh. I even tried to begin my first sentence while still walking, to give the effect of nonchalance, instead of coming to a halt in front of her before speaking, as at a court-martial.

'Is there any chance', I sang out, politely but with a certain subdued cheeriness, 'of my being able to get hold . . .'

These words brought me to within five feet of her black glass desk, and so great was the effort of gauging the exact distance at which I ought to stand, to show a proper respect, that it took all my attention and my voice petered out. She raised those lead-coloured, spike-fringed eyelids, to indicate that I had permission to exist, and I tried again.

'Mr Roper. Is he in town, d'you know?'

She looked at me calmly.

'Please,' I added, thinking that perhaps her silence was due to some dissatisfaction with the way I had worded my question.

The princess flickered her eyes momentarily towards the show-case of Blue Seal ware. The idea seemed to be that if I had to come in and pollute the showroom, it would at least be tactful for me to begin by placing an order for not less than five hundred pounds' worth of dinner-sets, and go on from there to work the conversation round to personal topics such as where I could get hold of the boss.

'It's a matter of some urgency,' I said.

The eyelids drooped, wearily, so that the azure pupils almost disappeared. I supposed, too late, that it was the mark of people like toilet-brush salesmen and football touts that they said things like that. I began to despair.

'They say the poodle-cut's going out of fashion,' I said. 'What do you think will come in?'

The princess thought for a moment and said, 'It could be anything. It could be either shoulder-length or semi-long.'

'Which would you rather it was?' I asked, encouraged at the sound of her voice. Get her talking, I thought, and before she knows where she is I'll trap her into saying where I can find Ned.

'Semi-long,' said the princess.

'But you could carry either, if you don't mind my saying so,' I said. 'You'd look fine with either . . . wait a minute though, I should need to look at your profile to make quite certain: would you mind just turning to face the show-case? I'd like to get all the significant angles.'

She turned. I studied her profile as it had never been studied before.

'On the whole I should say definitely shoulder-length,' I said at last. 'That's if you have to give up the poodle-cut, of course. Personally the poodle-cut is my favourite and always will be.'

'I'm sure she's glad to hear it,' said Ned, who had evidently leaned one finger against the revolving door and been decanted into the room. 'But what's the object of the exercise, I'd like to know?'

'I wanted to find out where you were.'

'Rather a roundabout way to go about it, wasn't it?'

'You don't understand Court procedure,' I said.

Ned looked baffled, but the princess lifted her livid lids and almost smiled. She understood.

'It worked anyway,' I said to Ned. 'You're here.'

He shrugged, then went round to the other side of the black glass desk and began showing the princess some sheets of paper which he got out of his brief-case. I naturally looked the other way. One doesn't talk about commonplace business with princesses, the kind that can be discussed in front of strangers.

I went over to the show-case and looked at the Blue Seal ware. It looked as expensive and cosmopolitan as ever. I could still not manage to imagine myself eating off it or drinking out of it, or doing anything with it except look at it while I waited for a princess to finish having a word with one of her envoys.

Then I heard Ned behind me. I didn't hear him approach me, naturally, but I heard him breathing. Even the carpet couldn't muffle the human nostril, though no doubt there would soon be some gadget on the market that did, and then Ned would have it installed.

'Coming?' he asked. We filtered ourselves through the swing-doors. The street looked different; more apologetic, as if aware that it didn't make much of an effect after the Blue Seal show-rooms and the princess. But I greeted it like an old friend.

We got into Ned's car without another word. It wasn't like Ned to be so taciturn; his character was The Man Who Never Has Moods or Behaves Unreasonably, and I could see there was something quite exceptionally on his mind with regard to me.

Then I realized. Of course! He was wondering whether I had heard the news yet, or whether he would have to break it to me. Now was my chance to spare him any further anxiety by saying at once that I had seen Robert and I did know.

I said nothing. I didn't mind if Ned had a bit more anxiety. I decided to be like the princess.

'Seen Robert lately?' he asked, offhand.

'Robert who?' I asked.

After that he gave up, and we drove in silence for some minutes.

'Where are you taking me?' I began again. It was a remark that I had often heard at the cinema theatre.

'Somewhere you've never been before,' he said tersely.

'Madame Tussaud's?' I asked.

He did not answer.

We drove down the King's Road, Chelsea, turned off, and threaded through a maze of tiny side-streets. When we stopped we were not far away from Chesterfield Mews, Robert's old slum. Not far from it as the crow flies, that is, but crows would never fly over this part of Chelsea. It was much too refined. Every neat little house breathed refinement and money and Soul. A worldly kind of Soul, the sort you acquire by trips to Italy and first editions and dinners that don't taste like much but cost a lot of money. But still, undeniably, Soul. It was the sort of place the princess might live in.

Ned got out a latchkey. 'Little place of mine,' he said.

I didn't know what to say. The only sensible question to ask was whether he had had it long, but that didn't seem too tactful under the circumstances. It involved itself too easily with another question – whether he had been entertaining Myra there while she was making up her mind whether of the two she preferred him or Robert. And that, of course, wasn't my business; though, if it wasn't, I failed to see why Ned had bothered to bring me here.

Altogether my feelings were in a pretty confused state as we went up the steps and Ned used his latchkey to open the front door. This door, by the way, was hedge-sparrow's-egg colour. Get the note: Chelsea, Mark I, superior.

We went up some rather narrow stairs and there we were. It seemed Ned didn't own all this house, just the first floor. That was a comfort at any rate.

He opened the door and went in first and held it open for me. From the way he watched my face as I walked the last couple of steps into the room, I knew Myra must be there and he was trying to get my reaction.

I didn't in the least know what to do, so I decided to follow my new-found rule of life and imitate the princess.

I walked into the room with my face immobile and slightly quizzical. At least, I hoped that was what it looked like to those who could see it. The first thing I saw was Myra on the divan with her feet prettily tucked under her. The second was that the room was furnished with lashings of Taste but not much taste, if you see what I mean.

Myra held out her hand to me with one of the gestures they taught her in ballet classes when she was sixteen. I didn't know whether I was meant to shake it, kiss it or get out a box of matches and light it for her.

'How nice to see an old friend,' she said.

'Yes, isn't it?' I said.

'You must be wondering what all this is about,' Ned put in, adopting his money-man's tone of directness and cackle-cutting. 'It must all seem pretty strange to you, Joe.'

'Oh, I don't know,' I said.

Myra began to speak, but Ned actually held up his hand, like a traffic policeman, to stop her. I had never seen a husband actually do this to a wife, though I had read about it in books. And these two weren't even husband and wife yet. It looked as if Ned had decided to treat Myra according to some rather old-fashioned ideas he had developed during his bachelor years. It seemed to be working, what's more, though I could see that Myra was only tolerating it because she was trying out a new pose – the Cleopatra-in-the-grip-of-Antony stuff. 'I wouldn't surrender to anyone else but you, you great big strong rich man,' I could feel her thinking, 'but seeing it's you, I'm going to surrender like the clappers.'

I was not quite sure which way to turn my head, or which one of them to look at, or what. It was turning out a confusing day. I also felt dirty and tired, not having had a wash since the

154

long drive down with Robert scaring the what's-it out of me in the Bristol. *I hear the angel voices calling,* I thought. *Poor old Joe.*

'The fact is, Myra's left Robert and she's going to marry me,' said Ned briskly, as if addressing a meeting of shareholders who had to be told of an important decision. His voice was full of confidence and steady assurance.

'I'll be there with the rice,' I said.

'Oh, it'll have to be at a register office this time, Joe darling,' Myra cooed, leaning forward. She smiled up at me. I seemed to have pleased her, for some reason, by talking about rice.

'No orange blossom?' I said earnestly.

'It's hard on Robert, of course,' Ned went on; he was trying to ignore the red herrings and get on with the story.

'Yes and no,' I said. 'It'll be a good thing for him in some ways.'

'I don't quite see what you mean, Joe,' said Ned sternly, almost threateningly. 'I shall have to ask you what you mean by that, old man.' He seemed to think I ought to join in drawing a picture of Robert on the verge of suicide with grief and despair.

'Look,' I said. 'If Myra wants to change husbands that's her affair. And if she changes to you that makes it your affair too; and as Robert's the one she's leaving behind, that makes it his affair too as well. But it's not my affair, so there's no reason why I should have any opinion at all. But if I *am* going to be asked what I think, I might as well say it without any evasions. All right?'

'All right,' he said. Myra watched us both tensely, but I knew that however hard she listened she was bound to miss the point.

'Robert didn't suit Myra,' I said. 'We know that because she's left him. Women don't leave men who suit them. They don't change just for the sake of variety, like men. Once they've found a man who suits them, they stick. So we know he didn't suit Myra. But I think Myra didn't suit him either.'

Myra jerked her trim little rear end up two inches and dropped it down on her heels again as if I had run a needle into it. To hear anyone suggest that she might not suit any man she chose to suit! It really stung her.

'Robert's an artist,' I went on. 'Most of the clap-trap that gets talked about an artist's special needs, and the duty of other people to minister to them, we can safely ignore. It's bunk and the people who talk it are the shams, not the genuine artists. But that doesn't mean that artists are just exactly the same as everyone else. They *do* have some special needs.'

'Like what?' Ned asked gruffly.

'Like not having their lives wrenched too far out of shape,' I said. 'Everyone's life has a sane shape, the shape it would grow into if it was left alone, like a tree. Most people tinker about with the shape and distort it more or less, either because they have to or because, for one reason or another, they want to. And usually they don't pay for this distortion very heavily; at least, I think they do, inside, and that they're usually unhappy in proportion to the amount of twisting out of shape they do; but at any rate they can go on with their work. If they're bus drivers they can still drive buses, and if they're accountants they can still account. But if they're artists they can't go on.'

'And you think Robert was twisting his life out of shape by marrying Myra?' Ned asked, still aggressively, as if to prove to Myra that he would defend her against any possibility of a slur.

'Not by that alone,' I said. 'But it confirmed him in a way of life that was kicking the foundations from under his art. It just wasn't him.'

'I didn't see any of that in his painting,' said Ned rather defensively.

'I can't help what you didn't see,' I said brutally. I was sick of being put in the wrong. 'It was there all the time, and it was getting worse – that thin, clever stuff without any warmth in it.'

'But I've got warmth in me,' Myra suddenly put in. I think she had been trying to follow what I was saying and had come up with the version that I was saying it was all her fault for having cold feet in bed, or something like that.

'Your temperature is ninety-eight point four degrees Fahrenheit,' I said to her. 'In fact you've probably got one of the nicest temperatures there is.' I smiled at her lasciviously to show that I meant it.

'Do you really believe all this stuff about twisting one's life out of shape, and trees, and all that?' Ned demanded.

'Give me a cigarette,' I said. I didn't see why I should waste my breath explaining that if I hadn't believed it I shouldn't have wasted my breath.

'Yes, he believes it,' said Myra, rather tenderly, I thought. 'He's really a philosopher, aren't you, Joe darling? I mean under your . . . under your . . .'

'Under my unprepossessing exterior,' I supplied.

Ned had been standing over by the window, holding himself rather tensely, and now he came across with his cigarette-case to offer me one. As he lit it for me he watched my face narrowly; it was almost as if he were using the light to help him examine my expression, as one might hold a candle up to a murky old oil-painting.

'So you don't really think I've injured Robert by taking Myra away from him?' he asked.

'Why?' I parried quickly. 'Did you want to injure him?'

Ned took a step back and looked at me in a different way; not as if he were studying a portrait but as if he were watching a cobra that seemed quiet enough at the moment but was apt to strike at any moment.

'Why should you say that, Joe? What possible motive could I have for wanting to injure Robert?'

'None, of course,' I said, breathing heavily through my cigarette. There was nothing to be done about him. I had too much sense to embark on another lecture.

'I've never been anything but loyal to Robert,' said Ned, as emphatically as if someone had denied it. 'Before he was successful – '

'Before he was successful you used to stand him nourishing meals,' I said. 'And that proves that you couldn't want to injure him now that he's successful.'

'Of course it does,' he said at once, whipping round to face me. Either the slight gloss of irony which I put on the words had escaped him altogether, or he preferred to let it go; I could not tell which, at the moment.

Myra drew her feet out from under her and put them on the floor and sat up straight. She had black ballet shoes on with little gold stars on the toes. She stood up and moved across the room in front of me to show me how gracefully she could walk. I thought as I watched her that she probably had little gold stars instead of nipples.

'Take me out to dinner, darling,' she said to Ned, turning on her husky voice to show what a fine wife she was going to be to him, with everything laid on. 'And tell that fat man over there that he can come with us.'

In reply he looked — I can't say deep into her eyes, because there wasn't anything deep about Myra's eyes. They were shallow. Anyway, he looked shallow into her eyes, registering strong-protective-husband emotion, and then turned to me.

'Where would you like to eat, Joe?'

Something malicious prompted me to say, 'I'm sick of restaurants. I'd like some home cooking. Let's stay here and Myra can go into the kitchen and cook us a nice little meal.'

She laughed daintily, the sort of laugh a budgerigar would give if it could laugh, and stood still for Ned to help her into her fur coat. She didn't even bother to say that she never did any cooking.

'I think I know a good place, if you don't mind leaving the choice to me,' said Ned, smiling his capable astute money-man's smile. He held the door open for Myra; she shimmered out, and he still stood holding the door open for me to go next.

They suit one another, I thought. And look at him preening himself. He's landed at the bottom of a ladder and gone up two dozen places and missed a lot of snakes. Suddenly I felt tired and old, sick of trying to explain, sick of eternally trying to mediate and see fair play.

I tried to remember why I had been in such a hurry to rush round and see Ned. To stop Robert from seeing him first and bitching it up — that was it. But when I tried to go further back and remember one good reason why I should care, why I should want them to be friends, why I should do more than shrug if they beat each other's brains out, nothing came up.

I made myself smile, and said, 'Take me where the good times are.' We went down the stairs and out of the egg-blue door. I kept the smile on my face, just to have something to do, but I knew that something bad had happened to me.

I had just finally realized that for people like me the good times were always somewhere else.

# X

The next day, about noon, I went into one of the Fleet Street pubs and there was Stocker. He had his hungry look on, and even though he was not looking in my direction I could see that his sunken little eyes were encircled with purple. He must have been tom-catting again.

I sat down next to him but he didn't notice me. We were at high stools with our elbows on the bar. Knowing Stocker I looked round for an attractive barmaid, but there was nobody serving except a moustached woman of about sixty and a morose man in a chef's cap, who was dishing out lunches – rollmops and ham and salad, that sort of stuff.

This man asked Stocker what he would have, and Stocker roused himself from a kind of trance and began ordering rather a lot of food, as if he felt his tissues needed restoring to an unusual extent. He ordered ham, salami, cheese, pickled onions and roll and butter. As the chef turned his back, Stocker drained his glass of stout and looked towards the moustached woman to order another. Then he saw me.

'Well, what next!' he said. 'I didn't expect to see you, Joe.'

Before I could answer, the woman with the moustache brought him some more stout, and he paid for it, looking carefully at the coins like someone using an unfamiliar currency. It was one of his bad days, all right.

'What brings you to town, as if I didn't know?' I asked.

He shrugged, and drank a lot of stout. 'I've got a bint down here.'

'One?' I said.

'A new one.'

We were silent for a moment. Stocker moved his glass so that the stout swished about and climbed up the sides. He stared down at it.

'Getting a bit old,' he said.

I wasn't sure whether he meant himself or his new girl, or perhaps even the stout, so I said nothing. In any case I had to give my attention to the chef and the woman with the moustache. My tissues needed restoring too, though probably not as much as his did.

By the time my lunch was put in front of me Stocker was half-way through his and he had taken the edge off his appetite sufficiently to want to talk.

'What I mean is that it isn't worth the candle, as you get older,' he said.

I still said nothing. Stocker prodded a piece of salami and said, 'It creases you.'

'Get off,' I said.

'Take this bint,' he said, ignoring me and speaking as if to himself. 'I picked her up on a train. I got her address out of her and when I found it was in London I made an excuse to get down there the next week. I'm not on holiday, you know.'

'No,' I said, eating.

'No, I'm not on holiday,' said Stocker. He passed his hand over his eyes. 'I have to do *some* work when I come here, and try to make it look a lot when I get back. So I just planned on a couple of days, or three at the most. It looked as if she might come up to form quickly, in which case there wouldn't be a lot of point in hanging about. But you know, you can't always tell, just from *looking* at them.'

'What else have you tried?' I asked.

'Anyway, this bint,' Stocker went on, drawing a meaningless pattern on the bar with his forefinger. 'She kept me hanging on for four whole days before the balloon went up.'

'Disgraceful,' I said.

'Four – whole – days – and – nights,' said Stocker impressively. 'But when it did go up it did go up.'

'Yes,' I said.

'Yes?' said Stocker huskily. He turned and stared at me as if wondering if I was understanding him.

I went on eating. Stocker slowly turned his head and began staring down into his glass again. His eyes searching its depths he resumed talking as if to himself.

'But even so,' he said, 'I was wondering all the time what I was doing it for. Pleasure, yes. But pleasure's a big word.'

'Only two syllables,' I said.

'A big word,' Stocker repeated. 'Covers a lot. And a lot of what it covers, Joe, is more like pain than pleasure.'

I could see this was going to be difficult. For a moment I almost wished I had not thrown my pipe away.

'With this bint, now,' said Stocker earnestly. 'It went off all right. If anything, better than all right. She messed my time-table up by keeping me waiting those four days, but what the hell, I thought, it's worth it.'

'Yes,' I said.

'At least, that's what I thought with half of my mind. With the other half I was thinking just the opposite. At least, that isn't quite accurate either. I don't think with my mind, Joe, you know. I think with my body.'

'So does everybody,' I said.

'My body does my thinking for me,' said Stocker, still ignoring me. 'I can't even say that my body was enjoying this bint and my mind was telling me I ought not to. In a queer way it was more like the other way round. My mind was telling me what a good time I was having and my body wasn't really agreeing. Only I haven't got any mind. It's just another part of my body.'

I thought it was time to supply him with a few terms in which he might have a chance of making his meaning clear. 'Different facets of the mind-body complex – ' I began.

'You don't understand me, I expect,' said Stocker. 'You just think I mean that I was out of condition, or tired, or something, so I couldn't enjoy it as much as I ought to have. That's not what I mean at all, Joe.'

'I know it isn't,' I said patiently.

'It's a funny thing, but I'm always like that nowadays,' said Stocker. 'All the time I'm working over them I'm wondering what I'm doing it for. Of course, I know it's a need and all that, but that argument doesn't work in my case. Nobody needs as much as I get.'

'Some people might,' I said.

Stocker shook his head. 'And it's worse than just having too much of something,' he said. 'It involves you in doing without other things that you need just as much. I never really get anything out of a girl because I'm always in such a hurry to move on to the next one. I sometimes wonder what they're really like.'

I began to be really afraid that he would settle down to a deep discussion of his fundamental problems. I didn't feel up to coping with one in the middle of the day, so I tried to head him off by saying lightly, 'Ah well, it's just one of those habits like smoking. There's no sensible reason for smoking and yet you can't imagine yourself doing without it.'

'I don't smoke,' said Stocker. He stared at me again, and I remembered that this was a fact that I had often noticed about lechers. On the whole it's the repressed people who smoke.

I took my cigarettes out and lit one.

'I think I'm going to give it all up,' said Stocker, waving his hand in a gesture of dismissal.

'When will you know?' I asked.

He thought for a bit and then turned towards me. His face was a mask of misery. It really brought home to me that remark of Wilde's – something about being interested in pleasure rather than happiness, because pleasure had tragic possibilities. I felt as I looked at Stocker that I was really seeing the tragic possibilities of pleasure. And yet that didn't give me any feeling of superiority over Stocker; I wasn't tempted to congratulate myself because my own life happened to be dull and respectable. Being tragic even gave Stocker a certain stature, as compared with me.

'I'll set myself a target,' he said, brightening up. 'I know well enough that I couldn't give up now. I'll name a figure and when my score reaches that figure I'll give up. Get married or go into a monastery or something.'

'What figure?' I asked, really wanting to know.

'A hundred,' said Stocker without hesitation. 'That's a nice round figure, like a barmaid's. When I've scored a century, I'll stop.'

'And what's the score now?'

He answered without having to think. 'Sixty-one.'

'You've got records?' I asked.

He shook his head. 'I don't remember names, places, even what they looked like sometimes. I don't even keep photographs. There's only one thing I'm never inaccurate about: numbers.'

I supposed this proved something, but I couldn't think what, at the moment. Too much had been happening lately and I needed some time to go and think it all over. I slid down from my stool.

'Remember that, Joe,' said Stocker. 'You're the witness. I guarantee to stop when I get to a hundred.'

'Don't bring me into it,' I said. 'It's like a drunkard wanting you to witness his signing the pledge. You feel personally responsible when they go back on it.'

'I shan't go back on it,' said Stocker. 'And I'll enjoy the

remaining thirty-nine all the more. I'll make them last.' His old grin had come back.

'Spread them out thin,' I said. I paid my bill to the moustached woman and went out into Fleet Street. For the rest of that day I couldn't see a girl walk past without wondering whether she would be one of Stocker's thirty-nine, and if so, how thin he would spread her out.

I went back home and settled down to work and endure the rest of the winter. By this time it was half-way through February and everyone was going about with that peculiar pinched, dour look that English people get after five months of their winter. They've withdrawn their energy from everything else and put it into one thing – holding on till the spring. Personal relationships come to a standstill, and so does work, except for day-to-day routine. It's rather like living in a besieged city with supplies running low; you don't even *expect* anyone to talk about anything but the possibility of being relieved.

One particularly vile morning, with a sour mist everywhere and the mud frozen in the streets, I had a picture postcard from Robert. He was in Italy, evidently at some Alpine resort; the card showed pines and snow and all the rest of it. As it lay on the breakfast-table it had the effect of making me wish, just for five minutes, that I was not Joe Shaw and fat and ordinary and content to work for a provincial newspaper and live through six months of fog and filth every year. It made me wish I were the kind of person who lashes out and leaves all that behind and couldn't be bribed by any degree of security to live the sort of life I lived.

Then my mother brought my bacon and eggs in and I listened to 'Morning Music' on the wireless and the fire crackled and spurted, and I was glad I was Joe Shaw again. Some like one thing, some another, I thought to myself. I'll go to the pictures tonight and you can keep the Dolomites.

The card just said, 'Having Wonderful Time Wish You Were Here' or some such thing. It didn't give any news. I suppose the fact that he was there was news enough; he had had enough of moping about in Hampstead, and had gone away to enjoy himself a bit and complete the process of regaining his balance that he had started during his few days with us.

Oddly enough it was that same day that I met Ned in the hotel. I had gone in for a whisky, no doubt to convince myself that one could be a bit self-indulgent without going off to the Dolomites; at any rate I felt a need to sit in a comfortable chair in a nicely warmed and carpeted bar and be served by a barman in a white coat, and I was prepared to pay another sixpence for my whisky to get those things. Ned was already in there, talking to a couple of thickset, bald-headed money-men in a corner. As soon as he saw me he excused himself and hurried over.

'Have a drink, Joe,' he said.

'It had crossed my mind,' I said.

'I particularly wanted to talk to you,' Ned went on, beckoning the barman. I ordered a double and let him pay. 'This place isn't exactly stiff with people I can talk to about the sort of problems I have just now.'

'I believe there's a Marriage Guidance Council been set up,' I said.

'There's the whole problem of where to live, for one thing,' he said, ignoring me as usual. 'I should find it very difficult to settle in London – after all, most of the work is centred here – and yet I can't see Myra coming up here to live, can you?'

I was glad he didn't say 'coming down here', so I answered kindly. 'Not quite her style,' I said.

'It isn't, by God,' said Ned angrily, looking round as if ready to lose his temper with the bar and everyone in it. 'For two pins I'd clear out and set up an entirely new business somewhere else. If I were in any other racket but potting I would too. But it's so damned centralized.'

'Get off,' I said.

'Mind you, it's got to be me that wears the trousers,' said Ned threateningly. 'She's going to be my wife and she's got to live where I want her to.' He looked at me as if expecting me to detect some logical flaw in this argument. When I didn't, he went on, 'Mind you, there's no question of bringing her up here until we're married. You know what this place is, Joe. Respectable lot of sods.'

'Well, get married – that'll stifle most of the scandal, anyway,' I said.

'Not very well up in the law, are you?' he said crushingly. 'Otherwise you'd know that it isn't possible to get divorced till you've been married three years.'

'Heard from Robert?' I asked, to change the subject.

'Yes, I should damned well think I have,' said Ned fiercely

and eagerly, as if I had at last given him permission to get it off his chest. 'He sent me a damn-fool letter from some Italian place. Didn't say anything about Myra, just that he was painting and seeing a lot of things freshly and making discoveries about himself as an artist, as if I cared.'

'I thought you did care.'

'Yes, but as if I cared at the moment, I mean. Then in a PS the fool says, as if it was the most casual thing on earth, that he wants to give Myra a divorce – when the time finally comes round, that is.'

'You mean frame it so that he looks like the guilty one?'

'Yes,' Ned sneered. 'The gentlemanly thing. As if Myra cared a damn.'

'Has she said she doesn't care a damn?'

He looked at me sternly, like an orator determined to crush a heckler before he gets out of hand. 'Myra hasn't said anything about it, one way or the other,' he said slowly and weightily, 'because Myra doesn't know anything about it. The letter came to me here and I haven't shown it to her. But I see what Robert's getting at.'

I could see what they were both getting at, for that matter. Robert wasn't going to do the usual injured husband stuff by suing for divorce on the grounds of Myra's adultery. He was going to make the big stylish gesture. And this was exactly what Ned didn't want Robert to do. It outpointed him, so to speak, and deflated him a little in front of Myra.

I must have grinned, because Ned snapped, 'I don't think it's so damned funny myself.'

'I do,' I said, and grinned a bit more. 'The two of you scuffling for position would be funny in any case, but when I think what position it is that you're both scuffling for, I just have to laugh. You both want to figure as the man with the initiative. Neither of you wants to look as if the other one had stolen a march on him.'

He looked at me old-fashioned, as we say up there.

'You always were one for seeing the funny side, Joe,' he said. 'But these things don't seem so funny when you're actually in them.'

I stopped grinning; not out of politeness but because what he said really did sober me up. He had a point there. I could sit about and see the funny side of other people's emotional problems because I hadn't got any myself. And why hadn't I

165

got any myself? Because I was Joe Shaw and fat and ordinary and content to work for a provincial paper and . . .

Ned went out and I sat on drinking whisky. There were beginning to be times when I wished something would *happen* to me. But then, the idea was so silly that I nearly started grinning again. Nearly but not quite.


The weeks passed, and slowly people began to realize that there would, after all, be an end to the winter. We got an occasional damp, muggy day with a mild wind that seemed to blow in from the wet countryside on purpose to make town life seem intolerably artificial. The sap began to rise. June changed her hair style and began losing ground even faster in her struggle against the English language, and no doubt in her struggle against Stocker too. Even I got pimples on the back of my neck.

One evening I was just leaving the office when Robert came through on the phone from London. He sounded strangely pleasant and relaxed; there was even a kind of schoolboyish glee in his voice.

'When are you coming to town?' he asked.

'About another ten days – I've not long been back.'

'Pity,' he said, but still cheerfully. It wasn't because he wanted me to help him out of a hole that he was asking – that was obvious. 'I've got a surprise for you, but it'll keep till you come.'

'Is it something to eat?' I asked.

He laughed richly, with a kind of gurgle. Even his laugh had changed. 'Not quite in the sense you mean,' he said.

'To hell with your riddles,' I said, and rang off. I was going through a stage of being a bit bad-tempered – perhaps it was traceable to the same causes as the pimples on the back of my neck – and I didn't want happy people flaunting their happiness in front of me. The only people I felt safe with were mediocrities, people who didn't ask anything from life and didn't get anything. And I can't complain that I had any lack of such people; on the contrary, they were all round me. For the next ten days I properly soaked myself in mediocrity and tameness. I went the rounds of the same pubs, cracked the same jokes, saw the same bleary faces. Sometimes of an evening I'd stand against the wall in the Conservative Club (that's the only place where you can get a drink after ten, and nobody need know you don't *vote* Conservative) and watch the bank managers and pot-bank executives playing billiards and smoking and drinking beer, and try to tell myself that this was the only world there was, that everything was like this and nobody ever went off to the mountains or painted pictures or even got to bed with girls like Myra. It didn't work, and I don't know why I tried it but I did.

The only person who stood out a bit was Stocker, though of course he was very much at home in that setting and the others all liked him. They enjoyed talking about him behind his back, telling stories about his prowess with the women, stories that even they must have known were exaggerated. It struck me that they were using him as Robert and Ned used Myra – as a symbol. They wanted to build him up into a kind of folk-hero, expiating their collective repression, avenging their collective defeat at the hands of the female sex.

He came up to me one night in the Conservative Club, wearing a grey suit and looking quite natty. His face had relaxed and no longer struck me as tragic. I dare say that like most people he just went in phases.

'Don't forget my resolution, Joe,' he said, winking at me. 'I depend on you to keep me to it.'

'All right,' I said. 'Let me know when you reach a century and I'll buy a sharp penknife.'

'That won't be necessary,' he said decisively. 'I've said it and I shall stick to it.' He really spoke as if he thought I should bother to castrate him.

Then he revealed the true reason why he had come up to me by saying, 'Did you see Robert and Myra when you were in London?'

'Robert was in Italy,' I said non-committally.

'Was Myra with him?' he persisted.

'What's it to you?' I countered aggressively.

Stocker looked at me and nodded his head slowly several times. 'All right, Joe,' he said. 'All right. You've told me all I want to know.'

'I've told you eff all,' I said hotly.

Stocker gave a knowing laugh. 'I always said it wouldn't last,' he said, enjoying himself.

'I don't remember you saying anything of the kind.'

'I didn't say it aloud,' said Stocker. 'I said it to myself. I knew Robert would never hold that bint.'

'And what else did you know?'

Stocker laid his finger on one side of his nose. It was a curiously old-fashioned gesture for such a modern-age person to make, but it suited him. It made him look like the Artful Dodger.

'It isn't what I knew then. It's what I know now that's interesting,' he said. 'I've got the rest of the jigsaw. Like me to piece it together and show you the picture?'

'Stick it on the wall,' I said and left him. I was angry, though I suppose, looking back, there was no reason why I should have concerned myself with it. It was clear what had happened: Stocker had seen Myra with Ned, and I had foolishly let it out that Robert was in Italy.

I went out into the night air, which was soft and mild. Rain had fallen while I had been in the club. I stood looking up at the sky. Robert had a surprise for me and Ned was going to bed with Myra and Stocker knew all about it, or enough to be going on with, and soon everybody would know and it would give them all something to talk about. Suddenly I hated them all and I hated Robert and Ned too. One kind of person seemed to exist just to talk and the other kind to give them something to talk *about*. And here was I trapped between the two kinds. As I got the Ford out of the car park and drove home to bed, it was really myself I was hating.

The next time I was in London I went round to Hampstead. To prove to myself that I was independent of Robert and his surprises, I didn't go until my second, and last, evening; I didn't depend on my eccentric friends to bring a bit of colour into my life. Still, it was only kindness to humour Robert; he was just a big child. As if to rivet this attitude firmly in place, I took my time about getting to Hampstead; I went on the trolley-bus to Pond Street terminus and walked up the hill past Keats's house. As I went past it I thought of Keats living in one half of the house and Fanny Brawne living in the other. I thought of him sitting up at night and spitting blood and writing poems about her, poems that did not even mention her name because he was too big an artist to need that self-indulgence. He would be coughing blood and looking at the wall and thinking of her on the other side of it. She was his Myra all right, I thought. I felt glad I wasn't a poet.

When I got to Robert's place I rang the bell and instead of Mrs Sienkiewicz it was a girl who came down and opened the door for me. I said could I see Mr Lamb, and she smiled and drew back with a gesture that invited me to step in. I realized then that she didn't speak English. This would have made me slightly curious about her in any case, but even before that I was staring at her as if I couldn't get enough of an eyeful. She wasn't beautiful in the way Myra had been, for instance, but to me there was no comparison between them. This girl was real in all the ways that Myra was artificial. She was about five and a half feet tall, not stocky but strongly built; it was as if nature had intended to make her slim and rather slight, but she had done a lot of hard work and it had broadened her shoulders. She had very clear greenish-blue eyes, and her hair was light brown, with lights in it that you could have called blonde.

All this was beside the point though. It was her face that fascinated me. She had the kind of beauty that goes with genuine goodness. You could see she had nothing at all to hide. And that was all, except that she had a very sweet little nose. And a very beautifully shaped chin. In fact the whole of her lower jaw was very elegantly shaped. Oh, and a very beautiful mouth too – I was forgetting that. And, of course, very pretty cheek-bones, rather pronounced. Did I say she had a lovely skin? Well, I meant to. And her hair looked soft as well as luxuriant.

As I say, that was all.

I went inside and shut the door behind me, still keeping my eyes on her. She turned and walked towards the stairs; then, pausing with one hand on the banister, she looked at me over her shoulder – just a routine glance, to see if I were following – and then went on up. I followed her, placing my feet by instinct because I couldn't take my eyes off her. It was the way she moved that was fascinating me now. To say that I had never seen a person move so gracefully would be to put it in the wrong terms. If I said that she was absolutely feminine, that would be even worse; you might think I meant she had a sexy slouch like a Hollywood cheese-cake queen. On the contrary, it was the essence of dignity, and what's more it was entirely natural. A girl like Myra knew how to move because she had been taught by expensively hired professionals; this girl just couldn't move in any other way than gracefully.

Of course, after thirty-six years of living among English girls, who don't ever know how to walk or hold themselves, or even how to sit down unless there's a horse under them, I was all the more ready to notice any woman who moved gracefully. But don't let's make that the point. This was something that anyone would have noticed.

As I followed her up the stairs I wondered if she was the surprise Robert had said he had got for me. All at once I twigged. This was something he had brought back from Italy. Probably she had replaced Mrs Sienkiewicz as housekeeper. I suppose it was nothing more noble than pure envy, but at that moment I really felt an impersonal, altruistic desire to murder Robert.

She led me into the studio and smiled at me and went off to fetch Robert. While I waited I tried hard to feel cynical. Don't be a fat Galahad, Joe, I said to myself. If she wasn't the kind of girl you treat like that, Robert wouldn't be treating her like that. She must have been willing to enter into the arrangement. You only think she's so good, I urged myself. But it was no use. I hated Robert for using her to console himself for losing Myra. It was like losing a glass bead and picking up a diamond as a second best. It didn't make sense.

Then I caught sight of a picture on the easel. It was where the drawing of Myra had stood, but that had gone now. This picture was a painting, probably not quite finished, of the Italian girl. There she was looking at you with those greenish-blue eyes; it showed her shoulders and arms, too, and Robert had somehow managed to convey that when she moved she would be graceful. As soon as I saw the painting I knew that Robert was not cynically making use of this girl. I knew he was in love with her.

When Robert came in, by himself, I said, 'I've seen the surprise.'

He laughed and said, 'In that case all there is left for me to do is to pour you a drink so that you can wish me happiness.'

'I should have thought you'd got that already,' I said, not seeing what he meant.

'I mean happiness in my marriage,' said Robert, smiling, and looking straight into my face.

For some reason I still didn't understand, and with a kind of stutter I asked, 'Which marriage?'

'Relax, Joe,' Robert said kindly. He came over to me and put a hand on my arm. 'You've been overworking, or perhaps it's just the winter that's been too much for you.'

'Damn the winter!' I shouted. 'What I want to know is what

you're – ' I was going to finish the sentence with 'talking about', but suddenly it struck me what he was talking about. 'Dash my rags,' I said. I suddenly felt I needed to sit down.

He was going to marry this girl.

'Where did you find her?' I asked.

Robert had poured out my whisky by this time, and he handed it to me. It was a stiff one, but I made it disappear in one swallow and handed him back the glass.

'You forgot the toast,' he said.

'I'll do that with the next one.'

As he crossed the room to get me another whisky I pursued him with my question.

'I suppose you found her in the Dolomites?'

'Madesimo isn't in the Dolomites,' said Robert, handing me my glass. 'It's in northern Italy. You reach it via Milan.'

'Here's wishing you everything,' I said. 'To me it'll always be in the Dolomites.' I drank half the whisky.

He looked at me sharply. 'It's not like you to have these fragments of undisciplined fantasy,' he said.

'Stow it,' I said. 'I'm the one that lectures you, not the other way round, remember?'

Robert settled down comfortably. I wanted him to fetch the girl in so that I could look at her instead of at him, but he seemed to want to give me the story first.

'It came about like this,' he began. 'That business about Myra and Ned shook me up rather. It made me feel for a time as if I'd lost my bearings, if you see what I mean.'

He looked at me seriously. I just nodded. It was obvious that he was one of those people who grow a kind of skin over any experience they don't enjoy. He had probably forgotten all about the night I had driven him home. It was a bad sign, I thought; people like that don't really learn from their experiences. They protect their egoism too well.

'I felt I had to make a fresh start,' said Robert. 'Those four days I spent with you – they started me along the right track, you know, Joe. I began to put first things first, as I used to do before I got . . .'

'Before you got successful,' I finished for him; for some reason he couldn't make himself utter the word.

'Put it that way if you like,' he said. 'Anyway, I felt I needed to leave London behind for a bit. For one reason and another I thought I'd go to the mountains. I had a feeling, suddenly, that I hadn't spent enough of my life in places like that. You know – simplicity . . . grandeur . . .'

'Yes,' I said. 'Snow. Pines. The treatment. You needn't explain.' I thought of the Conservative Club on a Saturday night.

'Anyway,' said Robert again, 'I went up to Madesimo and just stayed at a simple little hotel. I didn't have to take any special steps to be incognito; I mean I signed my right name in the book and all that, and it obviously didn't mean a thing to them.'

He waited, perhaps for me to say that this showed how ignorant they were.

'It wouldn't mean a thing to them if you were Picasso,' I said. 'When I write a gossip note about you in the *Sentry* I have to add each time that you're an artist. Why should they be any more aware of you in an Italian village?'

'Why should they, indeed?' he said brightly. 'And what does it matter anyway? If everyone in the world recognized me it wouldn't make me paint any better.' He said this emphatically, and yet in a curiously dead way.

'I'll tell you just how it came about,' he went on, cheering up at once as he got back to his story; it was as if he had been waiting to recount his experiences to me before he could feel that they had really happened. 'I settled quietly into this little hotel, as I was telling you, and I'd stayed there several days before I noticed Pepina.'

'Pepina?' I interrupted, snatching at the name.

'Yes. Short for Giuseppina.'

'I thought it was short for Ethel,' I said.

He went on, intent on the story. 'She didn't serve the food or anything like that; she was employed mostly on the linen, washing and mending it. To coin another few lire a week they did the laundry for everyone who stayed there, rather than let it be sent out into the village; they did it at cut rates and of course there were always rows about it, but that's neither here nor there. Pepina used to sit ironing for hours in a room opening off the entrance hall, so she could see the people coming in and out. It was about the only distraction she got. Talk about work! My God, Joe, I never knew what work was till I got to know her and saw how they worked her. All the staff were the same, of course. They literally did nothing at all except work. At the end of the day they'd just sit about for a bit and perhaps have a drink in the bar – it was very democratic in that way, we all just sat about together – and then they'd just collapse into bed about nine o'clock.'

'Doesn't sound like the ideal setting for a courtship,' I said.

'It wasn't, boy, it wasn't,' said Robert, 'but difficulties were made to be overcome.' His voice and expression were almost offensively cheerful and confident.

'Oh, that's what they were made for, is it?' I said.

'I couldn't pester her when she was working, and there was hardly any time when she wasn't working, except about half an hour at night,' Robert went on. 'My God, I got so that I longed for that half-hour. The other twenty-three and a half hours were just a pain. When she came into the bar at night I used to buy her a drink – at first she wouldn't let me, but after a time I managed to persuade her and then she got used to it.'

'What did the other people in the hotel think?' I asked foolishly.

'They thought I was a dirty old man, of course. They thought I must be hard up if I was reduced to trying it on with a girl who'd be too tired to do anything but sleep all night. Some of these damned swaggering city-bred Italians who were staying there used to look at me so that I nearly used my fists on them. But it never quite came to it, somehow. I was too intent on the matter in hand.'

'The whole thing was clear to you from the start?' I asked, wondering why I wanted to know. 'You knew all along that you were going to try to marry her?'

'No, I can't say it was very clear to me, at first,' said Robert, wrinkling his brow as he tried to put his memories into some sort of order. 'At first I just felt a need to talk to her. I didn't even feel physical desire for her, though I should have done, of course, if I'd let myself think about it. I just knew that she represented the thing I needed most. She represented the same thing as the mountains did. Everything that was the opposite of the life I'd been leading with Myra. I didn't stop to analyse it; I just found myself looking forward each day to having a few minutes with her in the evening, even with other people sitting all round us. And we didn't talk much either. I can speak a bit of Italian, as you know, Joe, but we didn't need to talk much.'

'What did you do, hold hands?' I asked.

173

'I showed her my drawings,' he said.

In that moment I understood again. He had talked to her in a language that she found immediately comprehensible and wonderful. Like all unsophisticated people, she would naturally relish the arts; it's only the debased town-dweller, surrounded by techniques, who declares himself bored by them. To her Robert had not had any snob appeal as an 'artist'; he was simply a man who could take a pencil in his hand and produce something that spoke to her. And, of course, if she was unusually sensitive to visual impressions, which she probably was, then the savagely truthful quality of Robert's drawing would speak to her immediately. No wonder she had fallen in love with him.

'These people respect an artist,' said Robert, quite unnecessarily following where my thoughts had already led the way. 'They take everybody at his face value. You don't carry your reputation about on your back like a snail's carapace. If Segovia walked into that bar and gave them a few tunes on his guitar, they wouldn't do like a city-bred crowd – feel nothing until they had found out his name and read about him in a newspaper; they'd say by God, this bastard knows how to play the guitar.'

'Yes,' I said patiently.

'If I'd been some dreary old professor of art history, who'd been able to talk to her about painting, she wouldn't have given a pig's turd,' said Robert. He was getting excited as his own explanation made things clearer to him. 'I could have flapped my mouth to all eternity, she'd have gone to bed and left me to it.'

'Get off,' I said.

'As it was, she began to – how can I put it? – to manifest a subtle but very intense kind of sympathy towards me,' said Robert, stabbing the air with a Gauloise. 'It was extraordinarily delicate, as a matter of fact. There was no sex in it, or rather no overt sex. She didn't give me the green light or anything like that, you understand.'

'Yes, I understand,' I said.

'She's told me since that she wasn't even in love with me, till I told her I loved her. She just never thought of me as attainable, and so she never fell in love with me because it just didn't strike her to think of me that way.' I thought, fleetingly, of the lecture Ned had treated us to that day in the train.

'That happens, you know, if you think of someone as simply unattainable.'

'Does it?' I said heavily.

'Yes,' said Robert. 'I've had it myself. But, of course, when once the barriers were down we both realized it.'

'What barriers?' I asked.

'Don't get me wrong,' said Robert. He searched my face for a moment, dragging on his Gauloise. 'It's not always easy to tell what you're thinking, Joe. For instance, I can't quite fathom the assumptions you're making just now.'

'Do you have to fathom them?'

'I'd like to, if you don't mind. After all, it matters to me what you think, Joe.' He gave me a wide, almost affectionate, smile.

'It matters to me what I think too,' I said.

'For instance,' he went on, 'I wouldn't mind betting that you think Pepina's living here as my mistress. Well, you're wrong. Mrs Sienkiewicz is still here and the whole thing's as orthodox as can be.'

'Whose fault's that, hers or yours?' I asked.

'Unworthy, Joe, unworthy,' said Robert, shaking his head. 'It isn't a situation in which the word "fault" can have any meaning. Still, as a matter of fact I don't mind telling you that it isn't mine. The divorce can't be for ages, of course, but it's going through and we shall be married the day it's completed. And Pepina's attitude is that as we are going to be married we might as well wait and make the ceremony mean something. She says that if I'd wanted her simply to be my mistress, she'd probably have consented, but as I've asked her to marry me she wants the wedding-day to be a genuine one. It's a Latin attitude, you know.'

'I thought it was an Eskimo attitude,' I said bad-temperedly.

'Here, drink this,' he said, sloshing three more fingers of whisky into my glass. 'You're not yourself tonight, Joe, old man. You seem irritable. It's not like you.'

'We all act out of character sometimes,' I said. 'It's not like you to marry an Italian laundress, if it comes to that.'

'Yes, it is,' he said fiercely, ready to quarrel with me. 'It's like any artist to know a good thing when he sees one.'

'Like Myra,' I sneered.

'By God, Joe, you're making me wonder why I ever liked you,' said Robert. He stood up. 'If you can't behave pleasantly, I needn't detain you in my house.'

I didn't know what to do. I was quite conscious of having behaved very badly, but it had been queerly involuntary, as if some force stronger than my own will had moved through me. It had been coming on all through those last wretched weeks of the end of the winter; all that dissatisfaction with myself and my surroundings, all the strange restiveness that came over me when I thought of people like Stocker, whom I'd always pitied for the mess they had made of their lives.

I was going to mumble out some sort of apology when Pepina came into the room. She smiled at me, as if to apologize for the fact that she couldn't speak English to me, then turned to Robert and asked him something in Italian. I gathered enough to know that she was asking if we would like some coffee and that it was all ready to bring in. Without waiting for Robert to translate for me, I addressed her directly, in French. It was taking a chance, but I thought most Italian hotel staff would be able to speak French.

I said I'd be very glad of some coffee and hoped it would do my temper good because I had just been very rude to her husband.

She said her husband had told her I was his best friend and that I was always very kind to everyone and she did not believe I had been rude, but if I would like some coffee she would bring me some very gladly.

She spoke the typical French of the Italian working class. All the vowels were given exactly as in Italian. As for me, I speak French like a drunken Arab. I speak it quite fluently, though, because I generally take my summer holidays in France.

So drunken-Arab French and Italian-hotel-staff French bridged the gap between us, and very nicely too. Pepina went out for the coffee, and I forgot to go on with my apology to Robert because I was too absorbed in thinking that a mannequin who could walk like her would sell any dress. This, as it turned out, mollified Robert more than any apology could have done. He caught the look on my face, and suddenly roared with laughter and punched me.

'You dirty old bastard, Joe,' he said, lapsing into the manner and accent of his boyhood. 'I know what's the matter with you: you're jealous!'

I laughed, very loudly.

'You've got your eye on her, you sod,' Robert shouted. 'I can see I shall have to watch you!'

'You've got me wrong,' I said, squawking. 'It was Myra I always had a lech for, didn't you know that?'

As we bawled and slapped each other Pepina opened the door and came across, with the tray in her hands, into the circle of our laughter.

# XI

≈≈≈≈≈≈≈≈≈≈≈≈≈≈≈≈≈≈≈

Spring had come. After that evening in Hampstead I had gone home and waited for it more impatiently than ever, and now at last it was here. Spring in North Staffordshire is much the same as spring anywhere else, so I won't bother to describe it. I was sitting in the bar of the hotel one evening; my day's work had ended at about the same time as anyone else's, for once, and by six I had been outside on the pavement, getting the old funny feeling that you get in April when it still feels strange to come out after a day's work and find that it's still light.

I had hardly got the first one lined up when Ned came in. We had a couple together, but he seemed restive and unable to keep up a conversation; finally he stood up and said, 'Look, Joe, come out to the house for dinner tonight. It seems a shame to waste this last bit of daylight, sitting in this hole.'

'I like it in here,' I said, drinking.

'No, you don't,' he corrected me authoritatively. 'You only think you do because it's one of your habits. We'll go out to the house, and while the finishing touches are put to the dinner, we'll stroll round the garden. Nature, Joe, Nature! See all the young things growing!'

'I feel safer with this,' I said, nodding towards the cactus that was as near as the bar ever got to Nature. 'What's come over you, Ned? Been reading books again?'

But I got my coat and went. In the car he said, 'I've been on the phone to the lawyers today. The divorce will be through in about two months from now.'

I didn't ask him whether he or Robert had won the tussle they had been having, about which was to have the honour of taking the blame for the ruckus. I trusted them to work it out with the maximum of inconvenience all round.

'And I want to talk to somebody about my plans for the wedding,' said Ned, turning to me with a satisfied smile.

'Talk to Myra about them,' I said.

'Naturally I shall,' said Ned. 'She's with me at the house. I decided to have her up here, for a time at least, and let the gossips do their worst. We shall be seeing her in a few minutes. I'll talk to you both at once.'

This arrangement seemed to strike him as the perfect one, because he went on smiling in the same satisfied way. I wondered if he was already finding Myra a bit hard to talk to, and needed somebody else there to help him keep the thread. Then I decided it was just the old display instinct. He didn't feel he was really talking to Myra unless he had someone there to see him talking to Myra. It was subjective idealism with a new slant; she didn't exist unless there was someone there to look at her, and that someone couldn't just be Ned, it had to be Ned plus. I was the plus for the moment. Robert had been a bit like that too, I remembered. It was something Myra seemed to do to her men.

The countryside was still the same as it had been last time I had ventured outside the city, about six months before. The trees were in the same places and there were the same number of fields. 'Nature,' I said.

'No, no,' said Ned impatiently. 'Wait till you get in my garden.' He seemed to be trying to claim that even Nature got more natural when he owned it.

Myra was certainly more Myra-ish, or Myresque, or whatever. She saw the car turning up the drive and waved from an upper window. Then she ran down and out of the front door and bounced into Ned's arms as he got out of the car.

'Darling, it's been such a long day without you!' she cried tragically.

'Same number of hours as all the rest, I think,' said Ned a bit curtly, trying to get his gloves off. He was too fond of the manner he assumed all day, the money-man's manner, to want to relinquish it immediately on getting home. He had to be given time to peel it off in strips.

'Why don't you kiss me? My psychiatrist says it would do me good,' I said, coming round the side of the car.

Myra laughed and brushed my cheek. 'It's sweet of you, darling, to bring Joe for me,' she said, still addressing Ned.

'I brought him for me as well,' said Ned over his shoulder,

moving away. 'Now run in and tell them to lay another place while I show him the garden.' It was clear that he was resisting her attempt to jockey them into a familiar grouping, a grouping whereby she was the queen who stayed at home and he was the roving knight who went out and found things and brought them back to lay at her feet. Or perhaps she just thought of them as Mother Squirrel and Father Squirrel. 'I'm the nut,' I said unintelligibly.

I followed Ned round the side of the house and went down a set of stone steps into the garden. As we walked across the lawn, I looked about me and tried to think of something to say about it all. He had given the garden the full treatment, with flowering shrubs and a kitchen garden and greenhouses, and an ornamental pool. Across the hedge I could see a man driving some cows home.

'Peaceful,' I said.

For some reason this seemed to annoy Ned. He positively scowled at me. He seemed on the point of asking me what I meant by saying such a thing about his garden.

'Quiet,' I faltered, trying to make him see what I meant, and if possible to cajole him into agreement.

His scowl deepened. 'Is that the first thing you notice?' he asked moodily.

The first thing I had actually noticed was that the garden must have cost him a lot of money in labour and materials, but I didn't want to start on that topic, so I said weakly, 'Yes, why not?' I was beginning to wish myself back in the hotel bar sitting next to the cactus, with a whisky glass in my hand. If I'd known what he was going to say in a few minutes I'd have wished myself sitting on the cactus, rather than with him.

'That's the first thing Myra noticed too,' said Ned. 'And the last, and all the ones in between. It's all she ever says – how quiet it is.' He brooded a bit, then added, 'What she really means is that she's bored.'

'Of course it isn't,' I said, not quite believing what I was saying. 'If she meant she was bored she'd say so. She wouldn't have any objection to using the word.'

We had wandered as far as a kind of rustic bench, and now we sat down on it. This ought to have relaxed Ned, but it didn't.

'You haven't heard her,' he said, shaking his head a lot of

times. 'It's the tone of voice that reveals the whole thing. She doesn't say, *Oh, darling, it's wonnnnnderfully quiet after all the horrible wear and tear of London*' – he brought this sentence out in a ludicrous parody of Myra's voice – 'she says it in a completely, a completely . . . well, as a matter of fact she never says anything at all, until I ask her, and then she just looks at me quite expressionlessly and says, *It's very quiet, isn't it?*'

I looked at him curiously. 'It's a bit early to get rattled, isn't it?' I couldn't help saying. 'Here you are not even married to the girl yet, still living in vice with her as a matter of fact, and you start being afraid that you're boring her. Why, at this stage it's what she – '

'I'm not in the least afraid that I'm boring her,' he interrupted me, very stiff and offended. 'That simply isn't in question. Of course I'm not boring her. But I'm a chap who likes to have his life organized, you know that, Joe. When I know I'm going to be faced with a problem, I start thinking how to meet it before it becomes acute; sometimes before it actually arises.'

'That's all right with business problems, but I shouldn't have thought it applied so well to emotional ones,' I said.

'That's where you reveal yourself, of course, as an unrealistic dreamer,' said Ned firmly. 'I feel sorry for you, Joe. At heart you're really no better organized than a chap like Robert.' He looked at me keenly, to see how I would take this, but I had my head down lighting a cigarette, cupping the match against the wind. He went on, 'It's just a fallacy that emotional problems have a special status. In reality they're subject to the same laws as business problems.'

'Profit and loss, you mean?' I said nastily.

'Precisely,' he said. 'I can see perfectly well that you're trying to take the piss out of me. Only it won't work. You think it's typically materialistic of me to say that emotional problems are subject to the laws governing profit and loss.' He was getting quite red in the face.

'Here's a bit of profit coming over to us,' I said, nodding to show him what I was looking at. 'I wish I could buy a few shares in it.'

He looked up and saw Myra bobbing towards us across the lawn. She had changed her dress, no doubt for the nth time that day, but I had to admit she had picked a good one. It fitted so tightly across her midriff that you could tell the shape of her navel. It was like a little sea-shell.

'Have you finished telling Joe about our plans, darling?' she asked, holding out both her hands to Ned as if wanting to be pulled out of a swimming pool. 'It's getting chilly: you must come in soon.'

'He hasn't started telling me about them yet,' I said.

'I was just going to, if you hadn't side-tracked me,' said Ned. He turned to me on the bench, his face suddenly very animated. 'You wait till I tell you all the details of our wedding, Joe!'

I gave a coarse laugh, and I noticed that Myra shied like a thoroughbred mare. But Ned plunged on.

'There are two possible alternatives open to me,' he said. 'One was to get married very quietly, with no one present except a couple of old friends to act as witnesses, and the other was to go to the opposite extreme and have a really big do.'

'So you chose the quiet one, of course,' I said.

'Like all hell I did,' said Ned fiercely. 'I scarcely even considered it, as a matter of fact. It only took me about ten minutes to make up my mind – and Myra agreed, didn't you, dear?'

'Dear' seemed a funny thing to call Myra, unless he meant 'expensive', but she answered all right. 'Yes,' she said. 'You know I'm quite happy to leave all that side of things to you, darling.'

'When we get married', Ned said to me almost threateningly, bringing his words out deliberately as if he were telling me what he'd do to me if ever he found me hanging about there again, 'we're going to have the reception of all time.'

'Oh,' I said feebly.

'Of all time,' he repeated. He stared at me. It was dusk now and his face wasn't very clearly visible. Also I was beginning to feel cold and to need something to drink and eat.

'Mind if we go in?' I asked.

'All the people who were at the first reception are coming to this,' Ned clarioned, raising his face to the streaky evening sky. He might have been saying that he held these truths to be self-evident, or something.

'The first – ?' I began, then suddenly realized what he meant. He was going to stage Myra's wedding all over again, as if to rub in the fact that the first one had been nothing but a dress rehearsal, and this time she was really getting married. I forgot to feel cold, or hungry, or thirsty. The horror of this thing gripped me to the exclusion of everything else.

'But you can't!' I cried out. I was really shaken.

'Watch me,' said Ned masterfully.

As if obeying him I turned and stared into his face. I was trying to fathom the thing that had got hold of him. It must be something of great destructive power, because it was really eating away the base of his character. With all his inadequacies, Ned had always been someone I rather admitted, and for him to make this steep dive into vulgarity – pointless and offensive vulgarity – really shook me.

'You mean to tell me', I said, 'that you're going to stage the whole bloody thing over again, with the same guests and all?'

'The same guests plus a few more,' he smiled.

'But for Christ's sake,' I said. 'Ned, don't you see . . .' I looked at him and opened and shut my mouth a few times. What terms could I find? If I said 'vulgarity', he'd just laugh. This thing that had got into him had already chewed up his sense of discrimination about things like that. If I said that he'd make a fool of himself, it would get through all right, but only to the extent of making him angry. He'd think I was just envious and was crabbing him.

I looked across him at Myra, who was now sitting on the bench with us. Was it because dusk was gathering that I failed to see anything written on that profile? Her posture was perfect, her expression was neither over-animated nor bored; she had her company manners on, perhaps as some form of defence, and it wasn't possible to see round them. But then, it came over me rather sickeningly, there probably wasn't anything to see: that was the simple truth. I looked at her profile again; all those straight lines, all that perfect but in the end meaningless regularity.

I felt powerless to do or say anything, and yet I couldn't go on just sitting there; a wave of something physical, something between nausea, fear and exhaustion, was sweeping over me. Looking back, I recognize it as pure dissatisfaction, a dissatisfaction so strong that it felt as tangible as a fire-hose played on me. For that one instant I was so sick of it all that I didn't see any way to go on living; sick of Ned, and therefore automatically sick of Robert, since I had long ago erected the two of them into a kind of joint totemistic sign, before which I had prostrated myself. They were the big men, the ones who did things, who counted for something; and I was . . . but I couldn't even bear to contemplate, however distantly, the role

I had cast myself for. I hated myself so much that it hurt like being flogged. All that false plain-man stuff, that dogginess, that anxious ordinariness! – all assumed because it was easier than trying to compete with Ned and Robert, because they were built on a bigger scale than I was.

And this was the bigger scale. This was the thing I had so played myself down to avoid competing with. The competition for an empty symbol, the reception held twice over with the same guests.

'Can we – go in?' I said, trying to keep my voice normal. 'It's gone rather cold, or perhaps it's just me . . . but I . . .'

'Let's go in and have a drink and then dinner will be ready,' said Myra, getting up from the bench. She performed the simple movement so perfectly, with such grace, that she made it look contrived. The way she put her feet on the ground, tilted her weight forward and at the same time straightened her back – it was incredible how easy she made it seem, as if just anybody could have done it. I was lost in admiration, and we were half-way across the lawn before I realized that Ned and I had got to our feet in much the same way. That was the effect Myra had on you.

We went into the house, and Myra was just about to shepherd us into the living-room for drinks, when Ned drew me aside.

'Just let me show you something, Joe,' he said, 'before we go in. It won't take a second. Upstairs.'

He called after Myra, 'Shan't be a minute, darling,' and started off up the stairs, beckoning me to follow. I trailed after him, feeling my tread heavy and inert; I was still physically stunned by the emotions of the last few minutes, and the turmoil they had set up in my mind. All the same, I had a grain of energy left over to wonder what he was going to show me. It seemed such a secretive business. We got to the top of the stairs and he went ahead down the landing. We seemed to be heading for what had once been the servants' quarters or something; smaller bedrooms and box-rooms and what-not. What was he keeping up here? A private zoo? A mad relative in a padded cell? A collection of erotica? A harmonium?

'In here,' he said. He held open the door of the last room along the passage.

I went in, and he followed me. For a second or two I couldn't see what I was supposed to find to interest me. There was a huge trestle-table, occupying most of the room, with a lot of small objects littered about on it, as I thought. Then I saw what it was. A model railway.

A tremendous, elaborate model railway. 'OO' gauge, electrically powered. Dozens of different lines, sidings, embankments, tunnels, and what not. Wooded countryside, made out of something like plasticine, for the trains to run through. And two fully equipped stations.

Ned went to a set of switches and began to flick them about expertly; obviously he could have controlled the thing blindfold. Powerful green-shaded lamps, like the ones they have over billiard-tables, came on and the little trains began to glide to and fro like mice, pulling strings of wagons. It was fascinating. But I wasn't fascinated.

'You can put them into reverse, of course, by remote control,' Ned started explaining. He was acting just as if I had asked to see his model railway, in the capacity of a fellow enthusiast. 'And when you get them assembled in the junction – you can – '

He was flicking the switches about and having a great time. I just stood there and looked. Sometimes I looked at the trains and sometimes at him. It was all too much for me.

'It must have taken you some time to build this up,' I said at last.

'Years,' he said happily.

Then I remembered the one room we hadn't been allowed into that night when we had been roaming the house storing Robert's pictures ready for the war. My facetious private guesses about that room had been inaccurate, but hardly more horrifying than the truth. There it had been all along, his private fantasy world; the world where *everything* arranged itself along foreseeable lines, and acted predictably according to the amount of power you played through it.

'I already had the nucleus of the thing before we left school,' said Ned, straightening up and looking at me squarely for the first time. 'But of course, one's funny about these things. At that age I never told anybody about this little hobby of mine. I suppose I'd have thought – you know how one does – that, well' – he laughed – 'it wouldn't have seemed quite grown up enough to be interested in model railways.'

'One's funny at that age,' I said, to help him to get it over.

'Yes,' he went on eagerly, 'and not only at that age. Would

it surprise you to know, Joe, that you're the first person I've ever shown this to? – outside my own family, of course.'

I just stared ahead of me. I couldn't say anything. He wanted me to be easy-going kindly old Joe, the understanding friend to whom he could reveal his little idiosyncrasy. That was how he had me docketed. And why shouldn't he, when it was the role I'd always acted up to? How could I suddenly tell him, now, that I wanted to escape from that role and I hated him for trying to confine me in it? How could I tell him that I hated his trains and his money and his Myra, and all the things he had piled on top of his poor little identity to hide it from the light?

I couldn't tell him any of this. So I said how nice his trains were, and after watching them trundle about a bit more we went downstairs to join Myra.

I suppose I must have been wrapped up in my thoughts a bit, because as she handed me my drink she said, 'You're very silent, Joe.'

'No wonder,' I said. 'I'm jealous of Ned. If I come to the reception I'll only have to keep going into the men's room to have a good cry.'

She gave me her party smile. Drinking my whisky, I began to wonder what was for dinner. The fresh air had made me hungry.

I went to bed that night with my mind very full of it all, dreading the reception, deploring the mess Ned seemed to have made of himself, wondering what Robert would do, and so on; but the next morning I got up and went to work without even giving it a thought. That's how one's mind works, of course. I'd thought about other people's lives enough, and now my own life took over for a bit; not that my own life consisted of anything more than going to work and coming home and sitting about drinking with bores.

That reminds me that it was Randall who brought the whole thing back to my mind. I went into the Grapes one day at about half past twelve and there he was, of course, propping up the bar and talking to himself with his hat over his eyes. He couldn't have been at school that morning, because it was the Easter holidays, but the old ruin had got so set in this habit of drinking in the Grapes every lunch time that he would have been lost without it. He must have come over from where he lived, which was a good couple of miles away, just to keep up his routine.

I ordered a beer and tried to get into a corner and drink it without his seeing me, but he was on to me like a flash. He wasn't a schoolmaster for nothing; he saw the corners of a room before he saw the centre.

'Shaw,' he said, coming across to me. His voice was thicker than I had remembered it, but otherwise much the same. 'I've got a lill problem for you.'

'Rest your mind,' I said.

He was fumbling in his inside pocket with exaggerated care, taking no notice of my attempts to fend him off. 'Lill problem,' he kept repeating, rather as some people will repeat a telephone number, in the interval between looking it up and dialling it, to stop it from getting lost. 'Lill problem. Ah, here it is.' He drew out a thick gold-edged card. 'Tell me what to think of this,' he said, pushing it under my nose and at the same time staring at me from the shelter of his downward-tilted hat and the subsidiary shelter of his thick sandy eyebrows. I could feel his eyes watching me from positions of safety, where I could not stare back into them. Only when he was satisfied that I was really reading the printing on the card did he take his gaze off me and swallow a long draught from his glass. He was drinking black and tan, I remember.

The card was to invite him to a reception at the hotel, following the wedding of Mrs Myra Lamb, née Chetwynd, and Mr Edward Roper.

'Why haven't I had one?' I said, blurting out the first thing that entered my head.

Randall turned that hooded stare on me, craftily.

'You'll get one,' he said. 'R comes before S.'

'Only one before.'

'What of it?' Randall countered, sneering gently. I could see he was rather pleased that I had not had an invitation and was only playing at cheering me up. 'They got as far as R and decided to pack up for the day. You'll get yours tomorrow. When I'm doing the fortnightly orders I often get about as far as R, then I feel justified in knocking off for the day. It sounds a lot but actually there's always a good deal to do still. You've always got a lot of the little bastards beginning with S. Smith, you know,' he went on, getting quite worked up, 'and Stevenson and that kind of – '

186

'Not to mention Thompson and Updyke and Valentine and Watkins and Xerxes and Young and Zacharias,' I said. 'I don't know how you get through it. What was it you wanted to ask me about this piece of cardboard?'

'Yes, the invitation,' Randall muttered, dropping his head so that his eyebrows hung down over his eyes like creepers. 'What's it all about, eh? What's going on, eh, Shaw?'

'Ned Roper's getting married,' I said.

'Don't be evasive, boy,' he snapped, bringing his head up so that I suddenly saw his eyes, and his hat nearly fell off the back of his head. I really think he slipped twenty years in that moment and had the pair of us back at school with me wearing short trousers. 'Answer the queshun I put you, not the queshun you'd like me to have put you.'

'The volume of a given mass of gas varies inversely as the pressure, the temperature remaining constant,' I intoned. 'What are you drinking?'

'Black and tan,' said Randall, coming back to the present. But he followed me over to the bar and went on with his prodding while we waited to be served. 'What's he playing at, marrying that other boy's wife?'

'Ever heard of divorce?' I asked.

'Divorce?' Randall echoed in a scandalized voice. 'Are you — ackshully — trying to tell me they're mixed up in that sort of thing?'

I hadn't been prepared for this; he seemed really shocked. I supposed he must be a Roman Catholic or something. Even after I had handed him his black and tan and he had downed half of it, he kept repeating, as he stood there swaying backwards and forwards (but holding his glass absolutely upright), 'You — ackshully trying to tell me they've swopped, passed her from one to the other — through the Divorsh Court?'

'Well, what about it if they have?' I couldn't help saying, in the end.

'I'll tell you what about it, Shaw!' Randall suddenly shouted. 'Ish damn disgrace, that's what about it!' He only slurred certain words; the rest he spoke exaggeratedly clearly, as if to make up for it. 'Boy's had a good education. Trouble was taken over their damn education. Was damn good, did it myself, some of it. And it's a *disgrace!*'

His voice rose to a shout again. 'A disgrace to the God-damned school, thash wharritish!'

'Easy now, easy now, Mr Randall,' said the landlord, coming up to our end of the bar.

'Finesh God-damn school inner nay-brood,' Randall insisted very loudly. He was really slurring badly now. 'Boys, carefully taught. Shetter good God-damn example. And now – *divorce*.' He spat the word out in a spray of black and tan.

I got him outside. Once we were in the open air he seemed to slump down inside himself. I started him going in the direction of where he lived, and he moved out of sight along the street quite quietly, putting his feet down one after the other in a straight line, and feeling in his inside pocket to make sure he still had his invitation.

As it happened, Randall was right; I did get my invitation the next day. What's more, Ned rang me up to make sure I wasn't going to slip out of it.

'Be sure and keep that date clear,' he ordered.

'Newspaper work's very uncertain,' I said shiftily. 'It's impossible to foresee what one might have to – '

Ned laughed in a bullying way. It sounded queer down the telephone. 'Don't come that stuff, Joe. If you were getting married yourself you could ask for a day off and be sure of getting it, couldn't you?'

'But I'm not getting married,' I hedged.

'No, but I am,' he said, and laughed again. 'Besides, you can call it work. You can go home afterwards and write the thing up in the paper.'

'Not much,' I said. 'I'd have to stay sober. We've got cub reporters for that kind of thing.' And I rang off, feeling uncomfortable. I didn't want any part of his silly reception. It was all so crass. If he had wanted to score off Robert there were so many better ways; much the best, I reflected, would have been simply to announce the thing in *The Times* and clear off on a long honeymoon; then people could wag their chins about it, and ask each other if they'd heard, which would be much more intriguing than having the thing paraded in front of them. However, there it was. I was going to meet all that gang again and what we were all going to say to each other, the dear only knew.

What annoyed me most was that so many people fell for it – or, from Ned's point of view, entered into the spirit of the thing. I suppose it was partly local pride. The idea of having the reception in the town I mustn't name, instead of in London, pleased people and really seemed to strike them as praiseworthy, the fools. Of course Ned played it up like blazes, giving his workpeople the day off so they would talk about his wedding a lot and also turn up in large droves at the register office door.

I really dreaded this reception so much that for several days beforehand I was going about in an acute state of nerves. But as I say, most people seemed to think it was a thing to bask in. My mother, for instance, she tried to conceal her interest, but it kept on breaking out, so to speak. Some days before the thing came off we had a note about it in the *Sentry* – 'Forthcoming Occasion' – that kind of thing. I noticed her studying this paragraph very intently one evening, when she thought I wasn't looking. She must have read it a dozen times in succession.

'You needn't pore over that so much,' I said bad-temperedly. 'I'll take you along and then you can see the circus for yourself.'

I think I expected her to refuse. Why, I don't know, except that I just thought of her as set in her ways, and this sort of thing certainly wasn't among her habits. But of course, looking back on it now, I can see that she acted as I might have foreseen. She jumped at it.

'I don't know that I've anything smart enough to wear,' she said, pursing her lips; this was to make me contradict her, which if I valued my life I had to do, but fast.

'Smart?' I choked. 'You'll stop the show. They'll run home and fetch their friends.' I was warming every minute to this sudden idea of taking her along. She was so genuine that she would be a wonderful talisman against all the phonies who would be there, and the falsity of the thing in general. 'You've got a better wardrobe than anyone in this city,' I went on. 'And what's more, you've got a lot of clothes in it too. What about the one you had made for Edward the Seventh's funeral? It wouldn't need much letting out.'

'You mean his wedding, don't you?' she said grimly. 'Are you going to take me to this reception or are you not?'

I went straight across to the telephone and rang up Ned and told him to get another place laid. After that there was no holding my mother. She was always up in her bedroom, laying out garments on the bed and looking at them critically; then she would go out for a conference with some crony of hers, or perhaps a dressmaker; then the pair of them would come back and go upstairs for another top-level conference. The cooking fell off remarkably; I remember I several times had to go out to a restaurant to quell my hunger.

Altogether I lived in a sort of limbo for about a week before this wretched thing came off. But in the end the day, as they say, 'dawned'. At any rate it was dark when I went to bed the previous night and light when I got up that morning, so I suppose it must have dawned. Perhaps they just switched it on. It was one of those artificially bright days in late spring, when the sunlight seems to take the colour out of everything, instead of putting it in as it does in the real summer-time. It flooded over the whole scene and just made it look drab.

Except my mother, who looked like Queen Salote of Tonga, only white, of course. I'd have had to say I liked her get-up whether I did or not, but as a matter of fact I did like it. She was dolled up without being over-dressed; and what I specially liked was that she didn't try to look any younger than she was. She had just that little touch of regality that seemed to say, 'I'm a survival and proud of it.'

When we got to the hotel it was like a bad dream. The wedding had already taken place, of course – I suppose it took about five minutes – and Myra and Ned were standing there shaking hands with everyone who came in. It was all got up in the prescribed fashion; a great fat flunkey asking for your name, and then shouting it out, and then getting rubber-stamped through by Myra and Ned. It was like a customs-shed.

As soon as we had got through I steered my mother over to where she could have a good view of the whole room, I got her something to drink, and stationed myself at her elbow. I wanted to hear her comments, which were bound to be satirical, on the other guests. But I soon noticed that she wasn't taking her eyes off Myra.

'So that's it, is it?' I heard her mutter, half to herself. I suppose 'it' in that context, was what they call a Complex Word; it meant 'so that's what they've been quarrelling over', and also, more deeply, 'so that's how they do it nowadays – that's a beautiful woman, contemporary version'. Right down at the core 'it' meant 'the old trouble, the one they'll never find a cure for'.

'That's it,' I said, leaning down.

She was silent, so I tried to nudge her into saying something.

'When Ned used to come round to our house after school,' I said, 'I suppose you never thought you'd see him in this sort of setting' – meaning, of course, with this kind of woman. But as soon as the words were out I saw that I had, as usually, been more naïve than my mother. She shook her head briefly.

'I wasn't so silly as to try to foresee what he'd do,' she said. 'And nothing that any boy grew up into would ever surprise me. A girl could surprise me – you can usually tell what a girl's going to grow up like, and if she does something unexpected then it is a surprise. Only generally they don't. If I'd seen her' – she nodded towards Myra – 'at ten years old, I'm pretty sure I should have foreseen all this.'

When she said 'all this' she spread her hand out to indicate, not only the huge room we were in, but the whole situation. She meant she could have foreseen Ned standing just inside the door with his morning suit fitting him just right, and the flunkey shouting people's names, and Robert doing God knew what somewhere else, and Randall already filling himself up in a corner, and Stocker making up to a woman who looked like a chartered accountant's wife, in the middle of the room. One look at Myra aged ten, and my mother could have foreseen all these things, because she would have seen the inner reality of which they were all fragments or facets.

These sombre reflections must have appeared on my face, because she said sharply, 'You ought to be mixing more. Go and wander round the room instead of standing there like Rasputin. Here's Mrs Nixon coming over to talk to me; you'd only be in the way.'

I lumbered off. It was about ten past twelve, and I gathered we were going to sit down to a terrific lunch at about one. I could have done with a nice brisk country walk, to get an appetite, instead of lounging about on a soft carpet with this bunch. That just showed, I reflected, how far this whole thing had knocked me off centre. Normally, offer me a brisk country walk and I start thinking how much nicer it is to lounge on a soft carpet. I was sick of the whole thing, I thought suddenly, sick of it before it had got started, and I had been a weak-kneed fool to come.

Then, of course, Stocker had to get hold of me. He actually took hold of my elbow as I was sidling past him.

'Well, what about it, Joe?' he grinned.

'What about what?'

'Looks like I was on the right track that night, when you bit my head off, in the Conservative Club,' he leered.

We had a bit more fencing over this, but neither of us was interested enough to carry it on for long and Stocker soon got back to his usual subject.

'See that bint I was just talking to?' he said, his hungry look coming back.

'I glimpsed her,' I said. 'She looked like a chartered accountant's wife.'

'Coal Board as a matter of fact,' said Stocker, always precise and literal where these things were concerned. 'She's only been married three years, but she comes to a do like this without her husband. Looks good, wouldn't you say?'

'Why isn't her husband here then?'

'Working,' said Stocker with a heavy wink. 'Sweating his guts out to keep her going. A well-turned-out little job, didn't you think? Got about two hundred quid on her back, I should say. And just ready for someone to admire it.'

I tried to move away, but he was relentless.

'And d'you know where she is now?' he pursued. 'In the women's room. Prinking herself up a bit extra, you can bet – not that she needs it. That's always a good sign. I paid her so many compliments she's gone to look in the mirror and see if any of it's true.'

'How do you know she hasn't got diarrhoea?' I said, grabbing a whisky from a passing tray. I was joking, but the suggestion really seemed to unsettle Stocker. Like most people, he couldn't even imagine the possibility of anyone's not taking his ruling passion as seriously as he took it himself.

'By God, I hope not,' he said earnestly. 'Spoil everything, that would. Because the way I've got it worked out is this. There's no time like the present. The booze is on the house, and it's good; I'll get her tanked up and then take her out in the car. Damn it, there's no need to do that, even. There's bound to be a quiet alcove somewhere, or a bathroom or something. I won't even take her out of the hotel, bejabers.' He paused to throw me a stern look. 'And don't give me any of that stuff about diarrhoea, Joe. If she'd got that she wouldn't have come at all.'

'You probably brought it on with your compliments,' I said.

'Yes, and that isn't all I'll bring on,' said Stocker grimly. He spoke about her as if he were going to murder her. 'I'll give her something she won't forget in a hurry,' he said, and went on to describe what he had in mind for this woman, ignoring my obvious wish to get away and continue my tour of the room. It was like listening to the Ancient Mariner. I was so uncomfortable that I was even glad to see Randall coming across to us.

'I've got another problem for you, Shaw,' he said heavily; no doubt he had sunk a bathful of whisky already. 'Prollem of identity. Prollem of nomenclature.'

Stocker tried to brush him aside; his outline of strategy had reached one of its vivid peaks. But I was so relieved that I said quickly, 'You mean you want me to tell you who somebody is?'

Randall nodded deliberately. 'Exactly, exactly,' he said. 'Exactly,' he went on nodding. He seemed to have forgotten who it was whose name he wanted to know, and also how to keep his head from nodding.

We stood there like three idiots with glasses in our hands. Stocker resumed his discourse to me in an urgent undertone and Randall stood there nodding, as if beating time. I was hating it all so much that I started sweating. Then I heard Myra's voice speaking right in my ear. She must have come up behind me.

'Joe,' she was saying rather earnestly, not at all in her party manner, 'have you heard from Robert lately?'

'Robert, no,' I said, as if I could offer her a wide selection of people I had heard from, and it was a pity she had just asked for the one I was out of. 'Not actually from Robert.' I wondered, bemusedly, why I was talking like a silly fool. Then I realized it was because of my embarrassment.

I looked at her. She must have thought I was drunk already, particularly as I was still partly under the drugging effect of Stocker's recital; my mind was full of the images he had thrown into it, and I couldn't help looking at Myra lasciviously.

'Good Christ,' I said, and passed my hand over my forehead.

'Please be serious, Joe,' Myra said crossly, perhaps not realizing that I had never been more serious in my life. 'I have to say this quickly, because Ned wouldn't like me to be telling you about it anyway, only I wanted to know how you'd react.'

'Well, react to what?' I said irritably, pulling myself together. Out of the corner of my eye I saw Stocker moving away in the direction of his quarry, who had just re-entered the room. *And I had forgotten to ask him what the score was!*

'Who do you think drew this?' Myra suddenly asked, taking a card from her handbag and pushing it under my nose. I looked at it. It was just an ordinary white card, of the kind you buy to write invitations to parties on, with some dotted lines and the words 'At Home' on one side and nothing on the other. Only in this case there was something on the other side. It was a hastily done but powerful drawing of a man fishing from a bridge. He had hooked an enormous fish, about twice as big as himself, and it was leaping up out of the water and snapping at him; he was starting back in terror. The thing had obviously been dashed off, but it consisted of just the right number of lines, with nothing wasted.

'Robert drew that,' I said.

She nodded and put it back in her handbag. Her eyes were very round.

'He did, didn't he?' she said. 'It just had a London postmark on it, Joe – do you think it's a *message* of some sort?'

Now what the hell was I going to say to that? Of course it was a message. But what was I going to say?

'Look, if you don't understand it, why should I?' I said plaintively.

'You know why, Joe,' she pleaded. It was the first time I had felt any humanity in her; perhaps it was the first time there had been any. 'I sometimes think you're the only person who understands either of my husbands. You know them both so deeply.'

'Not as deeply as you know them,' I said, still hedging, but I knew she was right. She still stood there, looking at me, waiting for me to say something that would help her, and for a wonder no one came to interrupt us, just when I could have done with it. We might have been on a desert island, the way we just stood there. In the brown stuff again, I thought. Joe Soap will now perform his popular self-mutilation act.

'If you want to know what I think, Myra,' I began wearily, 'there's only one thing for you to do. Just sit back and leave Ned and Robert to straighten this out between the pair of them.' It suddenly struck me that I had said something wise, so I went on eagerly, more and more interested in what I was saying. 'They were like this long before you ever came on the scene, and you just got caught up into it; there's no reason

194

why you should get hurt, necessarily, but you mustn't worry about it. After all, everyone who comes anywhere near these two gets drawn into this up-and-down relationship they have with one another – it's just something you have to take account of when considering them, either separately or together. That drawing of Robert's was a dig in the ribs for Ned. I can't say what it meant. What does any dig in the ribs mean? And I can't say exactly what spirit inspired it. Partly he wanted to hurt Ned – he wanted to say *All right, you've hooked your fish and now you'll find you're the bait yourself.* And partly he wanted to have a bit of a grin about it, a grin the two of them could share. And he didn't know how to do all that in words so he drew a picture. But it's nothing for you or me or anyone else in the world to worry about.'

'Who's talking about worrying?' said Ned heartily. He had come up to collect Myra, and caught the last words. 'That's Joe all over. Always carries his troubles with him. Never did know how to let himself go.' He took Myra's hand and beamed at me.

'You be thankful I don't,' I said, slipping back into the old jealousy act. 'For two pins I'd claim my *droit de seigneurie* right away.'

I didn't expect him to know what I meant, but he evidently did and looked at me old-fashioned. 'Anyway, come in to lunch,' he said, and led Myra off. So what with one thing and another I never had the chance to know how she felt about the advice I'd given her.

At lunch I found I had been put dangerously close to Justin Cartridge. I wasn't actually next to him, as, of course, the people on either side of me were women. One of them, in fact, was Stocker's prey, and as we were getting into our places I saw him signalling to me from down the table, beckoning and wagging his head about; it was clear enough he wanted me to change places with him. I tried to signal back that I wouldn't have minded if we could have done it a bit earlier, but it was too late now that we were all settled in our places. Of course it isn't really possible to convey anything so complicated by gesture alone, but he gathered that I wasn't going to move, and scowled at me.

When I had finished making signs to him, and brought my attention back to my own immediate surroundings, I saw Cartridge looking at me intently, leaning forward so as to see round the bosom of the coal-man's wife. I gave him a sickly grin; without changing his expression at all he continued to stare at me unwaveringly. I suppose he recognized me as the ex-convict, but he didn't show any sign of it. Suddenly it struck me what he was doing: this would be his first visit to the town I mustn't name, and he was solemnly engaged in studying the natives. No doubt he would go back to town and dine out on the story of how he had freely ventured into the very heart of the industrial provinces and rubbed shoulders with the aborigines. I felt like telling him he was welcome to rub my shoulders any time.

He leaned forward a bit further and I thought he was going to speak, but fortunately the coal-man's wife turned to me just at that moment and started some long, rambling monologue about how they had recently moved into the country and how she found it nicer in some ways and not nicer in others. She was already speaking rather fast and unsteadily, and no doubt she had chosen this neutral – indeed, boring – subject with the idea of getting her composure back and breathing out a bit of the alcohol Stocker had forced on her. I let her ramble. The food would do her good, and afterwards she'd have more of a chance against Stocker; it was nice to see fair play for once. Even so, Cartridge didn't give up watching me. I even caught him looking to see if I knew the right forks and things, as each course came on. I suppose all his life he'd thought we just grabbed our food with our fingers, or got down and lapped it up.

I chewed solidly through the stuff, glancing at my wrist-watch from time to time and waiting for the speeches; the sooner they began the sooner they would end. The coal-man's wife burbled on, stealing occasional glances at Stocker. Everyone seemed in a fairly good humour; what embarrassment they might have felt had been dispersed by alcohol, and it was obvious that they were enjoying the bean-feast for its own sake. Randall kept giving his peculiar choking laugh, a sound so rare that I only remembered hearing it four or five times in all the years I was at school; now, however, he kept it up almost continuously as he told some fool story to the people round him. It was like a pig being run over, a sort of agonized bubbling whoop. I noticed my mother looking at him with a kind of compassionate wonder.

Then the food was cleared away, large silver boxes of cigarettes and cigars began to circulate, and the speeches were on. I managed to make my mind a blank for about half an hour, even nodding off for a moment at one point; but finally it was Ned's turn, he was on his feet responding to the toast of The Happy Pair, and I began to attend. Like everyone else I was more than a bit curious to hear what he'd say.

In fact, I had quite an uncanny sensation as I looked round the room – sorry, the 'banqueting hall'. There they all were, invited for the second time to see Myra married – or, more precisely, to see her awarded. She was the prize, and this was the prize-giving day. There were two things Ned could do with this situation; one was to leave it alone, and just gracefully talk about nothing for a few minutes and then sit down; the other was to punch it over and make everything he could out of it. I knew which he'd do. The wrong one. The second one.

He went directly to the point, informing his guests that this was the second time they had been so kind as to celebrate Myra's wedding. And each time to a man of their own town. Evidently there was something about the breed that she found attractive. (Slightly strained silence.) He hoped it wouldn't turn into a habit. (Laughter, relaxing everyone.) A few more jokes, keeping everyone more or less chuckling, not so much at the wit as to enjoy the escape from tension. Then a sudden twist into seriousness. Why – he asked himself through them – was he making so much of the fact that Mrs Roper (a short, barking cheer from Randall) who had, after all, he thought he might say, plenty of choice (wild cheering and laughter), had chosen twice 'from among us'?

Then he started. I sat back and admired the way he did it. The whole opening section of the speech was just a lead to its real subject – local patriotism. Shorn of its festooning bullshit, the gist was this: Myra, who knew a thing or two about eligible men, had married two men from our town. And why? Because we knew how to breed 'em good. Where would old England be without us? Rough diamonds, we might be, but by God, we were the boys. We were resourceful, imaginative, tough, reliable. We were early to bed and early to rise, healthy, wealthy, and wise. He even brought in stuff about clay; semi-poetic stuff about the clay from which we grew, as if we were all a lot of rambler roses. He glossed over the fact, well known to his hearers, that the clay used for the better lines of pottery is actually brought up from Cornwall. They didn't care. It went over, but good.

Then I suddenly realized what Ned was doing. It wasn't only to please his hearers and reconcile his fellow citizens to his having grabbed Robert's wife that he was coming all this stuff. It was for his own benefit, to sketch in the *rationale* of his whole way of life, of which Myra was now a part. It was to claim the status of the non-prodigal son. He had stayed in the district and Robert hadn't. So much for Art and all the rest of it. He, Ned Roper, was going to stand by the district and see it through. And that proved he was in the right, didn't it, didn't it?

It was all rather frightening. He was talking to someone who wasn't there. The real point of everything he said was that it was aimed at Robert. I even felt, as he worked up to a peroration, an impulse to stand up and shout, 'Relax, Ned boy – he's not here!'

It's a good thing I didn't, though, because it wouldn't have been true. Robert *was* there. He and Pepina had arrived just as Ned started his speech and they had been waiting outside the room, listening to the speech through a chink in the big double doors. As Ned sat down and everybody applauded to show local solidarity, Robert pushed these doors open and came in, leading Pepina by the hand.

It would make a better story if I said that the applause stopped in an instant. Actually it just faded, as people caught sight of the two of them standing there. About twenty citizens at one table, placed where they couldn't see the door, kept on clapping for what seemed a quarter of an hour before they began to feel that there was something wrong and stopped. It was horrible.

Ned was one of the first to see Robert, and he was back on his feet in an instant. But neither of them moved until there was silence. Ned stood at his place at the table, holding a freshly lighted cigarette in his right hand, and Robert just went on with his Sandeman Port act by the door. Gradually the clapping ran down and all sound died away.

It was, I suppose, a moment of pure horror. If Robert had come in a little earlier, most of the guests would have been able to carry it off all right, but he had caught us smack off balance, just in the act of applauding a speech that – as we all knew only too well – had been thought out and delivered as a weapon against him. Against him personally, and against what he stood for. To be in the act of clapping such a speech, to have relaxed and deliberately allowed our critical faculties to slacken, to have accepted Ned's invitation to slip into the mood of warm self-congratulation – and then to have Robert standing there, having heard it all, Robert, the only man Jack of us who had got sufficiently away from himself to *create* anything, and who therefore had the right, if he felt like it, to despise us all. It was hell. At least, as I say, I suppose it was hell. I personally wasn't quite with it. The full impact of the situation has hit me often enough since, when I've thought about it, but at the time I side-stepped it. I was looking at Pepina. I don't think she saw me; she stood at Robert's right, about one pace to the rear and just looked round, warily but calmly. She had, obviously, not much idea what was going on, and wasn't concerned about putting on any act; she didn't care if the significance of this or that detail went over her head. For her the basis of the situation was that Robert was confronting these people, and in particular confronting Ned and Myra, and that her attitude to them was going to depend on how they treated him. She had submerged her will in Robert's, but without any abject abandonment of her own personality; on the contrary, it brought out her essential qualities. She was also shrewd enough, obviously, to grasp that she was being compared with Myra in everyone's mind, and not at all afraid of the comparison.

In fact, as we all sat there, the contest between the two women seemed to intensify, silently and without anyone's moving or speaking, until it dwarfed that between the men. Myra had by this time stood up, and the four of them were on their feet, facing one another. I suppose the tableau only went on for seven or eight seconds, but it seemed much longer. Even I had to draw my eyes away from Pepina and glance at Myra. And I had to admit they both came out of it pretty well. Myra was the finished product; take one vertebrate mammal, of the species *Homo sapiens*, feminine gender, and give her the treatment from end to end; all the teaching and the training and the deportment and ballet and everything else in the bag; round off at some fabulous finishing school, and dip a few times into the tub marked 'good society'. Result, Myra. Pepina was the product that was not merely not finished, but not started on. Recipe for Pepina: take one vertebrate mammal as before, and *don't spoil it*. It suddenly struck me that these must be two of the most beautiful women in the world. I looked them both over, in turn, trying to find a flaw like bad posture or a too long nose or else eyes too close together or blotchy skin or anything. But I couldn't. That didn't mean, of course, that I thought it was a photo-finish. For me Pepina was breaking the tape before Myra had left the starting-gate. But that part of it, I suppose, was personal.

All this, as I say, probably took a few seconds. It may be that Ned and Robert didn't even feel that the emphasis had shifted to the women. They were probably too much wrapped up in the psychological wrestling-match they were staging. At any rate, when they began to move and speak they did so without much reference to their respective partners. Ned welcomed Robert and said it was nice to see him at the reception, and that if he had known that he and Pepina would be in the neighbourhood they would certainly have been sent an invitation. Robert said they found themselves passing through and it was too much of a temptation to see how the reception was going, or some such palpable lie, which he uttered without any sign of embarrassment. Ned called the head waiter over and got him to lay a place for the two of them so that they could have some dessert and wine. In the course of moving them in, the introduction of Pepina was performed very smoothly. I listened all ears to see whether she would say anything in English: she said 'How do you do', as if it were something she had said a lot of times, but it didn't tell me whether she knew any more English. Then they sat down.

Conversation limply started up again. The party was at that moment like a flower that has not been watered for so long that you think it must surely be dead; it hangs right over the side of the pot in an attitude of utter hopelessness. But you water it just the same, and to your astonishment it begins slowly to straighten out. I even began saying something to the coal-man's wife.

But it was not to be. Heads began to turn, and people began to say 'Sh!' and things of that sort. Robert was on his feet. There was a certain amount of scraping of chairs, and I missed a word or two, but he was saying 'kindly permit me . . . give you a toast that isn't down in your list . . . but it's a toast that I'm sure you will readily join with me today in drinking.'

Everyone sat still, holding their glasses. Ned stared tensely up at Robert, not able, at that moment, even to manage a smile.

'I give you — *success!*'

Robert brought out the word with a harsh and resolute emphasis that was, at the same time, utterly empty. You couldn't tell, from the way he spoke, what sort of emotion lay behind it. And it was just that, of course, that gave the thing its deadliness. Because we all knew quite well what emotion did lie behind it. It was the exact verbal equivalent of his savage little drawing of the angler being menaced by the fish.

Success! We had been asked to drink a toast to success, in abstraction — not success to this or that person, but success itself. I don't think any one more devastating word could have been uttered in that situation — even some frightful obscenity would somehow have shattered us less. It was like a lash laid across our backs. We had been doing our bit of kow-towing to this success, in the person of Ned: all right, drink to it!

Nobody moved. I couldn't bear it. I had to do something to break the spell.

Pushing my chair back wildly, I got up. My glass was empty, but I lifted it as if it were full to the brim.

'Success!' I shouted. 'And lots of it — to both our distinguished friends!'

In ones and twos, and then all at once, the guests got to their feet. Amid a confused babbling, in which the word 'success' seemed to have some part, they drank — or, like me, pretended to drink. Disaster was averted.

We all sat down. I grabbed a cigarette with sweating hands and lit it. Justin Cartridge leaned across the coal-man's wife and said to me, 'I thought you showed presence of mind there.'

'Get off,' I said.

'No, really,' he said. He sat back, staring in front of him, and I knew he was already rehearsing the story he was going to make of all this when he got back to his club. I thought of the mess he was bound to make of it, and suddenly I felt happy and began smiling.

# XII

But smiling, as I'd discovered before, isn't something you can just keep on doing without fairly continuous renewal of the material you're smiling *about*. And the wedding reception was barely over, the last groups were only just breaking up in the foyer, when an unmistakable heaviness came down on me. I didn't feel quite happy about Robert. No, that wasn't it. I didn't feel quite happy about Ned and Robert. No, not that either. I didn't feel quite happy about Ned and Robert and Myra and Pepina. It was in there somewhere. But all I could put my finger on was a feeling that I'd like to speak to Robert before he pushed on to wherever he was pushing on to, and took Pepina with him. I got my mother into her coat and then dumped her on a sofa and asked her to wait a minute, and I ducked out of the hotel and scoured the car park for the Bristol. It wasn't there. But perhaps they hadn't come by car. The station was just across the road; I darted across and peered about, but there didn't seem to be anything unusual going on. If Robert was at large in a place there generally was *something* out of the ordinary happening; more noise and commotion, or a more deadly silence, or something. Still, I couldn't see much of the platform, from outside the barrier, and he might be there, so I went over to the machine to get a platform ticket. I was just fumbling for a penny when a voice said, 'Don't bother.'

It was the ticket-collector, grinning at me cheerily. He said, 'They've gone,' and jerked his thumb.

'Who have?' I asked.

'The 'appy couple,' he grinned. Of course he knew all about the wedding. I was about to tell him it was *another* happy couple I was after, but a sense of weariness descended on me. One happy couple had gone one way, and one happy couple another, and I was loitering about the happy station by my happy self.

'Took the express,' said the ticket-collector. 'Let 'em slip through y'fingers, eh?'

I understood. He knew I was on the *Sentry* and saw me as the baffled news-hound, arriving just too late to interview the happy couple before departing. He was wrong, but not all that wrong; somewhere along the journey I had arrived too late.

Shrugging heavily, I turned round and a man hurrying towards the barrier, with a woman following close behind, nearly bumped into me. Robert and Pepina.

'Well, hallo!' I said.

He scowled at me. 'Missed the blasted train,' he said peevishly, staring past me at the empty station. Pepina, coming to a halt at his side, took his arm, but his face didn't relax at all. She smiled at me a little. I wanted to speak to her but I had to speak to Robert first.

'Missed the train?' I said. 'You don't mean you were going to get on the same train as Ned and Myra?'

The ticket-collector, evidently not able to hear well enough, moved forward to get into the act. 'You're too late to see them off,' he said into a vacuum.

Robert looked at me irritably. His square, stocky form seemed to have gone smaller, as if he had defensively shrunk into himself, settling his bones more deeply into their sockets, as a protection against being shaken to pieces.

'The same train?' he snapped. 'Why not? We haven't got all evening to hang about here; it's bad enough as it is, having to waste a day. The only decent train we could get to come down on was the ten – '

He stopped, obviously ready to bite his tongue off for letting it out that they had come up for the day with no other motive than to horn in on Myra's second wedding. So that was it.

We looked at each other for an instant. There wasn't anything either of us could say. Pepina was looking about her like a person sightseeing. Probably the station seemed foreign and exotic, to her eyes. She was letting us bicker without bothering too much.

'When's the next fast train to London?' Robert asked the ticket man. On being told some impossible hour he turned away, gulping down huge nuggets of rage. 'Stuck here,' I heard him muttering.

He grated something in Italian to Pepina; she answered in English, 'We will wait,' and gestured towards the hotel. But Robert shook his head violently, and jerked out a few more fragments of Italian, in which I caught the word 'cinema'. They were going to fill the time in that way.

'Why not – ' I began, and stopped. I didn't quite know what I had intended to say. Something on the lines of, Why not come and have a cup of tea with me and my old mum? Why not sit and have a drink with the boys? Why not make a jolly day of it, with lots of good clean fun and memories of old times? *Why not walk up the steps of the town hall and blow your brains out?*

Robert saw me wavering about and searching for a formula, a way of keeping up my character as everybody's uncle. He had half turned away, with his hand on Pepina's arm, but he stopped for long enough to say, 'Do me a favour, Joe.'

'All right,' I said, and walked away quickly, without looking back. I knew that was the favour he meant, but I didn't want him to *say* it.

From then on I was on the griddle. The tension that built up inside me never stopped increasing. Sometimes I thought I would go off my nut completely, and then the only way to calm myself was to keep a firm grip on the fact that my uneasiness was, at any rate, traceable to a definite cause. People who have that kind of tension over nothing, or nothing that they can pin down, are the ones who really suffer. At least, I did know that I was on the stretch because of what I had seen written on Robert's face that evening, outside the station: the misery and impatience that he was making no attempt to hide. And what business was it of mine? Well, I didn't want to see Pepina suffer. Well, I needn't see her suffer. I could keep away. Yes, but I didn't want to think she was suffering that that I couldn't help. All right, but weren't there millions of people suffering, and could I help them? When it got round to this point, which happened about five times an hour, I used to take another sedative and another couple of stomach tablets and try to duck out of it that way. Sometimes I'd wash the mixture down with a whisky, and let them fight it out down there. I used to get palpitations a lot, I remember.

Finally, one evening, my mother said, 'It's no good, Joe. You'll have to attend to it.'

Actually, she didn't call me 'Joe'; she called me the name she gave me when I was born, but I've got this far without mentioning it.

'Attend to it?' I said, acting guilty. I didn't precisely *feel* guilty, but that's how you do tend to act when someone reads your thoughts.

'Yes,' she nodded, very firm. 'Get something done about it. I've watched you going through the mill with anxiety for as long as I can stand it. You'll be getting me in the same state next.'

'They always did say a boy's best friend was his mother, didn't they?' I said nastily. We wrangled for a bit and then I went out. And I hadn't walked ten yards before I had to laugh. Because the reason I had gone out was to get on to the telephone, in the box at the corner. Even while I was sarcastically fending off my mother's instructions I was automatically obeying them.

It was a warm summery evening, and when I got to the box there were a couple of chaps standing quite contentedly outside it, while a woman inside stared raptly before her, holding the instrument to her ear. I joined them and we struck up quite a friendship during those long minutes on the pavement. From the weather we passed on to international politics, economic affairs, sport and agriculture. One of them was a Scotsman, and he was able to add variety and breadth to our little symposium by giving the characteristic North British view. I began to question him keenly about the nationalist movement, and the extent to which he, personally, considered Home Rule desirable or feasible. Now and again we glanced at the woman inside the box; she didn't seem to be talking much – if she was, we could only conclude that she had learnt some technique of talking without moving her mouth; from a ventriloquist, no doubt. This led our discourse naturally into the realms of entertainment and the arts, our Caledonian friend contributing a spirited defence of the traditional songs and dances of his native heath. What sounded like a peal of laughter reached us through the glass; my fellow Englishman suggested that the lady's unseen interlocutor must be a witty fellow indeed. This stimulated me to a short comparison of fashions in epigram in our grandfather's and our own epochs respectively; I quoted (from memory but, I trust, accurately) a few of Oscar Wilde's celebrated gems of wit and wisdom, and heartening indeed was the frank, manly laughter that rang out. Two boys now joined us, and we modified our conversation so as to bring them within its orbit, now questioning them as to their school activities, now engaging in reminiscence of our own carefree youth. As the long, golden evening gradually yielded first to twilight and then to a deep dusk, through which we could barely discern each other's faces, we relived many memorable passages of our lives, and placed before the eager lads the garnered sheaves of our longer experience.

Suddenly, unable to stand it any longer, I went up to the kiosk and leaned against it, my face a few inches from the woman's. At first she did not see me, and I was able to study her intently as, shoulders hunched, she held the telephone in a tense grip jammed against her ear. Possibly through fatigue she was not standing, but leaning rigidly against the wall of the box; she looked like a roll of frozen linoleum in the hold of a liner. Her unseeing eyes were slightly raised as if staring at an imaginary horizon. In a flash I knew her secret. She was one of those women who are all soul, all fire and radiance. Nothing could assuage that wild thirst for beauty and profundity except the masterpieces of the great Russian novelists. But – child of a harsh civilization, ceaselessly denying the generous impulses of its people – she had never been taught to read. So each night she went to the telephone, and her cousin-in-law, the one with the stammer, read her half a dozen chapters of Dostoievsky.

Aflame with knowledge and sympathy I flung open the door of the box. But before I could find words to tell her that I knew her secret, and that it was safe with me, the woman put the telephone back in its rest.

'I can't get through,' she said wonderingly.

As we stared at each other, one of the waiting boys pushed his way into the box and pressed Button B. There was a loud rattle as the coins the woman had inserted were spat out of the apparatus. *It was true.* She had stood in the box till her feet had splayed out like a bird's and never heard one word. I tried to speak but nothing would come.

'Give her back that money,' said the Scotsman, appearing suddenly at my back. The boy, after one quick glance round for his missing companion, civilly handed the lady her three pennies and took himself off.

'Now if somebody'll start telephoning,' the Scotsman went on. He seemed to be looking at me; it was not my turn, but I had to make some move, and this was as good a one as any. The woman walked stiffly past me and I stepped into the box and closed the door. A moment later Robert's Hampstead number was ringing. And it was only then that I realized something.

I had no idea what I was going to say.

Feverishly I signalled through the glass to the Scotsman, trying to get him to come and take his turn. He only grinned broadly – dusk as it was, I saw the flash of his dentures – and the next thing I knew was that the ringing had stopped and Mrs Sienkiewicz was speaking.

'I must speak to Mr Lamb,' I jerked out.

'Nut at home,' came her voice.

'Mrs Lamb, then – I mean Miss – Signorina – '

'Nut at home as well.'

'Well, who is at home, for God's sake?'

'Nutbody,' she replied primly. I could imagine her getting ready to hang up on me.

'Where are they? It's important,' I shouted.

'I am wetting,' she said flatly. 'Since two days they are nut at home.'

Standing there in the box, exchanging gibberish with the housekeeper all those miles away, it came to me – the certain knowledge of catastrophe. I had known it in my belly, and now, though the woman could tell me nothing, I knew for certain that the volcano had gone up at last.

I slammed out of the box and walked on down the street. Neither Robert nor Pepina was at home, or had been for two days. I thought of this, and I saw again Robert's face, as it had looked when I saw him last; that angry impatience, that sense of loss and strain. He had come up, that day, to scorch his wings in the candle-flame. Perhaps he had hoped that one final glimpse of Myra would exorcise her spirit from his life; but, like a dram-drinker he had found that the last gulp never is the last. It wasn't that he loved her. It was simply that he had seen the cup awarded to the rival captain, and he just couldn't believe that there was to be no return fixture.

I was in the middle of the town now, and there were plenty of telephone boxes about. I went into a pub – there was just time to be served before they shut – and had a whisky so that I could get change for a pound note. Then, with a pocketful of silver and copper, I went into a box and started dialling numbers.

We'll skip the details. As a journalist I know where to go for information. Before my pound had run out, I had learnt, reliably, that Robert had taken a plane from London Airport to Paris two evenings ago. Paris being where Ned and Myra had gone for their honeymoon.

Robert had gone by himself. But natch. I hated him worse for that.

I walked home, got myself upstairs and into bed and took enough sleeping pills to duck me under for a few hours. When I woke the sun was shining in through the window. I got dressed and went downstairs, but my mother wasn't up yet, so I left her a note asking her to telephone the office and say I shouldn't be at work that day. 'Tell them anything,' I put. 'Back as soon as possible. Don't worry. Am doing what you told me – attending to things.'

There was an early train and I got it. At Euston I made myself slow down long enough to eat a roll and butter and drink some coffee. I had a long day coming.

First, though it was a waste of time and I knew it, I took a cab out to Hampstead. Mrs Sienkiewicz had gone to pieces under the strain; she knew Robert's unpredictable impulses, and was afraid of making a fool of herself and angering him if she made any move to trace either him or Pepina. The result was that her English had broken up into a mass of sharp splinters. I practically had to use deaf-and-dumb language, mime, lip reading and telepathy to get the simple story out of her. But I got it. Robert had banged out of the house, two afternoons previously, and stalked out of sight down the road with a travelling-bag. (In search of a taxi, obviously.) About an hour later she had heard sobbing from Pepina and had gone upstairs to see what she could do. But she had hardly got to the head of the stairs before Pepina had brushed past her, not seeing her, and gone out through the front door. Her face had been covered with tears and she had put on no outdoor clothes.

Mrs Sienkiewicz had shrugged and gone downstairs. A quarrel. By evening they would make it up. The sooner they got married the better.

'So you just let it go?' I asked. 'Sounds as if you were pretty well accustomed to seeing them quarrel.'

She shook her head powerfully. It was the first time she had known the peace broken. She had never seen tears in Pepina's eyes before. (As she pronounced it 'tares', she had me shaken at first with visions of some hellish injury.)

208

'Now, listen, this is important,' I said. 'Mr and Mrs Lamb went away separately. I mean Robert and Pepina. Wherever they are, they're not *together*. I know where he is – he's in Paris – and now I want to know where she is. Try and think where she's likely to be.'

A blank. It wasn't that the woman didn't want to tell me, it was simply that she'd no idea. Pepina didn't know anybody. She hadn't any friends in the neighbourhood – or further off, for that matter – that she might have gone to. She couldn't speak much English, for one thing. She'd been picking it up, but Robert wouldn't take seriously her wish to learn it; she suited him better when she stuck to Italian.

Of course. It made her seem more pastoral. The more she resembled an ordinary human being the less he could think of her as a special toy for himself, a 'find' that he'd brought back, at great expense, to keep by him as a permanent testimony to his love of natural simplicity.

You treated people like that, and this was what happened. Not that you cared, if you were Robert. Life was rough for you and you didn't see anything against its being rough for other people.

'Thank you, Mrs Sienkiewicz,' I said. Outside, down the street, round a couple of corners, and I was in the local cop-shop. It was still fairly early in the morning.

The trouble with the sergeant who handled my inquiry was that he had read in some book or other that a keen policeman always asks a lot of damn fool questions that don't concern the matter in hand. Nothing would satisfy him, for a start, but to know who I was. Then we went ahead, but I felt I was marked down from the start.

'You say this woman's disappeared,' he said, giving me his 'keen' look. As keen as a cork bath-mat.

'I don't only say it, I've been to find out, and it's true. She's been missing for two – '

'Never mind how long for the moment. We're coming to that. You say that the woman and her husband have both disappeared?'

It was true that I had described Robert as Pepina's husband, which by this time he could have been if he'd cared enough. I couldn't face all the maundering that would have followed if I'd tried to make clear their real relationship.

'Now what makes you so certain,' he followed up, treading

on the loud pedal when he reached the 'you', 'that they haven't gone off together in a perfectly ordinary way?'

I saw it was hopeless. But I had to soldier on, for a few more minutes at least. I thought of all those police stations, all those telephones, all those patrol cars, and all those big, healthy policemen with whistles and notebooks. I thought of how easily they could find her if I could only get them interested enough.

'Well, it'd take me too long to explain just what it is that makes me certain,' I began, 'but I know for a – '

Then he interrupted me. 'Just a moment,' he said, holding up a finger. I stopped, but he didn't say anything. Instead, he fumbled in his pocket for his spectacle-case, got it out, opened it, took his glasses out of it, and started to put them on. It seemed to take him about ten minutes. Probably he couldn't remember where his ears were, from one time to the next. Anyway, I knew, long before he spoke, that it was hopeless. I'd put him against me, and the rest of the time I spent there was going to be just wasted.

'You say the reason you can't explain why you're so anxious is that it would *take – too – long*,' he said, dropping each word like a brick on my toes. 'What d'you mean by that exactly? What's your idea of too long? Ten minutes? Half an hour? You come in here and you expect us to take up – '

I tried to tell him to save the rest, but he wouldn't stop.

' – a search job that's liable to take a lot of our time and the taxpayer's money, you want us to call the whole organization into play and when I ask you – '

Good manners were one thing, but I had something urgent to do. I started for the door before he had finished.

'Come BACK!' he shouted, really nasty, as soon as he saw me turn towards the door.

'I'm sorry, but I've got to go,' I said. 'I've left the taxpayer's money on the gas and it'll boil over and spoil the carpet.'

I was outside and there was London, there was England, there was the world, and somewhere in it was Pepina, without anyone to turn to. Well, she had, as of now. She had me.

Where would a girl go who couldn't speak much English, who had been accustomed to earning her living as an hotel worker? Don't let's all speak at once. I saw a taxi coming. I was waving and calling, I was in it, we were bowling along, we were stopping, I was out and paying, it had gone, I was there. Soho.

'Soho', they tell us, was once a hunting call. I felt like giving tongue to it. My lassitude had fallen away, leaving me buoyant. Last reel. Here comes the hero. Detective Inspector Joe Shaw, hero of the Yard. The scrap-yard. Always ready for a scrap. In two shakes he's solved the problem. Or shaken it, anyway. The girl's in Soho, somewhere. Working in some joint run by Italians. Hear that brain turning over? You don't need to hear it – you can smell the burning. Now all he's got to do is to force his way into every place run by Italians and ask where Pepina is. He doesn't know her second name. Well, get busy, Jack. Within a stone's-throw there must be four hundred places run by Italians, with an average of six girls called Pepina working in each. Get that stone ready.

I began by plunging into the café I happened to be standing outside as I reached this conclusion. I had some coffee and asked the proprietor if he had any Italian staff. He said no. I had no means of telling whether he was lying or not. He was English, and the two waitresses I could see were obviously English too. I paid for the coffee and went out. Perhaps Pepina was down in the kitchen, washing up. I didn't know how to find out. I went into the next place, and had some more coffee. There seemed to be a lot of Turks about. Was one of them the boss? I started asking the girl who served me what nationality most of the staff were. She drew away from me in horror, and I saw her talking about me to a rough-looking Turk, or perhaps he was just a Turkish-looking rough. He came over and asked me what I wanted. I said I was looking for a girl. He said there were plenty about. I said it was a special one I wanted. He said there were plenty of special ones about too, but would I get out of his café. I said he was not to misunderstand me. The girl I wanted was called Pepina. He closed one eye in a deep wink as if about to tell me some scandalous joke that we could both enjoy, then suddenly seized me by the arm and started pushing me towards the door. My foot caught on a table leg, and I nearly went over. For a wild second or two I had visions of myself lying on the floor while the Turks closed in and began kicking me to death. Looking back, I'm sure they wouldn't have bothered, but at the time I was a bit flustered. I found myself on the pavement, and went a few doors along to the next place. Here I walked in and asked for some coffee. I was beginning to hate the taste of coffee, so I didn't drink it when it came. I just paid for it and started questioning the waitress. She seemed to be a Greek. I got no change out of her, either literally or figuratively.

It was now getting on for the middle of the morning. 'Coffee time' as some people call it. I might have done, myself, once, but the term has dropped out of my vocabulary since that day. Anyway, about now I had a brainwave. I decided to overhaul my method. I had a card to say I worked for the *Staffordshire Sentry*. I'd use the privilege of the Fourth Estate. Just go in and show them the card and ask where Pepina was. Everyone's glad to help a newspaper reporter. They think it might lead to their grabbing a little of the publicity for themselves – and for some reason this appeals to them.

That's the theory, anyway. Actually I only tried it once. I went into the next snack-bar I came to and asked for the manager. A very hairy man came over and said quite frankly that he was the manager. He had a thick bushy moustache, a tremendous lot of hair on his head, and hairs all over the backs of his hands and as far as you could see up his sleeves. When he stripped he must have looked like an ape with a shaved face. I asked him about Pepina and showed him my card.

'What you after?' he asked me quietly. His English was good, with not much of an accent, but he never used any verbs. Perhaps they had only got as far as Lesson I, Nouns, when he had had to give up. He had mastered that part very well. He had lots of nouns, and a fair sprinkling of pronouns, adjectives, prepositions, and all that, but no verbs. I explained that I was looking for Pepina, that my paper had sent me to find her, and it was part of a complicated story.

'To my café, why?' he asked. 'Who?'

'Just at random,' I said. 'We – '

'Random,' he said quickly, catching at the name, storing it away in his memory as the name of the man who had informed on him.

'Now let me put it this way – ' I started.

'Nothing in my café,' he interrupted, shaking his bushy head.

'It's not a question of – '

'My café, nothing. *Nothing!*' he shouted.

'Well – '

'Good food! Good service! Everything good! All fine! Police, no.'

'No, certainly not' I assured him. 'No police.'

'No police! Good service!' he said loudly, staring at me. 'No papers! No questions! No police! Everything good!'

'For God's sake let me – ' I started off again. By this time I was convinced that the snack-bar was a front for a whore-house and he was terrified of any publicity. But I had to know whether Pepina was anywhere about.

'Pepina,' I said. 'Italian.'

That did it. I don't know why it should have, but it did. At the word 'Italian' he went over the edge. 'Everything good' and 'Nothing!' and things like that, together with the stuff about the service, began to pour out of him, and his hair-line crept down till it threatened to complete the circuit and join up with the hair on his chest.

'Italians, no!' he shouted. 'Everything good!'

'All right, all right,' I said, and backed out. After that I put my press card away, and in fact I abandoned my fixed plan and just wandered about. I stopped going into restaurants; I just looked in through the window. The only doors I went into now were backdoors, up entries; the ones that led to the kitchens and staff quarters. Sometimes I went up and down iron ladders on the outside walls of houses. It was hot and I got tired. I went and left my overcoat at the Left Luggage Office at Leicester Square tube station. It was afternoon. People were leaning against the walls, the vegetables were wilting on the barrows. The sky, glimpsed above brick, was a hard blue.

Perhaps the unusual weather helped to push reality to one side. Have you noticed how no English scene looks anything but artificial under a blue sky? These streets began to look like a film set, the people like eagerly performing extras; the houses had been built up and grouped by a panel of chefs, using wedding-cake and brown sugar. And suddenly I realized that my last pipeline to the real world had been cut. I had been counting this square mile of streets for hours – and now I *had forgotten which ones I had done*. I tried to remember by using individual landmarks; surely I had been into this café, that Espresso bar, the pub over there? But they had merged, by this time, into one amorphous globule. The dark men leaned at corners; the wreckage of a dozen languages ascended from basements; smells of cooking, laundry steam and thick silences wafted out of alleys. The shadows grew longer, and now at last I realized that I had finally passed through the barriers and was living in a dream. But it was a dream with a hole in its centre, a hole where Pepina should have been.

About the ninth hour of my wandering, the shadows rose and drowned everything. Under the lamps the hot, scented night proliferated like Borneo. The whores came out, the feline padding to and fro began, the shadows in the doorways were as deep as pit-shafts, and in the thick air we swam and swayed like creatures in a vaporous aquarium. I scarcely moved any more; I had become one of the men leaning at corners; quite soon I expected to fade backwards into the wedding-cake architecture. Fatigue fed me like a drug. I knew nothing. My mind had become a trapeze, swinging emptily under the Big Top, for any passing acrobat to seize and twirl on for a few seconds. Thoughts of people, of places, of states of mind, clambered and swung on my trapeze like apes. I thought of home, with its narrow crowded streets, its kilns and slag-heaps, its volatile grim comedians. I thought of Robert and Ned. All my life they had seemed big, they had always swaggered across the stage of my mind like enormous figures, one at a time because there was no room for both together. But now they had changed, dwindled. There was room and to spare for the two of them on my high swinging trapeze. Struggling, they dangled from the Big Top. Why had I thought them so big? They were big spenders, but too often their cheques bounced. Now that I was approaching the centre where the real coin was minted, their angry shadows fell away from me and I went forward alone.

I was ill; fever burned in my blood, banged round in my veins and hammered the inside of my forehead, trying to force it open. At times I held my hands cupped, ready to catch my eyes as they fell out, thumbed from their sockets by the bursting pressure behind them. My chief wish was to hide my illness; I walked and leaned, walked and leaned, avoiding the whores because I was afraid they might pity me. Inside my fat body my shrunken skeleton rattled like a folded-up tripod in a suitcase. Sweat ran down my face. A warm wind blew down the street, and I longed for the coolness of my overcoat. *An overcoat lined with ice!* I thought. What an invention! I longed for the morning so that the Patent Office would be open. I would hurry round and take out a patent for the ice-lined overcoat. I should be rich and happy always, cool in my overcoat with the ice lining. The walls melted and I sank into a sitting position on the pavement, but a policeman was standing not far off and I struggled up again. If he saw me falling over in the street he would take me off and have me locked up somewhere where I would never be able to patent my ice-lined overcoat. The authorities were jealous; if anyone breathed a word of my invention I might be kept in prison for the rest of my life. Prison! I thought of the thin blankets and the stone floors. How cold it would be! Looking up, I saw the grille already fastened. I put my hand tremblingly behind my back and touched the rough wall. I was inside! The policeman walked past, and as he went by he gave me a stern glance through the bars. He had informed on me, and had me arrested, all without moving from his spot on the street corner. He had done it by the power of thought! How could I fight against that?

I gave up. A sign said 'Hotel'. I must have got in, and seen someone to take my money and show me a room, though I don't remember it. When I woke, it was light, and had been for hours; I could tell that although my watch had stopped. I hurried out; I had been sleeping in my clothes, a practical arrangement, as it allowed me to be outside in the street in a minimum of seconds. I stood on the pavement in the cool of the morning, breathing gladly, and realized that my fever had gone. It must have been exhaustion. I began to move down the street, but before I had gone ten yards I passed a shop window that had a mirror in it, and my appearance pulled me up short. A shave, at least, I must have; if I went about looking like this no one would give me any information about Pepina. I moved on down the street looking out for a barber's. One of the first shops I passed was a horse-meat shop. There were white letters stuck in the window, and one of them had fallen off so that it read: HORSE MEAT FOR YOU DOGS.

I was the first customer in the little barber's shop, but the three men who worked there were all in readiness in their white coats. I wondered how three barbers could work at once in such a small shop. Perhaps they had a lot of midgets in the neighbourhood, who came in to be shaved. It would be possible to shave several midgets at once, or cut their hair.

While the barber worked on me I felt myself slowly tilting over and coming the right way up. A shave is the greatest of tonics, and these three added an extra dash of healing power to the mixture by talking to one another, ignoring me. There was a short one, a tall one, a fat one. The fat one was doing me.

As the mists cleared from my brain, I latched on to their conversation, knowing that if I hung on to it I should be pulled back across the frontier into the real world.

The Short One. Seems to be a lot more pests about this year. When I first started growin' vegetables, you didn't seem to get none of these pests, not so much as they do now, like.

The Tall One. If you want my explanation, it's all the atoms in the air.

The Fat One. What's that religion where they don't kill nothink?

The Short One. Quakers.

The Fat One. No, that one where they don't eat nothink that's alive, and that. They don't kill nothink.

The Tall One. Yerss. And suppose a gnat comes and lands on you. You brush him off, don't you? And durin' the brushin' process 'e gets killed.

By this time the shaving process was over. I straightened up and the fat barber said, 'You don't want any of our boss's specials?'

'What are they?' I asked.

'French letters,' he said and laughed until he coughed chestily.

While he was laughing I paid and went out, not taking any of their boss's specials.

My mood had changed again and now I was savage. As I walked through the streets, treading fast and carelessly, I felt my old, obsolete character crumbling away. I thought of this and it reminded me of the way gipsies eat hedgehogs – rolling them in clay, baking them and then cracking off the clay with the prickles baked into it. My coating of clay was hardening in the fire of my resolution, but there was a difference between me and the hedgehog; my spines were being exposed, for the first time, as the casing of timidity and sloth crumbled away.

Actually I must have been light-headed still, because I couldn't slow down for long enough to think of a plan of action. All I could do was to go on searching, alone, at random, like a man approaching a haystack with a piece of cotton in his pocket, ready to thread the first needle he finds with it. I had my cotton, and the needle would just have to be forthcoming; the fury of my impatience would compel it. As I walked I threatened the universe. If it did not come to heel soon, my reprisals would begin and they would be terrible.

Merely from an instinctive notion of avoiding the tangle of streets I had combed on the previous day, I allowed myself to cut through Covent Garden and generally work parallel with the Strand. Men were shouting and heaving sacks and baskets; amid a crowd of them I stood and drank several cups of hot dark tea, saturated with sugar. The smell of vegetables, the shirt-sleeved porters looking more like farm labourers than any kind of urban worker, the gum-booted men who had come in by lorry from the mist-hung villages before London was awake, all helped to increase my sense of unreality. Where was I? A provincial from a smoky bricked-up place far away, who had repeatedly dipped himself in metropolitan culture till all but the core of his mind was dyed in it, searching the capital city for a Latin girl from the impossibly distant mountains, drinking tea with this bunch of rustic Cockneys – and all this amid a sea of cabbage stalks, with a foreign-looking sun already striking burningly down through the Diesel-soaked London sky. It was too much of a mix-up. A *kaleidoscope*, I thought, but the word was too old-fashioned; the kaleidoscope had been a popular toy in Victorian times, but the spectacle of perpetually self-renewing chaos, always seeking new combination, is interesting only from the outside. Now we were on the inside of the kaleidoscope, looking out; I knew what I wanted to see but I had to find her first.

I took my overcoat to another Luggage Office. If this went on I should begin to measure the seasons, even the hours of the day, by whether I, or London Transport, had care of the garment. It was something to have one fixed point in my life, anyway. It gave me a little fibre of reality to cling on to; and in my rests from foot-slogging I could find recreation by reading the small print on the back of the ticket they gave me.

My wandering must have taken me somewhere towards Fleet Street. I remember seeing St Paul's, now and again, through openings in the houses that hemmed me in. But I never stopped to take a bearing. All I had the wit to do was to press on, steering from café to café. I had given up the habit of drinking coffee in each place; now, I just walked in, put my question bluntly, peered closely into the face of whoever answered, to try and assess whether they were hiding anything, and passed on. No one had any help to give me. London

217

contained nothing that concerned me in any way; its rooms, its floors, its millions of human beings, its machines, furnaces, landscapes, underground drains and cables, trees, flowers, radio waves, hair clippings, amputated limbs, wild animals, musical instruments waiting sadly in shop windows – all were indifferent to me, and I to them.

Then I met Stocker. Of all people, he was sitting quite close to me while I questioned the proprietor of a sandwich bar. He had undone his tie and slipped his jacket off, but it was hot in there, hotter even than out in the street, and he was sweating.

He said, 'Joe,' and I turned away from the boss and saw him. I felt no surprise, but he, on the other hand, looked at me with what seemed to be amazement.

'Hey, you look awful,' he said. 'You look bloody awful, Joe.'

'I've been working hard,' I said. 'Reporting important news.' All of a sudden I felt myself coming over crafty.

'In London? I thought you only did local news,' he said.

'*Social* news,' I said heavily. 'It's these duchesses who find this the best season for holding balls.'

He cackled, then said, 'Well, you look bloody awful.'

The proprietor went off to serve someone else who'd come in. I didn't feel like staying to waste any more time; he had denied any knowledge of Pepina, and if he was lying he was a good actor. So I started for the door, but Stocker pulled me back and said, 'Here, stay a minute. You'll have heat prostration if you charge about like this. Have a cup of coffee and rest for a bit. It's not like you to rush about.'

'No,' I said obscurely, 'but then I'm not going to be like me, in lots of ways, from now on.'

Still, I let him settle me on a stool and I let the proprietor bring me some coffee. I stared into it a bit and let Stocker talk. I didn't take any notice until suddenly it seemed to me that he was saying something very unexpected. I shook my head to clear it, and asked him, 'What was that?'

'Wish you'd listen. I was saying that I can definitely vouch for it that Robert and his Italian bint are washed up.'

My stomach bunched up like a fish, but I managed to keep my voice steady for long enough to say, 'Go on, tell.'

'I've had the most direct evidence you could possibly have,' said Stocker, his eyes shining in his soft, pallid face. 'I've *seen* her.'

After that we were busy for a minute or two, mopping up

my coffee, which had got itself all over the counter and down my suit. I suppose I gave a jerk when he said he had seen her.

'I was out Kentish Town way,' said Stocker, 'yesterday afternoon. I'm on the track of a bint there who works in the – '

'Never mind that.'

'Yes, but you ought to hear this, Joe. Ever since I told you I was aiming at a hundred up and then I was going to turn it in, I've been – '

'Never mind that, I said,' I said.

'Well, I'll tell you about Robert's bint first,' he agreed, relenting. 'I went into this café at about tea time – '

I interrupted him again and got the exact location of the café. As I slid down from my stool and began to fumble mechanically for the coins to pay for my coffee he was going on, ' . . . and of course there was no mistaking her. I had quite a long look at her before she saw me. When she did see me she went down into the kitchen – she seems to work partly down there and partly in the café, waiting. General work, I suppose. Anyway, I thought to myself, I wouldn't mind a packet of this myself. You know, Joe, that girl's very well built.'

'Get off,' I said, putting my sixpence on the table. I was not really listening.

'Yes. She's one of those girls who start out with rather a dainty sort of build – slight, even. But of course if they have any work to do, like she's had, it builds them up. That's what I liked about her. Dainty, and yet solid. Yes, solid.'

'Shut up,' I said.

He flexed his biceps and winked at me. 'Built like a brick shit-house,' he said.

Suddenly I had hit him and blood was coming away from the corner of his mouth.

'Blast you, Joe, what's that for?' he said, putting his hand up to his mouth and staring at me. Just as surprised, I stared back for an instant, then turned and went out. I was in a taxi, making for Kentish Town, before I even saw that my knuckles were grazed.

She hadn't gone far. The café was ten minutes' bus ride from Robert's. I walked in and found the place empty except for a man fatter than myself. If we had been advertising a slimming cure he could have represented the man who hadn't started on it yet. I could then have been the one who had been taking the cure for a bit. We could easily have found a thin man to stand in as the one who had successfully completed it.

This thought ran through my mind as I stood just inside the door, and for a moment I hesitated, unable to start talking, as he looked at me questioningly.

Then I said, 'I've got a message for Miss Pepina.'

'Who sent you?' he asked.

'That's the Italian girl who works here, isn't it?' I went on, overriding him. 'Where is she, downstairs?'

He nodded. 'We're slack just now,' he said as if it explained something. He pointed to where the stairs were. I liked him for being helpful and for being fatter than I was.

I went down the steep, uncarpeted stairs and there I saw her. There was no one else there, and she was kneeling down with her back to me, cleaning out a big gas stove. I wanted to go across to her and put my hands on her shoulders, but I was afraid of startling her, so I spoke to her from where I was standing at the foot of the stairs. 'Pepina,' I said.

She looked over her shoulder, saw me, and slowly got up. At first I thought she didn't recognize me, her face was so dead. But then I saw she knew who I was but just didn't care. She had turned so completely inwards, in her effort to escape the suffering. If she had any reaction at all it was to wish I'd go away.

'Did Robert send you?' she asked.

We spoke in our kind of French, but this was the substance of it.

'Robert didn't send me,' I said. 'He doesn't know where you are and he doesn't know I'm looking for you.'

She must have been going to ask me who had sent me, in that case; but she only opened her mouth and shut it again. It must have been obvious from my face that I had sent myself.

'Robert's in Paris, playing Ned in the Myra Cup Final,' I said. 'You won't be seeing him again – unless you specially want to.'

She shook her head, with a tired motion of the shoulders. She was still holding the wire brush she had been using to clean the oven; it was covered with flakes of black stuff, and she began to pick them off and let them fall on the floor.

'You mustn't stay here,' I said.

She looked up at me then, and I could see she was trying to read my mind. Then she went back to the brush again. 'Where can I go?' she said dully. 'I must work.'

I took her by the shoulders – I thought I'd waited long enough for it to be unstartling – and gave her a kiss, to help her read my mind. She was relaxed, moving neither towards nor away from me, but I could tell she got the idea.

I saw a plastic mackintosh hanging behind the door, and got it and put it round her. 'Anything else?' I asked. 'Any hat?'

She shook her head, still passive and lifeless. 'But I work here,' she said.

The man fatter than myself came down the stairs, blowing a lot. 'Don't keep her all day,' he said. 'She's got work to do.'

'You've got work to do, you mean,' I said. 'The oven wants cleaning, for a start.'

He was going to protest but I said, 'Look. How long has she worked for you?'

'Only three days,' he said reproachfully, as if he didn't mind his staff being abducted when he had had a chance to get to know them, but this was a bit thick.

'Well,' I said, 'you've had three days' work for nothing. You didn't give her any wages in advance, did you?'

He shook his head, and Pepina and I went on up the stairs and left him shaking it.

Outside, the sun was shining. Pepina's face was very pale, but the sun made it look golden. I had a question to ask her, but it could wait. I knew there was nothing to be gained from rushing it.

We walked a little and then she stopped. 'You say Robert is – ' she began and made a curious gesture, as if throwing something away. It meant, 'Robert is off on his eternal wild-goose chase.'

'Yes,' I said. 'And so is Ned. They're both – ' and I imitated her gesture. At that she laughed. And only ten minutes earlier you'd have said she would never laugh again.

I had a quick mental vision of Ned and Robert running down the Champs-Élysées passing Myra's head back and forth like a football. I suppose they were running towards the Arc de Triomphe to shoot at goal.

And at this I laughed, in my turn. Let them get on with it, I thought. For the first time since my childhood I felt free of them. An image flashed into my mind: muddy fields, a little boy on the verge of tears, and two figures in running-shorts loafing on a stile. How they had pounced on the child, in their endless search for an emblem, an emblem of their own importance and effectiveness. And they had dragged me into it all, so easily, that afternoon when it had all begun. The little boy was the Myra of that context, or Myra was the little boy of this – it didn't matter. My role had never changed; I had always been 'Joe'. 'We don't want any of your nonsense, Joe; of course you're coming with us.' 'It'll make the effect so much better.' Joe!

Pepina wriggled herself more deeply into her coat and accepted the arm I crooked towards her. 'You are taking me away,' she said wonderingly. 'And I come with you, without asking you anything – without knowing you.'

'You do know me,' I said.

'I only know your name. That is all I know of you: Joe Shaw.'

'And even that isn't true,' I said. 'That's just what people have been calling me. It's not my real name.'

'What is your name?' Pepina asked.

'Clarence Shaw,' I said.

It was like Ned showing me his trains. Only better, because it was the end of an epoch, an epoch that had gone on too long and had been too full of evasions.

'Where are we going?' said Pepina, in English.

And in English I said, 'Home.'